TERMS & CONDITIONS

Allows only one book at £7.99 per qualifying transaction. This voucher is valid from 1st October - 1st November 2009 subject to publication date. It can only be redeemed in WHSmith High Street Stores, airports and railways. Excludes Outlet stores, Online, motorway service stations, hospitals and work places. Subject to availability. Cannot be used in conjunction with any other promotional voucher or multi-buy promotion. Only one voucher can be redeemed per transaction and it must be surrendered upon use. No cash alternative. Photocopies will not be accepted and the voucher is not transferable. WHSmith reserves the right to reject any voucher it deems, in its sole discretion, to have been forged, defaced or otherwise tampered with.

Customers must retain their receipt as proof of pre-order and receipt must be presented, together with this voucher, upon collection of **The Unseen Academicals.** This voucher does not guarantee you a copy on day of release

<3411 9938>

TERMS & CONDITIONS

Both items must be purchased in the same transaction. Cheapest item is free. This voucher is valid from 1st October - 1st November 2009. Only applies to Terry Pratchett paperback books. It can only be redeemed in WHSmith High Street Stores, airports and railways. Excludes Outlet stores, Online, motorway service stations, hospitals and work places. Subject to availability. Cannot be used in conjunction with any instore multi-buy or promotional voucher. Only one voucher can be redeemed per transaction and it must be surrendered upon use. No cash alternative. Photocopies will not be accepted and the voucher is not transferable. WHSmith reserves the right to reject any voucher it deems, in its sole discretion, to have been forged, defaced or otherwise tampered with.

<3411 8238>

BOOKS BY TERRY PRATCHETT

FOR YOUNGER READERS

THE BROMELIAD TRILOGY
(containing *Truckers*, *Diggers* and *Wings*)
TRUCKERS ✣
DIGGERS ✣
WINGS ✣
THE CARPET PEOPLE ✣
ONLY YOU CAN
SAVE MANKIND ✣
JOHNNY AND THE DEAD ✣
JOHNNY AND THE BOMB ✣
THE JOHNNY MAXWELL TRILOGY
(containing *Only You Can Save Mankind*, *Johnny and the Dead* and *Johnny and the Bomb*)
JOHNNY AND THE DEAD
playscript (adapted by Stephen Briggs) ★

DISCWORLD FOR YOUNGER READERS

THE AMAZING MAURICE AND
HIS EDUCATED RODENTS ✣
THE AMAZING MAURICE AND
HIS EDUCATED RODENTS
playscript (adapted by Stephen Briggs) ★
THE WEE FREE MEN ✣
A HAT FULL OF SKY ✣
WINTERSMITH ✣

FOR ADULTS OF ALL AGES
THE DISCWORLD® SERIES

THE COLOUR OF MAGIC ✣
THE LIGHT FANTASTIC ✣
EQUAL RITES ✣
MORT ✣
SOURCERY ✣
WYRD SISTERS ✣
PYRAMIDS ✣
GUARDS! GUARDS! ✣
ERIC ✣ ●
MOVING PICTURES ✣
REAPER MAN ✣
WITCHES ABROAD ✣
SMALL GODS ✣
LORDS AND LADIES ✣
MEN AT ARMS ✣
SOUL MUSIC ✣
INTERESTING TIMES ✣
MASKERADE ✣
FEET OF CLAY ✣
HOGFATHER ✣
JINGO ✣
THE LAST CONTINENT ✣
CARPE JUGULUM ✣
THE FIFTH ELEPHANT ✣
THE TRUTH ✣
THIEF OF TIME ✣
NIGHT WATCH ✣
MONSTROUS REGIMENT ✣
GOING POSTAL ✣
THUD! ✣
MAKING MONEY ✣
THE COLOUR OF MAGIC –
GRAPHIC NOVEL
THE LIGHT FANTASTIC –
GRAPHIC NOVEL
MORT: A DISCWORLD BIG COMIC
(illustrated by Graham Higgins) ●
GUARDS! GUARDS!:
A DISCWORLD BIG COMIC
(adapted by Stephen Briggs,
illustrated by Graham Higgins) ●

SOUL MUSIC:
THE ILLUSTRATED SCREENPLAY

WYRD SISTERS:
THE ILLUSTRATED SCREENPLAY

MORT – THE PLAY
(adapted by Stephen Briggs)

WYRD SISTERS – THE PLAY
(adapted by Stephen Briggs)

GUARDS! GUARDS! – THE PLAY
(adapted by Stephen Briggs)

MEN AT ARMS – THE PLAY
(adapted by Stephen Briggs)

MASKERADE
(adapted for the stage by Stephen Briggs) ■

CARPE JUGULUM
(adapted for the stage by Stephen Briggs) ■

LORDS AND LADIES
(adapted for the stage by Irana Brown) ■

INTERESTING TIMES
(adapted for the stage by Stephen Briggs) ◆

THE FIFTH ELEPHANT
(adapted for the stage by Stephen Briggs) ◆

THE TRUTH
(adapted for the stage by Stephen Briggs) ◆

THE SCIENCE OF DISCWORLD
(with Ian Stewart and Jack Cohen) ✪

THE SCIENCE OF DISCWORLD II:
THE GLOBE
(with Ian Stewart and Jack Cohen) ✪

THE DISCWORLD COMPANION
(with Stephen Briggs) ●

THE STREETS OF
ANKH-MORPORK
(with Stephen Briggs)

THE DISCWORLD MAPP
(with Stephen Briggs)

A TOURIST GUIDE TO LANCRE –
A DISCWORLD MAPP
(with Stephen Briggs and Paul Kidby)

DEATH'S DOMAIN
(with Paul Kidby)

NANNY OGG'S COOKBOOK
(with Stephen Briggs, Tina Hannan and Paul Kidby)

THE PRATCHETT PORTFOLIO
(with Paul Kidby) ●

THE LAST HERO
(with Paul Kidby) ●

THE CELEBRATED DISCWORLD
ALMANAK
(with Bernard Pearson)

THE ART OF DISCWORLD
(with Paul Kidby)

WHERE'S MY COW?

THE UNSEEN UNIVERSITY
CUT-OUT BOOK
(with Bernard Pearson)

GOOD OMENS
(with Neil Gaiman)

STRATA

THE DARK SIDE OF THE SUN

THE UNADULTERATED CAT
(cartoons by Gray Jolliffe) ●

✤ also available in audio/CD ● published by Victor Gollancz

■ published by Samuel French ◆ published by Methuen Drama

✪ published by Ebury Press ★ published by Oxford University Press

THE WIT & WISDOM OF DISCWORLD

TERRY PRATCHETT

COMPILED BY
STEPHEN BRIGGS

CORGI BOOKS

TRANSWORLD PUBLISHERS
61-63 Uxbridge Road, London W5 5SA
A Random House Group Company
www.rbooks.co.uk

THE WIT AND WISDOM OF DISCWORLD
A CORGI BOOK: 9780552161879

First published in Great Britain
in 2007 by Doubleday
a division of Transworld Publishers
Corgi edition published 2008
This edition published exclusively for WHSmith 2009

A CIP catalogue record fro this book
is available from the British Library.

Addresses for the Randon House Group Ltd companies
outside the UK can be found at www.randomhouse.co.uk
The Random House Group Ltd Reg. No. 954009

The Random House Group Limited supports The Forest Stewardship Council (FSC), the leading international forest certification organisation. All our titles that are printed on Greenpeace approved FSC certified paper carry the FSC logo. Our paper procurement policy can be found at:
www.rbooks.co.uk/environment

Designed by Julia Lloyd
Typeset in Century Schoolbook
Printed and bound in the UK by
CPI Mackays, Chatham ME5 8TD

2 4 6 8 10 9 7 5 3 1

FSC
Mixed Sources
Product group from well-managed
forests and other controlled sources
www.fsc.org Cert no. TT-COC-2139
© 1996 Forest Stewardship Council

WIT & WISDOM

CONTENTS

INTRODUCTION

THROUGH THE WARDROBE INTO DISCWORLD®

IT WAS THE WIT OF TERRY PRATCHETT THAT FIRST ATTRACTED ME to the books, and which then led to my pushing past the fur coats and finding myself in his magical world – thankfully devoid of Turkish delight and talking beavers.

One of the big questions about Discworld for a newcomer is 'Where do I start?' This is a tricky one. For every diehard fan of Rincewind there's an advocate for *Small Gods*. For everyone who loves the 'Witch' or 'City Watch' books, there is another who prefers the 'one theme' books, such as *Soul Music* and *Moving Pictures*. I, as it happens, kicked off with *Mort*.

Terry writes fantasy – but his books are grounded firmly in reality. They contain heroes (not many), cowards, villains, bigots, crooks, the strong-willed and the weak-willed. Sometimes they are human. A lot of the time they are not. The series extends across many genres and deals with real issues. But Terry uses his wit to sharpen his pen; the humour in the books can be dark, and it can be so corny you may groan out loud as you read him on the train.

In producing this book, I have not tried to extract every single gag and witty exchange from the series. There are too many, and to do that, I might just as well have tied a set of the novels up with string and added a tag: 'The Complete Wit of Pratchett'.

What I *have* done is re-read every book in the canon, and pull out the extracts that appealed to me. Sometimes they'll be a page long, sometimes they'll be a single line of text. Sometimes a really good gag has been omitted because it needs the build-up that the novel can give but which would take too long to set up in a book of quotations. Here and there, I've had to change the *odd* word, or omit the *occasional* phrase, to help the quotation work outside its context in the novel.

The extracts are presented book by book, in the order in which they were published. Each book's section starts with the cover blurb (which in most cases was written by Terry), to give you the same sort of idea of the novel's plot as you'd get if you were browsing the shelves of your local bookstore.

IT'S A BIG BOOK

DO I HAVE TO READ IT ALL AT ONCE?

Don't panic: you don't need to sit and read this book section by section, from cover to cover. This is more of a 'dip into' book. If you're new to Terry's novels, this cornucopia of snippets may inspire you to go out and buy and read one – or more – of them. Oh, and the maps, diaries, audio books, scarf . . . As for you keen Discworld readers, what I hope is that, as you browse through this book – by torchlight under the covers last thing at night, smeared with sun lotion on a beach in Greece, on a long coach trip, sat on the privy – you'll find some of your favourite pieces from the Discworld canon. I haven't had the luxury of doing my research in any of these exotic locations – but I enjoyed the opportunity to wander once more through the roughly four million words which currently make up the series . . . around twice the complete wordage of the Bible and all Shakespeare's plays.

Stephen Briggs

www.stephenbriggs.com / www.studiotheatreclub.com

THE COLOUR OF MAGIC

ON a world supported on the back of a giant turtle (sex unknown), a gleeful, explosive, wickedly eccentric expedition sets out. There's an avaricious but inept wizard [Rincewind], a naive tourist [Twoflower] whose luggage moves on hundreds of dear little legs, dragons who only exist if you believe in them, and of course The Edge of the planet . . .

How it all began:

In a distant and second-hand set of dimensions, in an astral plane that was never meant to fly, the curling star-mists waver and part . . .

*

There was the theory that A'Tuin had come from nowhere and would continue at a uniform crawl, or steady gait, into nowhere, for all time. This theory was popular among academics.

An alternative, favoured by those of a religious persuasion, was that A'Tuin was crawling from the Birthplace to the Time of Mating, as were all the stars in the sky which were, obviously, also carried by giant turtles. When they arrived they would briefly and passionately mate, for the first and only time, and from that fiery union new turtles would be born to carry a new pattern of worlds. This was known as the Big Bang hypothesis.

*

The twin city of Ankh-Morpork, foremost of all the cities bounding the Circle Sea, was as a matter of course the home of a large number of gangs, thieves' guilds, syndicates and similar organizations. This was one of the reasons for its wealth.

*

The stranger smiled widely and fumbled yet again in the pouch. This time his hand came out holding a large gold coin. It was in fact slightly larger than an 8,000-dollar Ankhian crown and the design on it was unfamiliar, but it spoke inside Hugh's mind in a language he understood perfectly. My current owner, it said, is in need of succour and assistance; why not give it to him, so you and me can go off somewhere and enjoy ourselves?

*

If complete and utter chaos was lightning, then he'd be the sort to stand on a hilltop in a thunderstorm wearing wet copper armour and shouting 'All gods are bastards'.

Tourist, Rincewind had decided, meant 'idiot'.

At about this time a hitherto unsuccessful fortune-teller living on the other side of the block chanced to glance into her scrying bowl, gave a small scream and, within the hour, had sold her jewellery, various magical accoutrements, most of her clothes and almost all her other possessions that could not be conveniently carried on the fastest horse she could buy. The fact that later on, when her house collapsed in flames, she herself died in a freak landslide in the Morpork Mountains, proves that Death, too, has a sense of humour.

*

The Patrician of Ankh-Morpork smiled, but with his mouth only.

*

'I'm sure you won't dream of trying to escape from your obligations by fleeing the city . . .'

'I assure you the thought never even crossed my mind, lord.'

'Indeed? Then if I were you I'd sue my face for slander.'

*

'Ah, Gorphal,' said the Patrician pleasantly. 'Come in. Sit down. Can I press you to a candied starfish?'

'I am yours to command, master,' said the old man calmly. 'Save, perhaps, in the matter of preserved echinoderms.'

*

There are said to be some mystic rivers – one drop of which can steal a man's life away. After its turbid passage through the twin cities the Ankh could have been one of them.

*

That's what's so stupid about the whole magic thing . . . You spend twenty years learning the spell that makes nude virgins appear in your bedroom, and then you're so poisoned by quicksilver fumes and half-blind from reading old grimoires that you can't remember what happens next.

*

Death, on Discworld, is a character in his own right, and throughout the series is recognizable by always speaking IN BLOCK CAPITALS.

Death, insofar as it was possible in a face with no movable features, looked surprised. RINCEWIND? . . . WHY ARE YOU HERE?

'Um, why not?' said Rincewind.

I WAS SURPRISED THAT YOU JOSTLED ME, RINCEWIND. FOR I HAVE AN APPOINTMENT WITH THEE THIS VERY NIGHT.

'Oh no, not—'

OF COURSE, WHAT'S SO BLOODY VEXING ABOUT THE WHOLE BUSINESS IS THAT I WAS EXPECTING TO MEET THEE IN PSEUDOPOLIS.

'But that's five hundred miles away!'

YOU DON'T HAVE TO TELL ME, THE WHOLE SYSTEM'S GOT SCREWED UP AGAIN. I CAN SEE THAT.

*

I'LL GET YOU YET, CULLY, said Death, in a voice like the slamming of leaden coffin lids.

*

Death sat in His garden, running a whetstone along the edge of His scythe. It was already so sharp that any passing breeze that blew across it was sliced smoothly into two puzzled zephyrs.

*

'Run away and leave Hrun with that thing?' Twoflower said.

Rincewind looked blank. 'Why not?' he said. 'It's his job.'

'But it'll kill him!'

'It could be worse,' said Rincewind.

'What?'

'It could be *us*,' Rincewind pointed out logically.

*

'We've strayed into a zone with a high magical index,' Rincewind said. 'Don't ask me how. Once upon a time a really powerful magic field must have been generated here, and we're feeling the after-effects.'

'Precisely,' said a passing bush.

*

'You don't understand!' screamed the tourist, above the terrible noise of the wingbeats. 'All my life I've wanted to see dragons!'

'From the inside?' shouted Rincewind.

*

'You're your own worst enemy, Rincewind,' said the sword.

Rincewind looked up at grinning men.

'Bet?' he said wearily.

*

'Well,' said the voice. 'You see, one of the disadvantages of being dead is that one is released as it were from the bonds of time and therefore I can see everything that has happened or will happen, all at the same time except that of course I now know that Time does not, for all practical purposes, exist.'

'That doesn't sound like a disadvantage,' said Twoflower.

'You don't think so? Imagine every moment being at one and the same time a distant memory and a nasty surprise and you'll see what I mean.'

I'd rather be a slave than a corpse.

Plants on the Disc, while including the categories known commonly as *annuals*, . . . and *perennials*, . . . also included a few rare *reannuals* which, because of an unusual four-dimensional twist in their genes, could be planted this year to come up *last year*. The *vul* nut vine was particularly exceptional in that it could flourish as many as eight years prior to its seed actually being sown. *Vul* nut wine was reputed to give certain drinkers an insight into the future which was, from the nut's point of view, the past. Strange but true.

*

'We know all about you, Rincewind the magician. You are a man of great cunning and artifice. You laugh in the face of Death. Your affected air of craven cowardice does not fool me.'

It fooled Rincewind.

*

'What is your name?' he said.

'My name is immaterial,' she said.

'That's a pretty name,' said Rincewind.

*

'I hope you're not proposing to enslave us,' said Twoflower.

Marchesa looked genuinely shocked. 'Certainly not! Whatever could have given you that idea? Your lives in Krull will be rich, full and comfortable—'

'Oh, good,' said Rincewind.

'—just not very long.'

THE LIGHT FANTASTIC

As it moves towards a seemingly inevitable collision with a malevolent red star, the Discworld has only one possible saviour. Unfortunately, this happens to be the singularly inept and cowardly wizard called Rincewind, who was last seen falling off the edge of the world . . .

It is said that someone at a party once asked the famous philosopher Ly Tin Wheedle 'Why are you here?' and the reply took three years.

*

Cori Celesti, upon whose utter peak the world's quarrelsome and somewhat bourgeois gods lived in a palace of marble, alabaster and uncut moquette three-piece suites they had chosen to call Dunmanifestin. It was always a considerable annoyance to any Disc citizen with pretensions to culture that they were ruled by gods whose idea of an uplifting artistic experience was a musical doorbell.

*

Trymon didn't smile often enough, and he liked figures and the sort of organization charts that show lots of squares with arrows pointing to other squares. In short, he was the sort of man who could use the word 'personnel' and mean it.

*

'Do you think there's anything to eat in this forest?'

'Yes,' said the wizard bitterly, 'us.'

*

'[There are] some big mushrooms . . . Can you eat them?'

Rincewind looked at them cautiously. 'No, no good to eat at all.'

'Why?' called Twoflower. 'Are the gills the wrong shade of yellow?'

'No, not really . . .'

'I expect the stems haven't got the right kind of fluting, then.'

'They look okay, actually.'

'The cap, then, I expect the cap is the wrong colour,' said Twoflower.

'Not sure about that.'

'Well then, why can't you eat them?'

Rincewind coughed. 'It's the little doors and windows,' he said wretchedly, 'it's a dead giveaway.'

*

He moved in a way that suggested he was attempting the world speed record for the nonchalant walk.

*

'I said I hope it is a good party,' said Galder, loudly.

AT THE MOMENT IT IS, said Death levelly. I THINK IT MIGHT GO DOWNHILL VERY QUICKLY AT MIDNIGHT.

'Why?'

THAT'S WHEN THEY THINK I'LL BE TAKING MY MASK OFF.

He vanished, leaving only a cocktail stick and a short paper streamer behind.

*

When the first explorers from the warm lands around the Circle Sea travelled into the chilly hinterland they filled in the blank spaces on their maps by grabbing the nearest native, pointing at some distant landmark, speaking very clearly in a loud voice, and writing down whatever the bemused man told them. Thus were immortalized in generations of atlases such geographical oddities as Just A Mountain, I Don't Know, What? and, of course, Your Finger You Fool.

*

Cohen the Barbarian enters the Discworld canon:

The barbarian chieftain said: 'What then are the greatest things that a man may find in life?'

The man on his right spoke thus: 'The crisp horizon of the steppe, the wind in your hair, a fresh horse under you.'

The man on his left said: 'The cry of the white eagle in the heights, the fall of snow in the forest, a true arrow in your bow.'

The chieftain nodded, and said: 'Surely it is the sight of your enemy slain, the humiliation of his tribe and the lamentation of his women.'

Then the chieftain turned respectfully to his guest, and said: 'But our guest, whose name is legend, must tell us truly: what is it that a man may call the greatest things in life?'

The warriors leaned closer. This should be worth hearing.

The guest thought long and hard and then said, with deliberation: 'Hot water, good dentishtry and shoft lavatory paper.'

*

[He was] a very old man, the skinny variety that generally gets called 'spry', with a totally bald head, a beard almost down to his knees, and a pair of matchstick legs on which varicose veins had traced the street map of quite a large city . . .

*

'When I was a young man, carving my name in the world, well, then I liked my women red-haired and fiery.'

'Ah.'

'And then I grew a little older and for preference I looked for a woman with blonde hair and the glint of the world in her eye.'

'Oh? Yes?'

'But then I grew a little older again and I came to see the point of dark women of a sultry nature.'

He paused. Rincewind waited.

'And?' he said. 'Then what? What is it that you look for in a woman now?'

Cohen turned one rheumy blue eye on him.

'Patience,' he said.

*

Cohen [had] . . . spent his life living rough under the sky [and] knew the value of a good thick book, which ought to outlast at least a season of cooking fires if you were careful how you tore the pages out. Many a life had been saved on a snowy night by a handful of sodden kindling and a really dry book. If you felt like a smoke and couldn't find a pipe, a book was your man every time.

Cohen realized people wrote things in books. It had always seemed to him to be a frivolous waste of paper.

*

'If you kill me a thousand will take my place,' said the man, who was now backed against the wall.

'Yes,' said Cohen, in a reasonable tone of voice, 'but that isn't the point, is it? The point is, *you'll* be dead.'

*

Greyhald Spold, currently the oldest wizard on the Disc and determined to keep it that way, has been very busy. The servants have been dismissed. The doorways have been sealed with a paste made from powdered mayflies, and protective octograms have been drawn on the windows. Rare and rather smelly oils have been poured in complex patterns on the floor; in the very centre of the room is the eightfold octogram of Withholding, surrounded by red and green candles. And in the centre of that is a box, lined with red silk and yet more protective amulets. Because Greyhald Spold knows that Death is looking for him, and has spent many years designing an impregnable hiding place.

He has just set the complicated clockwork of the lock and shut the lid, lying back in the knowledge that here at last is the perfect defence against the most ultimate of all his enemies, although as yet he has not considered the important part that airholes must play in an enterprise of this kind.

And right beside him, very close to his ear, a voice has just said: DARK IN HERE, ISN'T IT?

*

Seven league boots are a tricksy form of magic at best, and the utmost caution must be taken in using a means of transport which, when all is said and done, relies for its effectiveness on trying to put one foot twenty-one miles in front of the other.

Cohen had heard of fighting fair, and had long ago decided he wanted no part of it.

Twoflower didn't just look at the world through rose-tinted spectacles, Rincewind knew – he looked at it through a rose-tinted brain, too, and heard it through rose-tinted ears.

*

There was no real point in trying to understand anything Twoflower said, and all anyone could do was run alongside the conversation and hope to jump on as it turned a corner.

'His name's Twoflower. He isn't from these parts.'

'Doeshn't look like it. Friend of yoursh?'

'We've got this sort of hate–hate relationship, yes.'

That's old Twoflower, Rincewind thought. It's not that he doesn't appreciate beauty, he just appreciates it in his own way. I mean, if a poet sees a daffodil he stares at it and writes a long poem about it, but Twoflower wanders off to find a book on botany. And treads on it.

*

Then they all heard it; a tiny distant crunching, like something moving very quickly over the snow crust.

...It was louder now, a crisp rhythm like someone eating celery very fast.

*

Rincewind was to magic what a bicycle is to a bumblebee.

*

Trolls were not unknown in Ankh-Morpork, of course, where they often got employment as bodyguards. They tended to be a bit expensive to keep until they learned about doors and didn't simply leave the house by walking aimlessly through the nearest wall.

*

There were many drawbacks to being a swordswoman, not least of which was that men didn't take you seriously until you'd actually killed them, by which time it didn't really matter anyway.

*

'It's the star, friend,' the man said. 'Haven't you seen it in the sky?'

'We couldn't help noticing it, yes.'

'They say that it'll hit us on Hogswatchnight and the seas will boil and the countries of the Disc will be broken and kings will be brought down and the cities will be as lakes of glass,' said the man. 'I'm off to the mountains.'

'That'll help, will it?' said Rincewind.

'No, but the view will be better.'

*

Ankh-Morpork!

Pearl of cities!

This is not a completely accurate description, of course – it was not round and shiny – but even its worst enemies would agree that if you had to liken Ankh-Morpork to anything, then it might as well be a piece of rubbish covered with the diseased secretions of a dying mollusc.

*

There have been bigger cities. There have been richer cities. There have certainly been prettier cities. But no city in the multiverse could rival Ankh-Morpork for its smell.

*

Ankh-Morpork, largest city in the lands around the Circle Sea, slept.

That statement is not really true.

On the one hand, those parts of the city which normally concerned themselves with, for example, selling vegetables, shoeing horses, carving exquisite small jade ornaments, changing money and making tables, on the whole, slept. Unless they had insomnia. Or had got up in the night as it might be, to go to the lavatory. On the other hand, many of the less law-abiding citizens were wide awake and, for instance, climbing through windows that didn't belong to them, slitting throats, mugging one another, listening to loud music in smoky cellars and generally having a lot more fun. But most of the animals were asleep, except for the rats. And the bats, too, of course. As far as the insects were concerned . . .

The point is that descriptive writing is very rarely entirely accurate and during the reign of Olaf Quimby II as Patrician of Ankh some legislation was passed in a determined attempt to put a stop to this sort of thing and introduce some honesty into reporting. Thus, if a legend said of a notable hero that 'all men spoke of his prowess' any bard who valued his life would add hastily 'except for a couple of people in his home village who thought he was a liar, and quite a lot of other people who had never really heard of him'. Poetic simile was strictly limited to statements like 'his mighty steed was as fleet as the wind on a fairly calm day, say about Force Three', and any loose talk about a beloved having a face that launched a thousand ships would have to be backed by evidence that the object of desire did indeed look like a bottle of champagne.

Quimby was eventually killed by a disgruntled poet during an experiment conducted in the palace grounds to prove the disputed accuracy of the proverb 'The pen is mightier than the sword', and in his memory it was amended to include the phrase 'only if the sword is very small and the pen is very sharp'.

Unseen University had never admitted women,

muttering something about problems with the plumbing, but the real reason was an unspoken dread that if women were allowed to mess around with magic they would probably be embarrassingly good at it . . .

The Octavo filled the room with a dull, sullen light, which wasn't strictly light at all but the opposite of light; darkness isn't the opposite of light, it is simply its absence, and what was radiating from the book was the light that lies on the far side of darkness, the light fantastic.

It was a rather disappointing purple colour.

*

It looked the sort of book described in library catalogues as 'slightly foxed', although it would be more honest to admit that it looked as though it had been badgered, wolved and possibly beared as well.

*

'All the shops have been smashed open, there was a whole bunch of people across the street helping themselves to musical instruments, can you believe that?'

'Yeah,' said Rincewind. 'Luters, I expect.'

'You know, I think I might re-enroll,' said Rincewind cheerfully.

'I think I could really make a go of things this time. I can really see myself getting to grips with magic and graduating really well. They do say if it's summa cum laude, then the living is easy—'

A Thaum is the basic unit of magical strength. It has been universally established as the amount of magic needed to create one small white pigeon or three normal-sized billiard balls.

EQUAL RITES

THE last thing the wizard Drum Billet did, before Death laid a bony hand on his shoulder, was to pass on his staff of power to the eighth son of an eighth son. Unfortunately for his colleagues in the chauvinistic (not to say misogynistic) world of magic, he failed to check on the new-born baby's sex . . .

The Discworld is . . .

. . . as round and flat as a geological pizza, although without the anchovies.

*

He came walking through the thunderstorm and you could tell he was a wizard, partly because of the long cloak and carven staff but mainly because the raindrops were stopping several feet from his head, and steaming.

*

There was a village tucked in a narrow valley between steep woods. It wasn't a large village, and wouldn't have shown up on a map of the mountains. It barely showed up on a map of the village.

*

Often there is no more than a little plaque to reveal that, against all gynaecological probability, someone very famous was born halfway up a wall.

*

Granny Weatherwax was a witch. That was quite acceptable in the Ramtops, and no one had a bad word to say about witches. At least, not if he wanted to wake up in the morning the same shape as he went to bed.

*

Granny had heard that broomsticks were once again very much the fashion among younger witches, but she didn't hold with it. There was no way a body could look respectable while hurtling through the air aboard a household implement. Besides, it looked decidedly draughty.

*

Although she was aware that somewhere under her complicated strata of vests and petticoats there was some skin, that didn't mean to say she approved of it.

*

The old woman had a flat, measured way of speaking sometimes. It was the kind of voice the Creator had probably used. Whether there was magic in it, or just headology, it ruled out any possibility of argument. It made it clear that whatever it was talking about was exactly how things should be.

*

The witch's cottage consisted of so many extensions and lean-tos that it was difficult to see what the original building had looked like, or even if there had ever been one.

*

Front doors in Bad Ass were used only by brides and corpses, and Granny had always avoided becoming either.

*

Granny had a philosophical objection to reading, but she'd be the last to say that books, especially books with nice thin pages, didn't have their uses.

*

'Do you know how wizards like to be buried?'

'Yes!'

'Well, how?'

Granny Weatherwax paused at the bottom of the stairs.

'Reluctantly.'

*

Esk felt that bravery was called for, but on a night like this bravery lasted only as long as a candle stayed alight.

*

Everyone knew there were wolves in the mountains, but they seldom came near the village – the modern wolves were the offspring of ancestors that had survived because they had learned that human meat had sharp edges.

*

'But,' Smith said, 'if it's wizard magic she's got, learning witchery won't be any good, will it? You said they're different.'

'They're both magic. If you can't learn to ride an elephant, you can at least learn to ride a horse.'

'What's an elephant?'

'A kind of badger,' said Granny. She hadn't maintained forest-credibility for forty years by ever admitting ignorance.

*

Granny grinned. 'That's one form of magic, of course.'

'What, just knowing things?'

'Knowing things that other people *don't know.*'

*

'Hoki's a nature god,' Granny said. 'Sometimes he manifests himself as an oak tree, or half a man and half a goat, but mainly I see him in his aspect as a bloody nuisance.'

*

A boxful of marzipan ducks on a nearby stall came to life and whirred past the stallholder to land, quacking happily, in the river (where, by dawn, they had all melted: that's natural selection for you).

No one can out-stare a witch, 'cept a goat, of course.

Granny, meanwhile, was two streets away. She was also, by the standards of other people, lost. She would not see it like that. She knew where she was, it was just that everywhere else didn't.

*

He had the kind of real deep tan that rich people spend ages trying to achieve with expensive holidays and bits of tinfoil, when really all you need to do to obtain one is work your arse off in the open air every day.

*

A person ignorant of the possibility of failure can be a halfbrick in the path of the bicycle of history.

If women were as good as men they'd be a lot better!

The air around them reeked of incense and grain and spices and beer, but mainly of the sort of smell that was caused by a high water-table, thousands of people, and a robust approach to drainage.

*

The Shades: an ancient part of the city whose inhabitants were largely nocturnal and never enquired about one another's business because curiosity not only killed the cat but threw it in the river with weights tied to its feet.

*

The lodgings were on the top floor next to the well-guarded premises of a respectable dealer in stolen property because, as Granny had heard, good fences make good neighbours.

*

At some time in the recent past someone had decided to brighten the ancient corridors of the University by painting them, having some vague notion that Learning Should Be Fun. It hadn't worked. It's a fact known throughout the universes that no matter how carefully the colours are chosen, institutional decor ends up as either vomit green, unmentionable brown, nicotine yellow or surgical appliance pink. By some little understood process of sympathetic resonance, corridors painted in those colours *always smell slightly of boiled cabbage* – even if no cabbage is ever cooked in the vicinity.

*

It wasn't that Granny could make herself invisible, it was just that she had this talent for being able to fade into the foreground so that she wasn't noticed.

*

Books tend to react with one another, creating randomized magic with a mind of its own . . .

One such accident had turned the librarian into an ape, since when he had resisted all attempts to turn him back, explaining in sign language that life as an orang-utan was considerably better than life as a human being, because all the big philosophical questions resolved themselves into wondering where the next banana was coming from. Anyway, long arms and prehensile feet were ideal for dealing with high shelves.

*

'You're wizards!' Esk screamed. 'Bloody well wizz!'

*

Cutangle stood with legs planted wide apart, arms akimbo and stomach giving an impression of a beginners' ski slope, the whole of him therefore adopting a pose usually associated with Henry VIII but with an option on Henry IX and X as well.

*

'Million-to-one chances,' Granny said, 'crop up nine times out of ten.'

*

She hit one, which had a face like a small family of squid, and it deflated into a pile of twitching bones and bits of fur and odd ends of tentacle, very much like a Greek meal.

*

But this was a storm of the Circle Sea plains, and its main ambition was to hit the ground with as much rain as possible. It was the kind of storm that suggests that the whole sky has swallowed a diuretic. The thunder and lightning hung around in the background, supplying a sort of chorus, but the rain was the star of the show. It tap-danced across the land.

*

'I was born up in the mountains. I get seasick on damp grass, if you must know.'

*

'You can't cross the same river twice, I always say,' [said Granny.]

Cutangle gave this some thought.

'I think you're wrong there,' he said. 'I must have crossed the same river, oh, thousands of times.'

'Ah, but it wasn't the same river.'

'It wasn't?'

'No.'

Cutangle shrugged. 'It looked like the same bloody river.'

*

. . . the endless rooftops of the University, which by comparison made Gormenghast look like a toolshed on a railway allotment . . .

*

One thing the water couldn't do was gurgle out of the ornamental gargoyles ranged around the roofs. This was because the gargoyles wandered off and sheltered in the attics at the first sign of rain. They held that just because you were ugly it didn't mean you were stupid.

*

'I don't think there's ever been a lady wizard before,' said Cutangle. 'I rather think it might be against the lore.'

MORT

DEATH comes to us all. When he came to Mort, he offered him a job. After being assured that being dead was not compulsory, Mort accepted. However, he soon found out that romantic longings did not mix easily with the responsibilities of being Death's apprentice...

Reannuals are plants that grow backwards in time. You sow the seeds this year and they grow last year.

A farmer who neglects to sow ordinary seeds only loses the crop, whereas anyone who forgets to sow seeds of a crop that has already been harvested twelve months before risks disturbing the entire fabric of causality, not to mention acute embarrassment.

*

Then there was the puzzle of why the sun came out during the day, instead of at night when the light would come in useful.

*

THANK YOU, BOY, said the skull. WHAT IS YOUR NAME?

'Uh,' said Mort, 'Mortimer . . . sir. They call me Mort.'

WHAT A COINCIDENCE.

*

'I suppose we were all young once.'

Death considered this.

NO, he said, I DON'T THINK SO.

*

Death leaned over the saddle and looked down at the kingdoms of the world.

I DON'T KNOW ABOUT YOU, he said, BUT I COULD MURDER A CURRY.

*

'Sir?'

YES?

'What's a curry?'

The blue fires flared deep in the eyes of Death.

HAVE YOU EVER BITTEN A RED-HOT ICE CUBE?

'No, sir,' said Mort.

CURRY'S LIKE THAT.

*

Ankh-Morpork is as full of life as an old cheese on a hot day, as loud as a curse in a cathedral, as bright as an oil slick, as colourful as a bruise and as full of activity, industry, bustle and sheer exuberant busyness as a dead dog on a termite mound.

*

'What are we going to do now?'

BUY YOU SOME NEW CLOTHES.

'These were new today.'

REALLY? IT CERTAINLY ADDS A NEW TERROR TO POVERTY.

*

They turned into a wider street leading into a more affluent part of the city (the torches were closer together and the middens further apart).

*

Although the Death of the Discworld is, in his own words, an ANTHROPOMORPHIC PERSONIFICATION, he long ago gave up using the traditional skeletal horses, because of the bother of having to stop all the time to wire bits back on.

*

Death was standing behind a lectern, poring over a map.

YOU HAVEN'T HEARD OF THE BAY OF MANTE, HAVE YOU? he said.

'No, sir,' said Mort.

FAMOUS SHIPWRECK THERE.

'Was there?'

THERE WILL BE, said Death, IF I CAN FIND THE DAMN PLACE.

*

Albert grunted. 'Do you know what happens to lads who ask too many questions?'

Mort thought for a moment.

'No,' he said eventually, 'what?'

There was silence.

Then Albert straightened up and said, 'Damned if I know. Probably they get answers, and serve 'em right.'

*

Mort remembered the woodcut in his grandmother's almanack, between the page on planting times and the phases of the moon section, showing Dethe thee Great Levyller Comes To Alle Menne. He'd stared at it hundreds of times when learning his letters. It wouldn't have been half so impressive if it had been generally known that the flame-breathing horse the spectre rode was called Binky.

*

WHY IS THERE A CHERRY ON A STICK IN THIS DRINK? . . . IT'S NOT AS IF IT DOES ANYTHING FOR THE FLAVOUR. WHY DOES ANYONE TAKE A PERFECTLY GOOD DRINK AND THEN PUT IN A CHERRY ON A POLE? . . . TAKE THESE THINGS, NOW, said Death, fingering a passing canape. I MEAN, MUSHROOMS YES, CHICKEN YES, CREAM YES, I'VE NOTHING AGAINST ANY OF THEM, BUT WHY IN THE NAME OF SANITY MINCE THEM ALL UP AND PUT THEM IN LITTLE PASTRY CASES? . . .

THAT'S MORTALS FOR YOU, Death continued. THEY'VE ONLY GOT A FEW YEARS IN THIS WORLD AND THEY SPEND THEM ALL IN MAKING THINGS COMPLICATED FOR THEMSELVES. FASCINATING.

*

'He doesn't look a *bad* king,' said Mort. 'Why would anyone want to kill him?'

SEE THE MAN NEXT TO HIM? WITH THE LITTLE MOUSTACHE AND THE GRIN LIKE A LIZARD? . . . HIS COUSIN, THE DUKE OF STO HELIT. NOT THE NICEST OF PEOPLE, said Death. A HANDY MAN WITH A BOTTLE OF POISON. FIFTH IN LINE TO THE THRONE LAST YEAR, NOW SECOND IN LINE. BIT OF A SOCIAL CLIMBER, YOU MIGHT SAY.

'My granny says that dying is like going to sleep,' Mort added, a shade hopefully.

I WOULDN'T KNOW. I HAVE DONE NEITHER.

This part of Ankh-Morpork was known as The Shades, an inner-city area sorely in need either of governmental help or, for preference, a flamethrower. It couldn't be called squalid because that would be stretching the word to breaking point. It was beyond squalor and out the other side, where by a sort of Einsteinian reversal it achieved a magnificent horribleness that it wore like an architectural award. It was noisy and sultry and smelled like a cowshed floor.

*

Even before it entered the city [the River Ankh] was slow and heavy with the silt of the plains, and by the time it got to The Shades even an agnostic could have walked across it. It was hard to drown in the Ankh, but easy to suffocate.

*

'Why do you trouble Igneous Cutwell, Holder of the Eight Keys, Traveller in the Dungeon Dimensions, Supreme Mage of—'

'Excuse me,' said Mort, 'are you really?'

'Really what?'

'Master of the thingy, Lord High Wossname of the Sacred Dungeons?'

'In a figurative sense.'

'What does that mean?'

'Well, it means no,' said Cutwell.

*

'Is it possible to walk through walls?' said Mort desperately.

'Using magic?'

'Um,' said Mort, 'I don't think so.'

'Then pick very thin walls,' said Cutwell.

'What time's sunset around here?' 'We normally manage to fit it in between night and day.'

He felt as if he'd been shipwrecked on the *Titanic* but in the nick of time had been rescued. By the *Lusitania*.

*

'. . . and the princesses were beautiful as the day is long and so noble they, they could pee through a dozen mattresses—'

'What?'

Albert hesitated. 'Something like that, anyway.'

*

She looked around slowly and met the impertinent gaze of the doorknocker. It waggled its metal eyebrows at her and spoke indistinctly through its wrought-iron ring.

'I am Princess Keli, heir to the throne of Sto Lat,' she said haughtily . . . 'And I don't talk to door furniture.'

'Fwell, *I'm* just a doorknocker and I can talk to fwhoever I please,' said the gargoyle pleasantly. 'And I can ftell you the fmaster iff having a trying day and duff fnot fwant to be disturbed. But you could ftry to use the magic word,' it added. 'Coming from an attractiff fwoman it works nine times out of eight.'

'Magic word? What's the magic word?'

The knocker perceptibly sneered. 'Haff you been taught nothing, miss?'

She drew herself up to her full height, which wasn't really worth the effort.

'I have been *educated*,' she informed it with icy precision, 'by some of the finest scholars in the land.'

The doorknocker did not appear to be impressed.

'Iff they didn't teach you the magic word,' it said calmly, 'they couldn't haff fbeen all that fine.'

Keli reached out, grabbed the heavy ring, and pounded it on the door. The knocker leered at her.

'Ftreat me rough,' it lisped. 'That'f the way I like it!'

'You're disgusting!'

'Yeff. Ooo, that waff nife, do it again . . .'

The door opened a crack. There was a shadowy glimpse of curly hair.

'Madam, I said we're cl—'

Keli sagged.

'*Please* help me,' she said. 'Please!'

'See?' said the doorknocker triumphantly. 'Sooner or later *everyone* remembers the magic word!'

*

'The first thing you learn when you enroll at Unseen University, I'm afraid, is that people don't pay much attention to that sort of thing. It's what their minds tell them that's important.' . . .

'Actually it's not the *first* thing you learn when you enroll,' he added. 'I mean, you learn where the lavatories are and all that sort of thing before that. But after all that, it's the first thing.'

*

Keli drummed her fingers on the table, or tried to. It turned out to be difficult. She stared down in vague horror.

Cutwell hurried forward and wiped the table with his sleeve.

'Sorry,' he muttered, 'I had treacle sandwiches for supper last night.'

*

You can tell from the following exchange that these two are made for each other.

'I don't want to get married to anyone yet,' Mort added. 'And certainly not to you, no offence meant.'

'I wouldn't marry you if you were the last man on the Disc,' Ysabell said sweetly.

'At least I don't look like I've been eating doughnuts in a wardrobe for years,' he said, as they stepped out on to Death's black lawn.

'At least I walk as if my legs only had one knee each,' she said.

'*My* eyes aren't two juugly poached eggs.'

Ysabell nodded. 'On the other hand, *my* ears don't look like something growing on a dead tree. What does juugly mean?'

'You know, eggs like Albert does them.'

'With the white all sticky and runny and full of slimy bits?'

'Yes.'

'A good word,' she conceded thoughtfully. 'But *my* hair, I put it to you, doesn't look like something you clean a privy with.'

'Certainly, but neither does mine look like a wet hedgehog.'

'Pray note that my chest does not appear to be a toast rack in a wet paper bag.'

Mort glanced sideways at the top of Ysabell's dress, which contained enough puppy fat for two litters of Rottweilers, and forbore to comment.

'*My* eyebrows don't look like a pair of mating caterpillars,' he hazarded.

'True. But *my* legs, I suggest, could at least stop a pig in a passageway.'

'Sorry—?'

'They're not bandy,' she explained.

'Ah.'

'Enough?' she said.

'Just about.'

'Good. Obviously we shouldn't get married, if only for the sake of the children.'

*

History unravels gently, like an old sweater. It has been patched and darned many times, reknitted to suit different people, shoved in a box under the sink of censorship to be cut up for the dusters of propaganda, yet it always – eventually – manages to spring back into its old familiar shape. History has a habit of changing the people who think they are changing *it*. History always has a few tricks up its frayed sleeve. It's been around a long time.

'Would you like a strawberry?'

Mort glanced at the small wooden punnet in the wizard's hands.

'In mid-winter?'

'Actually, they're sprouts with a dash of enchantment.'

'They taste like strawberries?'

Cutwell sighed. 'No, like sprouts.'

'I shall die nobly, like Queen Ezeriel,' [said Keli.]

Mort's forehead wrinkled. History was a closed book to him.

'Who's she?'

'She lived in Klatch and she had a lot of lovers and she sat on a snake,' said Cutwell.

'She meant to! She was crossed in love!'

'All I can remember was that she used to take baths in asses' milk. Funny thing, history,' said Cutwell reflectively. 'You become a queen, reign for thirty years, make laws, declare war on people and then the only thing you get remembered for is that you smelled like yoghurt and were bitten in the—'

*

The most famous inn on Discworld used to be called the Broken Drum (Broken Drum – You Can't Beat It!). Renamed after a particularly bad fire.

The Mended Drum in Filigree Street, foremost of the city's taverns. It was famed not for its beer, which looked like maiden's water and tasted like battery acid, but for its clientele. It was said that if you sat long enough in the Drum, then sooner or later every major hero on the Disc would steal your horse.

*

Ysabell was heavily into frills. Even the dressing table seemed to be wearing a petticoat. The whole room wasn't so much furnished as lingeried.

*

Mort is reading from a very old book in the Library of Death:

'. . . turnered hys hand, butt was sorelie vexed that alle menne at laste comme to nort, viz. Deathe, and vowed hymme to seke Imortalitie yn his pride . . . It's written in Old,' he said. 'Before they invented spelling.'

*

Death visits a job centre:

'It would seem that you have no useful skill or talent whatsoever,' Keeble said. 'Have you thought of going into teaching?'

Death's face was a mask of terror. Well, it was always a mask of terror, but this time he meant it to be.

They opened the ledger.

They looked at it for a long time.

Then Mort said, 'What do all those symbols mean?'

'Sodomy non sapiens,' said Albert under his breath.

'What does that mean?'

'Means I'm buggered if I know.'

Harga's House of Ribs down by the docks is probably not numbered among the city's leading eateries, catering as it does for the type of beefy clientele that prefers quantity and breaks up the tables if it doesn't get it. They don't go in for the fancy or exotic, but stick to conventional food like flightless bird embryos, minced organs in intestine skins, slices of hog flesh and burnt ground grass seeds dipped in animal fats; or, as it is known in their patois, egg, soss and bacon and a fried slice.

*

'Rincewind!' bawled Albert. 'Take this thing away and dispose of it.'

The toad crawled into Rincewind's hand and gave him an apologetic look.

'That's the last time that bloody landlord gives any lip to a wizard,' said Albert with smug satisfaction. 'It seems I turn my back for a few hundred years and suddenly people in this town are encouraged to think they can talk back to wizards, eh?'

'As the bursar of this university I must say that we've always encouraged a good neighbour policy with respect to the community,' mumbled a wizard, trying to avoid Albert's gimlet stare.

'You spineless maggots! I didn't found this university so you could lend people the bloody lawnmower!'

*

The Rite of AshkEnte, quite simply, summons and binds Death. Students of the occult will be aware that it can be performed with a simple incantation, three small bits of wood and 4cc of mouse blood, but no wizard worth his pointy hat would dream of doing anything so unimpressive; they knew in their hearts that if a spell didn't involve big yellow candles, lots of rare incense, circles drawn on the floor with eight different colours of chalk and a few cauldrons around the place then it simply wasn't worth contemplating.

*

The wizards have escaped unscathed from an encounter with their long-dead founder, whose statue had hitherto graced the campus.

'I propose here and now we replace the statue [said the bursar]. And to make sure no students deface it in any way I suggest we then erect it in the deepest cellar.

'And then lock the door,' he added. Several wizards began to cheer up.

'And throw away the key?' said Rincewind.

'And *weld* the door,' the bursar said. 'And then brick up the doorway.' There was a round of applause.

'And throw away the bricklayer!' chortled Rincewind, who felt he was getting the hang of this.

The bursar scowled at him. 'No need to get carried away,' he said.

*

The princess sprang to her feet and launched herself at her uncle, but Cutwell grabbed her.

'No,' he said, quietly. 'This isn't the kind of man who ties you up in a cellar with just enough time for the mice to eat your ropes before the flood-waters rise. This is the kind of man who just kills you here and now.'

*

'It's not that I mind being a duke,' said Mort. 'It's being married to a duchess that comes as a shock.'

I WASN'T CUT OUT TO BE A FATHER, AND CERTAINLY NOT A GRANDAD. I HAVEN'T GOT THE RIGHT KIND OF KNEES.

The Disc's greatest lovers were undoubtedly Mellius and Gretelina, whose pure, passionate and soul-searing affair would have scorched the pages of History if they had not, because of some unexplained quirk of fate, been born two hundred years apart on different continents.

*

Ankh-Morpork had dallied with many forms of government and had ended up with that form of democracy known as One Man, One Vote. The Patrician was the Man; he had the Vote.

SOURCERY

THERE was an eighth son of an eighth son. He was, naturally, a wizard. And there it should have ended. However (for reasons we'd better not go into), he had seven sons. And then he had an eighth son ... a wizard squared ... a source of magic ... a Sourcerer.

Far below, the sea sucked on the shingle as noisily as an old man with one tooth who had been given a gobstopper.

*

'Children are our hope for the future.'

THERE IS NO HOPE FOR THE FUTURE, said Death.

'What does it contain, then?'

ME.

'Besides you I mean!'

Death gave him a puzzled look. I'M SORRY?

*

'What is there in this world that makes living worth while?'

Death thought about it.

CATS, he said eventually, CATS ARE NICE.

*

There was no analogy for the way in which Great A'Tuin the world turtle moved against the galactic night. When you are ten thousand miles long, your shell pocked with meteor craters and frosted with comet ice, there is absolutely nothing you can realistically be like except yourself.

So Great A'Tuin swam slowly through the interstellar deeps like the largest turtle there has ever been, carrying on its carapace the four huge elephants that bore on their backs the vast, glittering waterfall-fringed circle of the Discworld, which exists either because of some impossible blip on the curve of probability or because the gods enjoy a joke as much as anyone.

*

Spring had come to Ankh-Morpork. It wasn't immediately apparent, but there were signs that were obvious to the cognoscenti. For example, the scum on the River Ankh, that great wide slow waterway that served the double city as reservoir, sewer and frequent morgue, had turned a particularly iridescent green. The city's drunken rooftops sprouted mattresses and bolsters as the winter bedding was put out to air in the weak sunshine, and in the depths of musty cellars the beams twisted and groaned when their dry sap responded to the ancient call of root and forest. Birds nested among the gutters and eaves of Unseen University, although it was noticeable that however great the pressure on the nesting sites they never, ever, made nests in the invitingly open mouths of the gargoyles that lined the rooftops, much to the gargoyles' disappointment.

*

Books of magic have a sort of life of their own. Some have altogether too much; for example, the first edition of the *Necrotelicomnicon* has to be kept between iron plates, the *True Arte of Levitatione* has spent the last one hundred and fifty years up in the rafters, and *Ge Fordge's Compenydyum of Sex Majick* is kept in a vat of ice in a room all by itself and there's a strict rule that it can only be read by wizards who are over eighty and, if possible, dead.

*

In most old libraries the books are chained to the shelves to prevent them being damaged by people. In the Library of Unseen University, of course, it's more or less the other way about.

The Librarian ambled back down the aisles. He had a face that only a lorry tyre could love.

There are eight levels of wizardry on the Disc; after sixteen years Rincewind has failed to achieve even level one. In fact it is the considered opinion of some of his tutors that he is incapable even of achieving level zero, which most normal people are *born* at; to put it another way, it has been suggested that when Rincewind dies the average occult ability of the human race will actually go up by a fraction.

*

On top of the wardrobe, wrapped in scraps of yellowing paper and old dust sheets, was a large brass-bound chest. It went by the name of the Luggage. Why it consented to be owned by Rincewind was something only the Luggage knew, and it wasn't telling, but probably no other item in the entire chronicle of travel accessories had quite such a history of mystery and grievous bodily harm. It had been described as half suitcase, half homicidal maniac. It had many unusual qualities . . . but currently there was only one that set it apart from any other brass-bound chest. It was snoring, with a sound like someone very slowly sawing a log.

*

The Luggage might be magical. It might be terrible. But in its enigmatic soul it was kin to every other piece of luggage throughout the multiverse, and preferred to spend its winters hibernating on top of a wardrobe.

*

But it wasn't the sight of the cockroaches that was so upsetting. It was the fact that they were marching in step, a hundred abreast . . . There was something particularly unpleasant about the sound of billions of very small feet hitting the stones in perfect time.

Rincewind stepped gingerly over the marching column . . . The Luggage, of course, followed them with a noise like someone tap-dancing over a bag of crisps.

*

There was a lot of beer about. Here and there red-faced wizards were happily singing ancient drinking songs which involved a lot of knee-slapping and cries of 'Ho!' The only possible excuse for this sort of thing is that wizards are celibate, and have to find their amusement where they can.

*

The higher levels of wizardry are a perilous place. Every wizard is trying to dislodge the wizards above him while stamping on the fingers of those below; to say that wizards are healthily competitive by nature is like saying that piranhas are naturally a little peckish.

*

One of Rincewind's tutors had said of him that 'to call his understanding of magical theory *abysmal* is to leave no suitable word to describe his grasp of its practice'.

*

The reason that wizards didn't rule the Disc was quite simple. Hand any two wizards a piece of rope and they would instinctively pull in opposite directions. Something about their genetics or their training left them with an attitude towards mutual co-operation that made an old bull elephant with terminal toothache look like a worker ant.

*

The last thing Rincewind saw before he was dragged away was the Librarian. Despite looking like a hairy rubber sack full of water, the orang-utan had the weight and reach of any man in the room and was currently sitting on a guard's shoulders and trying, with reasonable success, to unscrew his head.

*

'I said come on,' she repeated. 'What are you afraid of?'

Rincewind took a deep breath. 'Murderers, muggers, thieves, assassins, pickpockets, cutpurses, reevers, snigsmen, rapists and robbers,' he said.

Down these mean streets a man must walk, he thought. And along some of them he will break into a run.

It might be thought that the Mended Drum was a seedy disreputable tavern. In fact it was a *reputable* disreputable tavern. Its customers had a certain rough-hewn respectability – they might murder each other in an easygoing way, as between equals, but they didn't do it vindictively. A child could go in for a glass of lemonade and be certain of getting nothing worse than a clip round the ear when his mother heard his expanded vocabulary. On quiet nights, and when he was certain the Librarian wasn't going to come in, the landlord was even known to put bowls of peanuts on the bar.

*

'Is he a fair and just ruler?'

'I would say that he is unfair and unjust, but scrupulously even-handed. He is unfair and unjust to everyone, without fear or favour.'

*

The current Patrician, head of the extremely rich and powerful Vetinari family, was thin, tall and apparently as cold-blooded as a dead penguin. Just by looking at him you could tell he was the sort of man you'd expect to keep a white cat, and caress it idly while sentencing people to death in a piranha tank; and you'd hazard for good measure that he probably collected rare thin porcelain, turning it over and over in his blue-white fingers while distant screams echoed from the depths of the dungeons. You wouldn't put it past him to use the word 'exquisite' and have thin lips. He looked the kind of person who, when they blink, you mark it off on the calendar.

Practically none of this was in fact the case, although he did have a small and exceedingly elderly wire-haired terrier called Wuffles that smelled badly and wheezed at people. It was said to be the only thing in the entire world he truly cared about. He did of course sometimes have people horribly tortured to death, but this was considered to be perfectly acceptable behaviour for a civic ruler and generally approved of by the overwhelming majority of citizens. The people of Ankh are of a practical persuasion, and felt that the Patrician's edict forbidding all street theatre and mime artists made up for a lot of things. He didn't administer a reign of terror, just the occasional light shower.

*

'I can't swim,' [said Rincewind.]

'What, not a stroke?'

'About how deep is the sea here, would you say? Approximately?' he said.

'About a dozen fathoms, I believe.'

'Then I could probably swim about a dozen fathoms, whatever they are.'

*

Abrim laughed. It wasn't a nice sound. It sounded as though he had had laughter explained to him, probably slowly and repeatedly, but had never heard anyone actually do it.

*

'They'll throw you into a seraglio!'

Conina shrugged. 'Could be worse.'

'But it's got all these spikes and when they shut the door—' hazarded Rincewind.

'That's not a seraglio. That's an Iron Maiden. Don't you know what a seraglio is?'

'Um . . .'

She told him. He went crimson.

*

It was said that everything in Ankh-Morpork was for sale except for the beer and the women, both of which one merely hired.

*

Of course, Ankh-Morpork's citizens had always claimed that the river water was incredibly pure in any case. Any water that had passed through so many kidneys, they reasoned, had to be very pure indeed.

*

The shape of DNA, it is popularly said, owes its discovery to the chance sight of a spiral staircase when the scientist's mind was just at the right receptive temperature. Had he used the lift, the whole science of genetics might have been a good deal different.†

*

In the bathtub of history the truth is harder to hold than the soap, and much more difficult to find . . .

†Although, possibly, quicker. And only licensed to carry fourteen people.

*

'Death walks abroad,' added Nijel helpfully.

'Abroad I don't mind,' said Rincewind. 'They're all foreigners. It's Death walking around here I'm not looking forward to.'

*

'If we get a chance,' whispered Rincewind to Nijel, 'we run, right?'

'Where to?'

'From,' said Rincewind, 'the important word is *from*.'

*

Nijel was one of those people who, if you say 'don't look now', would immediately swivel his head like an owl on a turntable. These are the same people who, when you point out, say, an unusual crocus just beside them, turn round aimlessly and put their foot down with a sad little squashy noise. If they were lost in a trackless desert you could find them by putting down, somewhere on the sand, something small and fragile like a valuable old mug that had been in your family for generations, and then hurrying back as soon as you heard the crash.

*

Rincewind tries to explain a wizard's inbuilt desire to construct a tower:

'Wizards always used to build a tower around themselves, like those . . . what do you call those things you find at the bottom of rivers?'

'Frogs.'

'Stones.'

'Unsuccessful gangsters.'

'Caddis flies is what I meant,' said Rincewind.

*

Rincewind wasn't very good at precognition; in fact he could barely see into the present.

*

There came a thunderous knock at the door.

There is a mantra to be said on these occasions. It doesn't matter if the door is a tent flap, a scrap of hide on a wind-blown yurt, three inches of solid oak with great iron nails in or a rectangle of chipboard with mahogany veneer, a small light over it made of horrible bits of coloured glass and a bellpush that plays a choice of twenty popular melodies that no music lover would want to listen to even after five years' sensory deprivation.

One wizard turned to another and duly said: 'I wonder who that can be at this time of night?'

*

The astro-philosophers of Krull once succeeded in proving conclusively that all places are one place and that the distance between them is an illusion, and this news was an embarrassment to all thinking philosophers because it did not explain, among other things, signposts. After years of wrangling the whole thing was then turned over to Ly Tin Wheedle, arguably the Disc's greatest philosopher, who after some thought proclaimed that although it was indeed true that all places were one place, that place was *very large*.

*

The Four Horsemen of the Disc's Apocralypse have had three of their horses stolen while they were in an inn.

WEIGHT DOESN'T COME INTO IT. MY STEED HAS CARRIED ARMIES. MY STEED HAS CARRIED CITIES. YEA, HE HATH CARRIED ALL THINGS IN THEIR DUE TIME, said Death. BUT HE'S NOT GOING TO CARRY YOU THREE.

'Why not?'

IT'S A MATTER OF THE LOOK OF THE THING.

'It's going to look pretty good, then, isn't it,' said War testily, 'the One Horseman and Three Pedestrians of the Apocralypse.'

*

'If we're going to die anyway, I'd rather die like this. Heroically,' [said Nijel.]

'Is it heroic to die like this?' said Conina.

'*I* think it is,' he said, 'and when it comes to dying, there's only one opinion that matters.'

WYRD SISTERS

WITCHES are not by nature gregarious, and they certainly don't have leaders. Granny Weatherwax was the most highly regarded of the leaders they didn't have. But even she found that meddling in royal politics was a lot more difficult than certain playwrights would have you believe . . .

Granny Weatherwax paused with a second scone halfway to her mouth.

'Something comes,' she said.

'Can you tell by the pricking of your thumbs?' said Magrat earnestly. Magrat had learned a lot about witchcraft from books.

'The pricking of my ears,' said Granny.

*

'I didn't become a soldier for this. Not to go round killing people.'

*

'If I was you, I'd become a sailor,' said Granny thoughtfully. 'Yes, a nautical career. I should start as soon as possible. Now, in fact. Run off, man. Run off to sea where there are no tracks. You will have a long and successful life, I promise.' She looked thoughtful for a moment, and added, 'At least, longer than it's likely to be if you hang around here.'

*

Lancre Castle was built on an outcrop of rock by an architect who had heard about Gormenghast but hadn't got the budget. He'd done his best, though, with a tiny confection of cut-price turrets, bargain basements, buttresses, crenellations, gargoyles, towers, courtyards, keeps and dungeons; in fact, just about everything a castle needs except maybe reasonable foundations and the kind of mortar that doesn't wash away in a light shower.

*

'There is a knocking without,' the porter said.

'Without what?' said the Fool.

'Without the door, idiot.'

The Fool gave him a worried look. 'A knocking without a door?' he said suspiciously. 'This isn't some kind of Zen, is it?'

*

'How many times have you thrown a magic ring into the deepest depths of the ocean and then, when you get home and have a nice bit of turbot for your tea, there it is?'

They considered this in silence.

'Never,' said Granny irritably. 'And nor have you.'

*

It was one of the few sorrows of Granny Weatherwax's life that, despite all her efforts, she'd arrived at the peak of her career with a complexion like a rosy apple and all her teeth. No amount of charms could persuade a wart to take root on her handsome if slightly equine features, and vast intakes of sugar only served to give her boundless energy.

*

Granny explains her view on the proposition that replicas can be more convincing than the real thing:

'Things that try to look like things often do look more like things than things.'

*

The best you could say for Magrat was that she was decently plain and well-scrubbed and as flat-chested as an ironing board with a couple of peas on it.

*

The duke has sent some guards to arrest a witch. They come back empty-handed.

'Admit it – she offered you hedonistic and licentious pleasures known only to those who dabble in the carnal arts, didn't she?'

'No, sir. She offered me a bun.'

'A bun?'

'Yes, sir. It had currants in it.'

Felmet sat absolutely still while he fought for internal peace. Finally, all he could manage was, 'And what did your men do about this?'

'They had a bun too, sir. All except young Roger, who isn't allowed fruit, sir, on account of his trouble. He had a biscuit, sir.'

*

'Fool?'

'Marry, sir—' said the Fool nervously.

'I am already extremely married. Advise me, my Fool.'

'I'faith, nuncle—' said the Fool.

'Nor am I thy nuncle. I feel sure I would have remembered,' said Lord Felmet, leaning down until the prow of his nose was a few inches from the Fool's stricken face. 'If you preface your next remark with nuncle, i'faith or marry, it will go hard with you.'

'How do you feel about Prithee?'

The duke knew when to allow some slack. 'Prithee I can live with,' he said. 'So can you.'

*

Magrat tried. Every morning her hair was long, thick and blond, but by the evening it had always returned to its normal worried frizz. To ameliorate the effect she had tried to plait violets and cowslips in it. The result was not all she had hoped. It gave the impression that a window box had fallen on her head.

*

The Fool fumbled in his sleeve and produced a rather soiled red and yellow handkerchief embroidered with bells. The duke took it with an expression of pathetic gratitude and blew his nose. Then he held it away from him and gazed at it with demented suspicion.

'Is this a dagger I see before me?' he mumbled.

'Um. No, my lord. It's my handkerchief, you see. You can sort of tell the difference if you look closely. It doesn't have as many sharp edges.'

*

On the crest of the moor . . . was a standing stone . . .

The stone was about the same height as a tall man, and made of a bluish tinted rock. It was considered intensely magical because, although there was only one of it, *no one had ever been able to count it.*

*

Granny, Nanny and Magrat have summoned a demon.

'Who're you?' said Granny, bluntly.

'My name is unpronounceable in your tongue, woman,' it said.

'I'll be the judge of that,' warned Granny.

'Very well. My name is WxrtHltl-jwlpklz,' said the demon smugly.

'We haven't got time to bandy legs with you all night,' said Granny.

Magrat blurted out, 'You know the Fool, who lives up at the castle?' . . .

'It's a steady job,' said Nanny. 'I'll grant you that.'

'Huh,' said Granny. 'A man who tinkles all day. No kind of husband for anyone, I'd say.'

*

Nanny Ogg was also out early. She hadn't been able to get any sleep anyway, and besides, she was worried about Greebo. Greebo was one of her few blind spots. While intellectually she would concede that he was indeed a fat, cunning, evil-smelling multiple rapist, she nevertheless instinctively pictured him as the small fluffy kitten he had been decades before. The fact that he had once chased a female wolf up a tree and seriously surprised a she-bear who had been innocently digging for roots didn't stop her worrying that something bad might happen to him. It was generally considered by everyone else in the kingdom that the only thing that might slow Greebo down was a direct meteorite strike.

*

The books said that the old-time witches had sometimes danced in their shifts. Magrat had wondered about how you danced in shifts. Perhaps there wasn't room for them all to dance at once, she'd thought.

*

Nanny Ogg is being held captive in a torture chamber.

The duchess leaned forward until her big red face was inches away from Nanny's nose.

'This insouciance gives you pleasure,' she hissed, 'but soon you will laugh on the other side of your face!'

'It's only got this side,' said Nanny.

The duchess fingered a tray of implements lovingly. 'We shall see,' she said, picking up a pair of pliers.

*

'It's gone too far this time,' said a peasant. 'All this burning and taxing and now this. I blame you witches. It's got to stop. I know my rights.'

'What rights are they?' said Granny.

'Dunnage, cowhage-in-ordinary, badinage, leftovers, scrommidge, clary and spunt,' said the peasant promptly. 'And acornage, every other year, and the right to keep two-thirds of a goat on the common. Until he set fire to it. It was a bloody good goat, too.'

*

Hour gongs were being struck all across the city and nightwatchmen were proclaiming that it was indeed midnight and also that, in the face of all the evidence, all was well. Many of them got as far as the end of the sentence before being mugged.

*

The River Ankh, the cloaca of half a continent, was already pretty wide and silt laden when it reached the city's outskirts. By the time it left it didn't so much flow as exude. Owing to the accretion of the mud of centuries the bed of the river was in fact higher than some of the low lying areas and now, with the snow melt swelling the flow, many of the low-rent districts on the Morpork side were flooded, if you can use that word for a liquid you could pick up in a net.

*

'You know, Hwel, I reckon responsible behaviour is something to get when you grow older. Like varicose veins.'

*

Vitoller shifted uneasily. 'I already owe Chrystophrase the Troll more than I should.'

'He's the one that has people's limbs torn off!' said Tomjon.

'How much do you owe him?' said Hwel.

'An arm and a leg.'

*

The dwarf playwright Hwel is leaving actor-manager Vitoller's company.

'I'll miss you, laddie. I don't mind telling you. You've been like a son to me. How old are you, exactly? I never did know.'

'A hundred and two.'

'You've been like a father to me, then,' Vitoller said.

*

'When's this play going to be, then?' Magrat said, moving closer.

'Marry, I'm sure I'm not allowed to tell you,' said the Fool. 'The duke said to me, he said, don't tell the witches that it's tomorrow night.'

'I shouldn't, then,' agreed Magrat.

'At eight o'clock.'

'I see.'

'But meet for sherry beforehand at seven-thirty, i'faith.'

*

Nanny . . . leaned towards the empty seat. 'Walnut?'

'No, thank you,' said King Verence [a ghost], waving a spectral hand. 'They go right through me, you know.'

PYRAMIDS

BEING trained by the Assassins' Guild in Ankh-Morpork did not fit Teppic for the task assigned to him by fate. He inherited the throne of the desert kingdom of Djelibeybi rather earlier than he expected (his father wasn't too happy about it either), but that was only the beginning of his problems...

All assassins had a full-length mirror in their rooms, because it would be a terrible insult to anyone to kill them when you were badly dressed.

*

He . . . had also heard that only one student in fifteen actually became an assassin. He wasn't entirely certain what happened to the other fourteen, but he was pretty sure that if you were a poor student in a school for assassins they did a bit more than throw the chalk at you, and that the school dinners had an extra dimension of uncertainty.

*

Djelibeybi really was a small, self-centred kingdom. Even its plagues were half-hearted. All self-respecting river kingdoms have vast supernatural plagues, but the best the Old Kingdom had been able to achieve in the last hundred years was the Plague of Frog.†

*

It was said that life was cheap in Ankh-Morpork. This was, of course, completely wrong. Life was often very expensive; you could get death for free.

*

'What's your name, kiddo?'

Teppic drew himself up. 'Kiddo? I'll have you know the blood of pharaohs runs in my veins!'

The other boy looked at him unabashed, with his head on one side and a faint smile on his face.

'Would you like it to stay there?' he said.

[My mother] died when I was young . . . She went for a moonlight swim in what turned out to be a crocodile.

. . . Ptraci, his favourite handmaiden. She was *special*. Her singing always cheered him up. Life seemed so much brighter when she stopped.

*

The Ankh . . . drained the huge silty plains all the way to the Ramtop mountains, and by the time it had passed through Ankh-Morpork, pop. one million, it could only be called a liquid because it moved faster than the land around it; being sick in it would probably make it, on average, marginally cleaner.

† It was quite a big frog, however, and got into the air ducts and kept everyone awake for weeks.

*

One of the two legends about the founding of Ankh-Morpork relates that the two orphaned brothers who built the city were in fact found and suckled by a hippopotamus.

The other legend, not normally recounted by the citizens, is that at an even earlier time a group of wise men survived a flood sent by the gods by building a huge boat, and on this boat they took two of every type of animal then existing on the Disc. After some weeks the combined manure was beginning to weigh the boat low in the water so – the story runs – they tipped it over the side, and called it Ankh-Morpork.

*

'Cats are sacred,' said Dios.

'Long-legged cats with silver fur and disdainful expressions are, maybe,' said Teppic. 'I'm sure sacred cats don't leave dead ibises under the bed. And I'm certain that sacred cats that live surrounded by endless sand don't come indoors and do it in the king's sandals, Dios.'

*

Descendants! The gods had seen fit to give him one son who charged you for the amount of breath expended in saying 'Good morning', and another one who worshipped geometry and stayed up all night designing aqueducts. You scrimped and saved to send them to the best schools, and then they went and paid you back by getting educated.

*

'Why are you here?'

The man hung his head. 'I spoke blasphemy against the king.'

'How did you do that?'

'I dropped a rock on my foot. Now my tongue is to be torn out.'

The dark figure nodded sympathetically.

'A priest heard you, did he?' he said.

'No. I told a priest. Such words should not go unpunished,' said the man virtuously.

The old king told me once that the gods gave people a sense of humour to make up for giving them sex.

It's a fact as immutable as the Third Law of Sod that there is no such thing as a good Grand Vizier. A predilection to cackle and plot is apparently part of the job spec.

*

'Would your sire still be honouring us with the capping-out ceremony? There's drinks,' Ptaclusp stuttered. 'And a silver trowel that you can take away with you. Everyone shouts hurrah and throws their hats in the air.'

'Certainly,' said Dios. 'It will be an honour.'

'And for us too, your sire,' said Ptaclusp loyally.

'I *meant* for you,' said the high priest.

*

Pyramids are dams in the stream of time. Correctly shaped and orientated, with the proper paracosmic measurements correctly plumbed in, the temporal potential of the great mass of stone can be diverted to accelerate or reverse time over a very small area, in the same way that a hydraulic ram can be induced to pump water *against the flow*.

The original builders, who were of course ancients and therefore wise, knew this very well and the whole point of a correctly built pyramid was to achieve absolute null time in the central chamber so that a dying king, tucked up there, would indeed live forever – or at least, never actually die. The time that should have passed in the chamber was stored in the bulk of the pyramid and allowed to flare off once every twenty-four hours.

After a few aeons people forgot this and thought you could achieve the same effect by a) ritual b) pickling people and c) storing their soft inner bits in jars.

This seldom works.

He . . . liked my singing. Everyone else said it sounded like a flock of vultures who've just found a dead donkey.

He knew about tortoises. They could be called a lot of things – vegetarians, patient, thoughtful, even extremely diligent and persistent sex-maniacs – but never, up until now, fast. Fast was a word particularly associated with tortoises because they were not it.

*

The fastest *insect* is the .303 bookworm. It evolved in magical libraries, where it is necessary to eat extremely quickly to avoid being affected by the thaumic radiations. An adult .303 bookworm can eat through a shelf of books so fast that it ricochets off the wall.

*

Kings who hadn't got a kingdom any more were not likely to be very popular in neighbouring countries. There had been one or two like that in Ankh-Morpork – deposed royalty, who had fled their suddenly dangerous kingdoms . . . carrying nothing but the clothes they stood up in and a few wagonloads of jewels. The city, of course, welcomed anyone – regardless of race, colour, class or creed – who had spending money in incredible amounts, but nevertheless the inhumation of surplus monarchs was a regular source of work for the Assassins' Guild. There was always someone back home who wanted to be certain that deposed monarchs stayed that way. It was usually a case of heir today, gone tomorrow.

The Ephebians made wine out of anything they could put in a bucket, and ate anything that couldn't climb out of one.

He pushed the food around on his plate. Some of it pushed back.

'The diameter divides into the circumference, you know. It ought to be three times. But does it? No. Three point one four one and lots of other figures. There's no end to the buggers . . . It tells me that the Creator used the wrong kind of circles.'

*

Someone was just putting a torch to the lighthouse, which was one of the More Than Seven Wonders of the World and had been built to a design by Pthagonal using the Golden Rule and the Five Aesthetic Principles. Unfortunately it had then been built in the wrong place because putting it in the right place would have spoiled the look of the harbour, but it was generally agreed by mariners to be a very beautiful lighthouse and something to look at while they were waiting to be towed off the rocks.

*

Ptraci didn't just derail the train of thought, she ripped up the rails, burned the stations and melted the bridges for scrap.

*

It was another nice day in the high desert. It was always a nice day, if by nice you meant an air temperature like an oven and sand you could roast chestnuts on.

*

It is now known to science that there are many more dimensions than the classical four. Scientists say that these don't normally impinge on the world because the extra dimensions are very small and curve in on themselves, and that since reality is fractal most of it is tucked inside itself. This means either that the universe is more full of wonders than we can hope to understand or, more probably, that scientists make things up as they go along.

*

Teppic takes a novel approach to the age-old Riddle of the Sphinx:

'What goes on four legs in the morning, two legs at noon, and three legs in the evening?' said the Sphinx smugly.

Teppic considered this.

'That's a tough one,' he said, eventually.

'You'll never get it.'

'You're right.' Teppic stared at the claws.

'The answer is: "A Man",' said the Sphinx.

'What do you mean, a man?'

'It's easy,' said the Sphinx. 'A baby crawls in the morning, stands on both legs at noon, and at evening an old man walks with a stick. Good, isn't it?'

Teppic bit his lip. 'We're talking about *one day* here?' he said doubtfully.

There was a long, embarrassing silence.

'It's a wossname, a figure of speech,' said the Sphinx irritably. 'Nothing wrong with the riddle. Damn good riddle. Had that riddle for fifty years, sphinx and cub.' It thought about this. 'Chick,' it corrected.

'It's a good riddle,' Teppic said soothingly. 'But is there internal consistency within the metaphor? Let's say for example that the average life expectancy is seventy years, okay?'

'Okay,' said the Sphinx, in the uncertain tones of someone who has let the salesman in and is now regretfully contemplating a future in which they are undoubtedly going to buy life insurance.

'*Right*. Good. So noon would be age 35, am I right? Now considering that most children can toddle at a year or so, the four legs reference is really unsuitable, wouldn't you agree? I mean, most of the morning is spent on two legs. According to your analogy . . . only about twenty minutes immediately after 00.00 hours, half an hour tops, is spent on four legs. Am I right? Be fair.'

'Well—' said the Sphinx.

'By the same token you wouldn't be using a stick by six p.m. because you'd be only, er, 52,' said Teppic, scribbling furiously. 'In fact you wouldn't really be looking at any kind of walking aid until at least half past nine, I think . . . I'm sorry, it's basically okay, but it doesn't work . . . You just need to alter it a bit, that's all.'

'Okay,' it said doubtfully. 'I suppose I could ask: What is it that walks on four legs—'

'Metaphorically speaking,' said Teppic.

'Four legs, metaphorically speaking,' the Sphinx agreed, 'for about—'

'Twenty minutes, I think we agreed.'

'—okay, fine, twenty minutes in the morning, on two legs—'

'But I think calling it "in the morning" is stretching it a bit,' said Teppic. 'It's just after midnight. I mean, technically it's the morning, but in a very real sense it's still last night . . . Let's just see where we've got to, shall we? What, metaphorically speaking, walks on four legs just after midnight, on two legs for most of the day—'

'—barring accidents,' said the Sphinx, pathetically eager to show that it was making a contribution.

'Fine, on two legs barring accidents, until at least suppertime, when it walks with three legs—'

'I've known people use two walking sticks,' said the Sphinx helpfully.

'Okay. How about: when it continues to walk on two legs or with any prosthetic aids of its choice?'

The Sphinx gave this some consideration.

'Ye–ess,' it said gravely. 'That seems to fit all eventualities.'

*

The city of the dead lay before Teppic. After Ankh-Morpork, which was almost its direct opposite (in Ankh, even the bedding was alive) it was probably the biggest city on the Disc.

GUARDS! GUARDS!

THIS is where the dragons went. They lie ... not dead, not asleep, but ... dormant. And although the space they occupy isn't like normal space, nevertheless they are packed in tightly. They could put you in mind of a can of sardines, if you thought sardines were huge and scaly. And presumably, somewhere, there's a key ...

The Library was the greatest assemblage of magical texts anywhere in the multiverse. Thousands of volumes of occult lore weighted its shelves.

It was said that, since vast amounts of magic can seriously distort the mundane world, the Library did not obey the normal rules of space and time. It was said that it went on *forever*. It was said that you could wander for days among the distant shelves, and that there were lost tribes of research students somewhere in there.

Wise students in search of more distant volumes took care to leave chalk marks on the shelves as they roamed deeper into the fusty darkness, and told friends to come looking for them if they weren't back by supper.

*

Not many people these days remarked upon the fact that the Librarian was an ape. The change had been brought about by a magical accident, always a possibility where so many powerful books are kept together, and he was considered to have got off lightly. After all, he was still basically the same shape. And he had been allowed to keep his job, which he was rather good at, although 'allowed' is not really the right word. It was the way he could roll his upper lip back to reveal more incredibly yellow teeth than any other mouth the University Council had ever seen before that somehow made sure the matter was never really raised.

*

The figure rapped a complex code on the dark woodwork. A tiny barred hatch opened and one suspicious eye peered out.

' "The significant owl hoots in the night," ' said the visitor, trying to wring the rainwater out of its robe.

' "Yet many grey lords go sadly to the masterless men," ' intoned a voice on the other side of the grille.

' "Hooray, hooray for the spinster's sister's daughter," ' countered the dripping figure.

' "To the axeman, all supplicants are the same height." '

' "Yet verily, the rose is within the thorn." '

' "The good mother makes bean soup for the errant boy," ' said the voice behind the door.

There was a pause, broken only by the sound of the rain. Then the visitor said, 'What?'

' "The good mother makes bean soup for the errant boy." '

There was another, longer pause. Then the damp figure said, 'Are you sure the ill-built tower doesn't tremble mightily at a butterfly's passage?'

'Nope. Bean soup it is. I'm sorry.'

'What about the cagèd whale?' said the soaking visitor, trying to squeeze into what little shelter the dread portal offered.

'What about it?'

'It should know nothing of the mighty deeps, if you must know.'

'*Oh*, the cagèd *whale*. You want the *Elucidated* Brethren of the Ebon Night. Three doors down.'

*

The Supreme Grand Master rapped his gavel for attention. 'I call the Unique and Supreme Lodge of the Elucidated Brethren to order,' he intoned. 'Is the Door of Knowledge sealed fast against heretics and knowlessmen?'

'Stuck solid,' said Brother Doorkeeper. 'It's the damp. I'll bring my plane in next week, soon have it—'

'All right, all *right*,' said the Supreme Grand Master testily. 'Just a yes would have done.'

*

Minor thief Zebbo Mooty has just been incinerated by a dragon.

'Do you know, a fortune-teller once told me I'd die in my bed, surrounded by grieving great-grandchildren,' said Mooty. 'What do you think of that, eh?'

I THINK SHE WAS WRONG.

*

The Patrician nodded.

'I shall deal with the matter momentarily,' he said. It was a good word. It always made people hesitate. They were never quite sure whether he meant he'd deal with it *now*, or just deal with it *briefly*. And no one ever dared ask.

*

You came to [the Patrician] with a perfectly reasonable complaint. Next thing you knew, you were shuffling out backwards, bowing and scraping, relieved simply to be getting away. You had to hand it to the Patrician, he admitted grudgingly. If you didn't, he sent men to come and take it away.

The Patrician gave him a sweet smile. 'Thank you for coming to see me. Don't hesitate to leave.'

The Watch hadn't liked it, but the plain fact was that the thieves were far better at controlling crime than the Watch had ever been. After all, the Watch had to work twice as hard to cut crime just a little, whereas all the Thieves' Guild had to do was to work less.

*

The only reason you couldn't say that Nobby was close to the animal kingdom was that the animal kingdom would get up and walk away.

*

Nobby was a small, bandy-legged man, with a certain resemblance to a chimpanzee who never got invited to tea parties.

*

Sergeant Colon owed thirty years of happy marriage to the fact that Mrs Colon worked all day and Sergeant Colon worked all night. They communicated by means of notes. He got her tea ready before he left at night, she left his breakfast nice and hot in the oven in the mornings. They had three grown-up children, all born, Vimes had assumed, as a result of extremely persuasive handwriting.

*

You could describe Sergeant Colon like this: he was the sort of man who, if he took up a military career, would automatically gravitate to the post of sergeant. You couldn't imagine him ever being a corporal. Or, for that matter, a captain. If he didn't take up a military career, then he looked cut out for something like, perhaps, a sausage butcher; some job where a big red face and a tendency to sweat even in frosty weather were practically part of the specification.

*

Every town in the multiverse has a part that is something like Ankh-Morpork's Shades. It's a sort of black hole of bred-in-the-brickwork lawlessness. Put it like this: even the *criminals* were afraid to walk the streets.

*

You need a special kind of mind to rule a city like Ankh-Morpork, and Lord Vetinari had it. But then, he was a special kind of person.

You had to get up very early in the morning to get the better of the Patrician; in fact, it was wiser not to go to bed at all.

But he was popular, in a way. Under his hand, for the first time in a thousand years, Ankh-Morpork *operated*. It might not be fair or just or particularly democratic, but it worked. It was said that he would tolerate absolutely anything apart from anything that threatened the city† . . .

Ankh-Morpork!

Brawling city of a hundred thousand souls! And, as the Patrician privately observed, ten times that number of actual people.

From a high point of vantage, Ankh-Morpork looked as though someone had tried to achieve in stone and wood an effect normally associated with the pavements outside all-night takeaways.

† And mime artists. It was a strange aversion, but there you are. Anyone in baggy trousers and a white face who tried to ply their art anywhere within Ankh's crumbling walls would very quickly find themselves in a scorpion pit, on one wall of which was painted the advice: Learn The Words.

*

The Librarian rolled his eyes. It was strange, he felt, that so-called intelligent dogs, horses and dolphins never had any difficulty indicating to humans the vital news of the moment, e.g., that the three children were lost in the cave, or the train was about to take the line leading to the bridge that had been washed away or similar, while he, only a handful of chromosomes away from wearing a vest, found it difficult to persuade the average human to come in out of the rain.

*

'A book has been taken. A book has been taken? You summoned the Watch,' Carrot drew himself up proudly, 'because someone's taken a *book*? You think that's worse than murder?'

The Librarian gave him the kind of look other people would reserve for people who said things like 'What's so bad about genocide?'

*

Jimkin Bearhugger's Old Selected Dragon's Blood Whiskey. Cheap and powerful, you could light fires with it, you could clean spoons. You didn't have to drink much of it to be drunk, which was just as well.

*

It was the usual Ankh-Morpork mob in times of crisis; half of them were here to complain, a quarter of them were here to watch the other half, and the remainder were here to rob, importune or sell hot-dogs to the rest.

*

Vimes looked into the grinning, cadaverous face of Cut-Me-Own-Throat Dibbler, purveyor of absolutely anything that could be sold hurriedly from an open suitcase in a busy street and was guaranteed to have fallen off the back of an oxcart.

*

'Anti-dragon cream. Personal guarantee: if you're incinerated you get your money back, no quibble.'

'What you're saying,' said Vimes slowly, 'if I understand the wording correctly, is that if I am baked alive by the dragon you'll return the money?'

'Upon personal application,' said Cut-Me-Own-Throat.

*

Vimes'd had a look at Cut-Me-Own-Throat Dibbler's dragon detectors, which consisted solely of a piece of wood on a metal stick. When the stick was burned through, you'd found your dragon. Like a lot of Cut-Me-Own-Throat's devices, it was completely efficient in its own special way while at the same time being totally useless.

*

Ankh-Morpork did not have many hospitals. All the Guilds maintained their own sanitariums, but by and large medical assistance was nonexistent and people had to die inefficiently, without the aid of doctors. It was generally thought that the existence of cures encouraged slackness and was in any case probably against Nature's way.

It was a plate stacked high with bacon, fried potatoes and eggs. Vimes could hear his arteries panic just by looking at it.

Captain Vimes limped forward from the shadows.

A small and extremely frightened golden dragon was clamped firmly under one arm. His other hand held it by the tail.

The rioters watched it, hypnotized.

'Now I know what you're thinking,' Vimes went on, softly. 'You're wondering, after all this excitement, has it got enough flame left? And, y'know, I ain't so sure myself . . .'

He leaned forward, sighting between the dragon's ears, and his voice buzzed like a knife blade:

'What you've got to ask yourself is: Am I feeling lucky?'

*

Vimes gave his men his usual look of resigned dismay.

'My squad,' he mumbled.

'Fine body of men,' said Lady Ramkin. 'The good old rank and file, eh?'

'The rank, anyway,' said Vimes.

*

It is difficult for an orang-utan to stand to attention. Its body can master the general idea, but its skin can't. The Librarian was doing his best, however, standing in a sort of respectful heap at the end of the line and maintaining the kind of complex salute you can only achieve with a four-foot arm.

*

'Do you think picking someone up by their ankles and bouncing their head on the floor comes under the heading of Striking a Superior Officer?' said Carrot.

*

'Ah, pageantry,' said the monarchist, pointing with his pipe. 'Very important. Lots of spectacles.'

'What, free?' said Throat.

'We–ell, I think maybe you have to pay for the frames,' said the monarchist.

*

Books bend space and time. One reason the owners of those aforesaid little rambling, poky second-hand bookshops always seem slightly unearthly is that many of them really *are*, having strayed into this world after taking a wrong turning in their own bookshops in worlds where it is considered commendable business practice to wear carpet slippers all the time and open your shop only when you feel like it. You stray into L-space at your peril.

*

The truth is that even big collections of ordinary books distort space, as can readily be proved by anyone who has been around a really old-fashioned second-hand bookshop, one of those that look as though they were designed by M. Escher on a bad day and have more staircases than storeys and those rows of shelves which end in little doors that are surely too small for a full-sized human to enter. The relevant equation is: Knowledge = power = energy = matter = mass; a good bookshop is just a genteel Black Hole that knows how to read.

*

People were stupid, sometimes. They thought the Library was a dangerous place because of all the magical books, which was true enough, but what made it really one of the most dangerous places there could ever be was the simple fact that it was a library.

Energy equals matter . . .
Matter equals mass.

And mass distorts space. It distorts it into polyfractal L-space.

So, while the Dewey system has its fine points, when you're setting out to look something up in the multidimensional folds of L-space what you really need is a ball of string.

*

The three rules of the Librarians of Time and Space are: 1) Silence; 2) Books must be returned no later than the last date shown; and 3) Do not interfere with the nature of causality.

*

The Summoning of Dragons. Single copy, first edition, slightly foxed and extremely dragoned.

*

Vimes strolled along for breakfast at Harga's House of Ribs. Normally the only decoration in there was on Sham Harga's vest and the food was good solid stuff for a cold morning, all calories and fat and protein and maybe a vitamin crying softly because it was all alone.

*

Time could bifurcate, like a pair of trousers. You could end up in the wrong leg, living a life that was actually happening in the *other* leg, talking to people who weren't in your leg, walking into walls that weren't there any more. Life could be horrible in the wrong trouser of Time.

*

'Never build a dungeon you wouldn't be happy to spend the night in yourself,' said the Patrician.

*

Vimes landed in damp straw and also in pitch darkness.

Never trust any ruler who puts his faith in tunnels and bunkers and escape routes. The chances are that his heart isn't in the job.

Eventually Great A'Tuin would reach the end of the universe. Eventually the stars would go out. Eventually Nobby might have a bath, although that would probably involve a radical rethinking of the nature of Time.

*

'Oh, you think you're so clever, so in-control, so *swave*, just because I've got a sword and you haven't!'

*

The Patrician steepled his hands and looked at Vimes over the top of them.

'Let me give you some advice, Captain,' he said. 'It may help you make some sense of the world. I believe you find life such a problem because you think there are the good people and the bad people. You're wrong, of course. There are, always and only, the bad people, *but some of them are on opposite sides*.'

He waved his thin hand towards the city and walked over to the window.

'A great rolling sea of evil. Shallower in some places, of course, but deeper, oh, so much *deeper* in others. But people like you put together little rafts of rules and vaguely good intentions and say, this is the opposite, this will triumph in the end. Amazing. Down there,' he said, 'are people who will follow any dragon, worship any god, ignore any iniquity. All out of a kind of humdrum, everyday badness. Not the really high, creative loathsomeness of the great sinners, but a sort of mass-produced darkness of the soul. Sin, you might say, without a trace of originality. They accept evil not because they say *yes*, but because they don't say *no*. I'm sorry if this offends you,' he added, patting the captain's shoulder, 'but you fellows really need us. We're the only ones who know how to make things work.

You see, the only thing the good people are good at is overthrowing the bad people. And you're *good* at that, I'll grant you. But the trouble is that it's the *only* thing you're good at. One day it's the ringing of the bells and the casting down of the evil tyrant, and the next it's everyone sitting around complaining that ever since the tyrant was overthrown no one's been taking out the trash. Because the bad people know how to *plan*. It's part of the specification, you might say. Every evil tyrant has a plan to rule the world. The good people don't seem to have the knack.'

ERIC

ERIC is the Discworld's only demonology hacker. Pity he's not very good at it. All he wants is his three wishes granted. Nothing fancy – to be immortal, rule the world, have the most beautiful woman in the world fall madly in love with him, the usual stuff.

But instead of a tractable demon, he calls up Rincewind, probably the most incompetent wizard in the universe, and the extremely *in*tractable and hostile form of travel accessory known as the Luggage.

With them on his side, Eric's in for a ride through space and time that is bound to make him wish (quite fervently) again – this time that he'd never been born.

Like all beekeepers, Death wore a veil.

It wasn't that he had anything to sting, but sometimes a bee would get inside his skull and buzz around and give him a headache.

No enemies had ever taken Ankh-Morpork. Well, *technically* they had, quite often; the city welcomed free-spending barbarian invaders, but somehow the puzzled raiders always found, after a few days, that they didn't own their own horses any more, and within a couple of months they were just another minority group with its own graffiti and food shops.

*

'All right. I give in. We *will* try the Rite of AshkEnte.'

The Rite of AshkEnte is the most serious ritual eight wizards can undertake. It summons Death . . .

It took place in the mid-night in the University's Great Hall, in a welter of incense, candlesticks, runic inscriptions and magic circles, none of which was strictly necessary but which made the wizards feel better. Magic flared, the chants were chanted, the invocations were truly invoked.

The wizards stared into the magic octogram, which remained empty. After a while the circle of robed figures began to mutter amongst themselves.

'We must have done something wrong.'

'Oook.'

'Maybe He is out.'

'Or busy . . .'

'Do you think we could give up and go back to bed?'

WHO ARE WE WAITING FOR, EXACTLY?

*

Rincewind wanted to say: Look, what you should do is stop all this messing around with chemicals in dark rooms and have a shave, a haircut, a bath, make that *two* baths, buy yourself a new wardrobe and get out of an evening and then – but he'd have to be honest, because even washed, shaved and soaked in body splash Thursley wasn't going to win any prizes – and then you could have your face slapped by any woman of your choice.

I mean, it wouldn't be much, but it would be body contact.

*

If there is one thing a wizard would trade his grandmother for, it is power. But . . . any wizard bright enough to survive for five minutes was also bright enough to realize that if there was any power in demonology, then it lay with the demons. Using it for your own purposes would be like trying to beat mice to death with a rattlesnake.

*

Lord Astfgl's patience, which in any case had the tensile strength of putty, snapped at this point.

*

Rincewind tried some. It was a bowl of cereal, nuts, and dried fruit. He didn't have any quarrel with any of that. It was just that somewhere in the preparation something had apparently done to these innocent ingredients what it takes a million gravities to do to a neutron star. If you died of eating this sort of thing they wouldn't have to bury you, they would just need to drop you somewhere where the ground was soft.

*

Pre-eminent amongst Rincewind's talents was his skill in running away, which over the years he had elevated to the status of a genuinely pure science; it didn't matter if you were fleeing from or to, so long as you were fleeing. It was flight alone that counted. I run, therefore I am; more correctly, I run, therefore with any luck I'll still *be*.

But he was also skilled in languages and in practical geography. He could shout 'help!' in fourteen languages and scream for mercy in a further twelve.

*

The Tezuman Empire in the jungle valleys of central Klatch is known for its organic market gardens, its exquisite craftsmanship in obsidian, feathers and jade, and its mass human sacrifices in honour of Quezovercoatl, the Feathered Boa, god of mass human sacrifices. As they said, you always knew where you stood with Quezovercoatl. It was generally with a lot of people on top of a great stepped pyramid with someone in an elegant feathered headdress chipping an exquisite obsidian knife for your very own personal use.

'Why do you keep saying wossname?' said Rincewind.

'Limited wossname. Doodah. Thingy. You know. It's got words in it,' said the parrot.

'Dictionary?' said Rincewind.

'It's their god Quezovercoatl. Half man, half chicken, half jaguar, half serpent, half scorpion and half mad.'

*

Rincewind and companions have been tied up and left.

'In fact,' said da Quirm, 'I think—' He rolled from side to side experimentally, tugging at the vines which were holding him down. 'Yes, I think when they did these ropes up – yes, definitely, they—'

'What? What?' said Rincewind.

'Yes, definitely,' said da Quirm. 'I'm absolutely sure about it. They did them up very tightly and professionally. Not an inch of give in them anywhere.'

*

They were discussing strategy when Rincewind arrived. The consensus seemed to be that if really large numbers of men were sent to storm the mountain, then enough might survive the rocks to take the citadel. This is essentially the basis of all military thinking.

*

'It's probably some kind of magic, or something,' Rincewind said. 'There's no air. That's why there's no sound. All the little bits of air sort of knock together, like marbles. That's how you get sound, you know.'

'Is it? Gosh.'

'So we're surrounded by absolutely nothing,' said Rincewind. 'Total nothing.' He hesitated. 'There's a word for it,' he said. 'It's what you get when there's nothing left and everything's been used up.'

'Yes. I think it's called the bill,' said Eric.

*

Hell, it has been suggested, is other people.

This has always come as a bit of a surprise to many working demons, who had always thought hell was sticking sharp things into people and pushing them into lakes of blood and so on.

This is because demons, like most people, have failed to distinguish between the body and the soul.

The fact was that, as droves of demon kings had noticed, there was a limit to what you could do to a soul with, e.g., red-hot tweezers, because even fairly evil and corrupt souls were bright enough to realize that since they didn't have the concomitant body and nerve endings attached to them there was no real reason, other than force of habit, why they should suffer excruciating agony. So they didn't. Demons went on doing it anyway, because numb and mindless stupidity is part of what being a demon is all about, but since no one was suffering they didn't enjoy it much either and the whole thing was pointless. Centuries and centuries of pointlessness.

*

Astfgl had achieved in hell a particularly high brand of boredom which is like the boredom you get which a) is costing you money, and b) is taking place *while you should be having a nice time.*

*

The speaker was Duke Vassenego, one of the oldest demons. How old, no one knew. But if he didn't actually invent original sin, at least he made one of the first copies.

*

Rincewind looked down at the broad steps they were climbing. They were something of a novelty; each one was built out of large stone letters. The one he was just stepping on to, for example, read: I Meant It For The Best.

The next one was: I Thought You'd Like It.

Eric was standing on: For The Sake Of The Children.

'Weird, isn't it?' he said. 'Why do it like this?'

'I think they're meant to be good intentions,' said Rincewind. This was a road to hell, and demons were, after all, traditionalists.

Old Tom was the single cracked bronze bell in the University bell tower.

The clapper dropped out shortly after it was cast, but the bell still tolled out some tremendously sonorous silences every hour.

MOVING PICTURES

THE alchemists of the Discworld have discovered the magic of the silver screen. But what is the dark secret of Holy Wood hill?

It's up to Victor Tugelbend ('Can't sing. Can't dance. Can handle a sword a little') and Theda Withel ('I come from a little town you've probably never heard of') to find out . . .

This is space. It's sometimes called the final frontier.

(Except that of course you can't have a *final* frontier, because there'd be nothing for it to be a frontier *to*, but as frontiers go, it's pretty penultimate . . .)

*

The Discworld is as unreal as it is possible to be while still being just real enough to exist.

*

There's a saying that there's a saying that all roads lead to Ankh-Morpork.

And it's wrong. All roads lead *away* from Ankh-Morpork, but sometimes people just walk along them the wrong way.

Meat pies! Hot sausages! Inna bun! So fresh the pig hasn't noticed they're gone!

Unseen University had had many different kinds of Archchancellor over the years. Big ones, small ones, cunning ones, slightly insane ones, extremely insane ones – they'd come, they'd served, in some cases not long enough for anyone to be able to complete the official painting to be hung in the Great Hall, and they'd died. The senior wizard in a world of magic had the same prospects of long-term employment as a pogo stick tester in a minefield.

*

The name might change occasionally, but what *did* matter was that there always was *an* Archchancellor . . .

At the time, it had seemed a really good idea to elect an Archchancellor who hadn't set foot in the University in forty years. A search of the records turned up Ridcully the Brown. He looked ideal . . .

A messenger had been sent. Ridcully the Brown had sighed, cursed a bit, found his staff in the kitchen garden where it had been supporting a scarecrow, and had set out.

Within twelve hours of arriving, Ridcully had installed a pack of hunting dragons in the butlers' pantry, fired his dreadful crossbow at the ravens on the ancient Tower of Art, drunk a dozen bottles of red wine, and rolled off to bed at two in the morning singing a song with words in it that some of the older and more forgetful wizards had to look up.

And then he got up at five o'clock to go duck hunting down in the marshes on the estuary.

And came back complaining that there wasn't a good trout fishin' river for miles. (You couldn't fish in the river Ankh; you had to jump up and down on the hooks even to make them sink.)

And he ordered beer with his breakfast.

And told *jokes*.

On the other hand, at least he didn't interfere with the actual running of the University. Ridcully the Brown wasn't the least interested in running anything except maybe a string of hounds. If you couldn't shoot arrows at it, hunt it or hook it, he couldn't see much point in it.

*

A full moon glided above the smoke and fumes of Ankh-Morpork, thankful that several thousand miles of sky lay between it and them.

The Alchemists' Guildhall was new. It was always new.

It had been explosively demolished and rebuilt four times in the last two years, on the last occasion without a lecture and demonstration room in the hope that this might be a helpful move.

By and large, the only skill the alchemists of Ankh-Morpork had discovered so far was the ability to turn gold into less gold.

*

The Patrician's stare had him pinned. It was a good stare, and one of the things it was good at was making people go on talking when they thought they had finished.

*

'Well, what you do is, you take some corn, and you put it in, say, a Number 3 crucible, with some cooking oil, you see, and then you put a plate or something on top of it, and when you heat it up it goes bang, I mean, not *seriously* bang, and when it's stopped banging you take the plate off and it's metamorphosed into these, er, things . . . If you put butter and salt on it, it tastes like salty butter . . . I just call it banged grains.'

*

When you became a wizard you were expected to stop shaving and grow a beard like a gorse bush. Very senior wizards looked capable of straining nourishment out of the air via their moustaches, like whales.

*

Victor eyed the glistening tubes in the tray around Dibbler's neck. They smelled appetizing. They always did. And then you bit into them, and learned once again that Cut-Me-Own-

Throat Dibbler could find a use for bits of an animal that the animal didn't know it had got. Dibbler had worked out that with enough fried onions and mustard people would eat *anything*.

*

Most people think in curves and zigzags. For example, they start from a thought like: I wonder how I can become very rich, and then proceed along an uncertain course which includes thoughts like: I wonder what's for supper, and: I wonder who I know who can lend me five dollars?

Whereas Throat was one of those people who could identify the thought at the other end of the process, in this case *I am now very rich*, draw a line between the two, and then think his way along it, slowly and patiently, until he got to the other end.

Not that it worked. There was always, he found, some small but vital flaw in the process. It generally involved a strange reluctance on the part of people to buy what he had to sell.

*

'Mr Dibbler can even sell sausages to people that have bought them off him *before* . . . And a man who could sell Mr Dibbler's sausages twice could sell anything.'

*

There was a dog sitting by his feet.

It was small, bow-legged and wiry, and basically grey but with patches of brown, white and black in outlying areas . . .

It looked up slowly, and said 'Woof?'

Victor poked an exploratory finger in his ear. It must have been a trick of an echo, or something. It wasn't that the dog had gone 'woof!', although that was practically unique in itself; most dogs in the universe *never* went 'woof!', they had complicated barks like 'whuuugh!' and 'hwhoouf!'. No, it was that it hadn't in fact *barked* at all. It had *said* 'woof'.

'Could have bin worse, mister. I could have said "miaow".'

He was aware of a strange smell. It was hard to place, but could perhaps have been a very old and slightly damp nursery rug.

'Woof bloody woof,' said Gaspode the Wonder Dog.

Dibbler gave Gaspode a long, slow stare, which was like challenging a centipede to an arse-kicking contest. Gaspode could outstare a mirror.

*

'I never had a chance, you know. I mean, look at the start I had in life. Frone inna river inna sack. An actual sack. Dear little puppy dog opens his eyes, looks out in wonder at the world, style of fing, he's in this sack.' The tears dripped off his nose. 'For two weeks I thought the brick was my mother.' . . .

'Just my luck they threw me in the Ankh,' Gaspode went on. 'Any other river, I'd have drowned and gone to doggy heaven.'

*

Victor was aware of a cold sensation against his leg. It was as though a half-melted ice cube was soaking through his trousers. He tried to ignore it, but it had a definite unignorable quality.

He looked down.

''scuse me,' said Gaspode.

*

Mrs Marietta Cosmopilite of 3 Quirm Street, Ankh-Morpork, believed the world was round, that a sprig of garlic in her underwear drawer kept away vampires, that it did you good to get out and have a laugh occasionally, that there was niceness in everyone if you only knew where to look, and that three horrible little dwarfs peered in at her undressing every night.†

*

'Well, of course,' said Silverfish, 'a lot of very talented people want to be in moving pictures. Can you sing?'

†She was right about that, but only by coincidence.

'A bit. In the bath. But not very well,' Victor conceded.

'Can you dance?'

'No.'

'Swords? Do you know how to handle a sword?'

'A little,' said Victor.

'I see,' said Silverfish gloomily. 'Can't sing. Can't dance. Can handle a sword a little.'

You would have to go a long way to find air that was realer than Ankh-Morpork air.

You could tell just by breathing it that other people had been doing the same thing for thousands of years.

'I don't understand her,' he said. 'Yesterday she was quite normal, today it's all gone to her head.'

'Bitches!' said Gaspode, sympathetically.

'Oh, I wouldn't go that far,' said Victor. 'She's just aloof.'

'Loofs!' said Gaspode.

*

The *Necrotelicomnicon* was written by a Klatchian necromancer known to the world as Achmed the Mad, although he preferred to be called Achmed the I Just Get These Headaches.

It contained forbidden knowledge.

Well, not actually *forbidden*. No one had ever gone so far as forbidding it. Apart from anything else, in order to forbid it you'd have to know what it was, which was forbidden. But it definitely contained the sort of information which, once you knew it, you wished you didn't.

'Come *on*,' said Gaspode. 'It's not right, you being alone in a lady's boodwah.'

'I'm not alone,' Victor said. 'She's with me.'

'That's the point,' said Gaspode.

'Did I hear things, or can that little dog speak?' said Dibbler.

'He says he can't,' said Victor.

Dibbler hesitated. 'Well,' he said, 'I suppose he should know.'

*

The universe contains any amount of horrible ways to be woken up, such as the noise of the mob breaking down the front door, the scream of fire engines, or the realization that today is the Monday which on Friday night was a comfortably long way off. A dog's wet nose is not strictly speaking the worst of the bunch, but it has its own peculiar dreadfulness which connoisseurs of the ghastly and dog owners everywhere have come to know and dread. It's like having a small piece of defrosting liver pressed lovingly against you.

*

As the magic of the movies infects everyone, there are spillages from our own roundworld.

'I don't know what it's called, but we're doing one about going to see a wizard. Something about following a yellow sick toad,' a man in one half of a lion suit explained to a companion in the queue.

*

A Man and A Woman Aflame With Passione in A Citie Riven by Sivil War!

Brother against brother! Women in crinoline dresses slapping people's faces! A mighty dynasty brought low!

A great city aflame!

All it needed was a title. Something with a ring to it. Something that people would remember. Something – Dibbler scratched his chin with the pen – that said that the affairs of ordinary people were so much chaff in the great storms of history. Storms, that was it. Good imagery, a storm. You got thunder. Lightning. Rain. Wind.

Wind. That was it!

He crawled up to the top of the sheet and, with great care, wrote:

BLOWN AWAY.

*

Soll was standing over the artist who lettered the cards . . .

The lettering artist tugged at his sleeve.

'I was just wondering, Mr Soll, what you wanted me to put in the big scene now—'

'Don't worry me now, man!'

'But if you could just give me an idea—'

Soll firmly unhooked the man's hand from his sleeve. 'Frankly,' he said, 'I don't give a damn,' and he strode off towards the set.

The artist was left alone. He picked up his paintbrush. His lips moved silently, shaping themselves around the words.

Then he said, 'Hmm. Nice one.'

*

According to the history books, the decisive battle that ended the Ankh-Morpork Civil War was fought between two handfuls of bone-weary men in a swamp early one misty morning and, although one side claimed victory, ended with a practical score of Humans 0, ravens 1,000, which is the case with most battles.

*

The real city had been burned down many times in its long history – out of revenge, or carelessness, or spite, or even just for the insurance. Most of the big stone buildings that actually made it a *city*, as opposed simply to a load of hovels all in one place, survived them intact and many people considered that a good fire every hundred years or so was essential to the health of the city since it helped to keep down the rats, roaches, fleas and, of course, people not rich enough to live in stone houses.

Inside every old person is a young person wondering what happened.

There's a bar like it in every town. It's dimly lit and the drinkers, although they talk, don't address their words to one another and they don't listen, either. They just talk the hurt inside. It's a bar for the derelict and the unlucky and all of those people who have been temporarily flagged off the racetrack of life and into the pits.

*

Yetis are a high-altitude species of troll, and quite unaware that eating people is out of fashion. Their view is: if it moves, eat it. If it doesn't, then wait for it to move. And then eat it.

*

An inviolable rule about buildings for the showing of moving pictures, applicable throughout the multiverse, is that the ghastliness of the architecture around the back is inversely proportional to the gloriousness of the architecture in the front. At the front: pillars, arches, gold leaf, lights. At the back: weird ducts, mysterious prolapses of pipework, blank walls, fetid alleys.

And the window to the lavatories.

*

'*Fascinating*,' said the Patrician. He had not got where he was today by bothering how things worked. It was how people worked that intrigued him.

*

''Twas beauty killed the beast,' said the Dean, who liked to say things like that.

'No it wasn't,' said the Chair. 'It was it splatting into the ground like that.'

All dwarfs have beards and wear many layers of clothing.

Their courtships are largely concerned with finding out, in delicate and circumspect ways, what sex the other dwarf is.

The flooded stairs lay in front of them.

'Can you swim?' said Victor.

'Not very well,' said Ginger.

'Me neither,' he said . . .

'Still,' he said, taking her hand. 'We could look on this as a great opportunity to improve really *quickly*.'

REAPER MAN

DEATH is missing – presumed . . . er . . . gone. Which leads to the kind of chaos you always get when an important public service is withdrawn.

Meanwhile, on a little farm, far, far away, a tall dark stranger is turning out to be really good with a scythe. There's a harvest to be gathered in . . .

> Not a muscle moved on Death's face, because he hadn't got any.

The shortest-lived creatures on the Disc were mayflies, which barely make it through twenty-four hours. Two of the oldest zigzagged aimlessly over the waters of a trout stream, discussing history with some younger members of the evening hatching.

'You don't get the kind of sun now that you used to get,' said one of them.

'You're right there. We had proper sun in the good old hours. It were all yellow. None of this red stuff.'

'It were higher, too.'

'It was. You're right.'

'And nymphs and larvae showed you a bit of respect.'

'They did. They did,' said the other mayfly vehemently.

'I reckon, if mayflies these hours behaved a bit better, we'd still be having proper sun.'

The younger mayflies listened politely.

'I remember,' said one of the oldest mayflies, 'when all this was fields, as far as you could see.'

The younger mayflies looked around.

'It's still fields,' one of them ventured, after a polite interval.

'I remember when it was *better* fields,' said the old mayfly sharply.

'Yeah,' said his colleague. 'And there was a cow.'

'That's right! You're right! I remember that cow! Stood right over there for, oh, forty, fifty minutes. It was brown, as I recall.'

'You don't get cows like that these hours.' . . .

'What were we doing before we were talking about the sun?'

'Zigzagging aimlessly over the water,' said one of the young flies. This was a fair bet in any case.

'No, before that.'

'Er . . . you were telling us about the Great Trout.'

'Ah. Yes. Right. The Trout. Well, you see, if you've been a good mayfly, zigzagging up and down properly—'

'—taking heed of your elders and betters—'

'—then eventually the Great Trout—'

Clop

Clop

'Yes?' said one of the younger mayflies.

There was no reply.

'The Great Trout what?' said another mayfly, nervously.

They looked down at a series of expanding concentric rings on the water.

'The holy sign!' said a mayfly. 'I remember being told about that! A

Great Circle in the water! Thus shall be the sign of the Great Trout!'

*

Whereas the oldest things on the Discworld were the famous Counting Pines.

The six Counting Pines in this clump were listening to the oldest, whose gnarled trunk declared it to be thirty-one thousand, seven hundred and thirty-four years old. The conversation took seventeen years, but has been speeded up.

'I remember when all this wasn't fields.'

'What was it, then?' said the nearest pine.

'Ice. If you can call it ice. We had *proper* glaciers in those days. Not like the ice you get now, here one season and gone the next. It hung around for ages.'

'Wow. That was a sharp one.'

'What was?'

'That winter just then.'

'Call that a winter? When I was a sapling we had winters—'

Then the tree vanished.

After a shocked pause for a couple of years, one of the clump said: 'He just went! Just like that! One day he was here, next he was gone!'

Since the trees were unable even to sense any event that took place in less than a day, they never heard the sound of axes.

*

Death's pale horse's name was Binky. He was a real horse. Death had tried fiery steeds and skeletal horses in the past, and found them impractical, especially the fiery ones, which tended to set light to their own bedding and stand in the middle of it looking embarrassed.

Killing off a wizard of a higher grade was a recognized way of getting advancement in the orders.

Wizards don't believe in gods in the same way that most people don't find it necessary to believe in, say, tables. They know they're there, they know they're there for a purpose, they'd probably agree that they have a place in a well-organized universe, but they wouldn't see the point of *believing*, of going around saying, 'O great table, without whom we are as naught'. Anyway, either the gods are there whether you believe or not, or they exist only as a function of the belief, so either way you might as well ignore the whole business and, as it were, eat off your knees.

*

The Bursar . . . didn't eat much, but lived on his nerves. He was certain he was anorectic, because every time he looked in a mirror he saw a fat man. It was the Archchancellor, standing behind him and shouting at him.

*

Mustrum Ridcully was, depending on your point of view, either the worst or the best Archchancellor that Unseen University had had for a hundred years.

There was too much of him, for one thing. It wasn't that he was particularly big, it was just that he had the kind of huge personality that fits any available space. He'd get roaring drunk at supper and that was fine and acceptable wizardly behaviour. But then he'd go back to his room and play darts all night and leave at five in the morning to go duck hunting. He shouted at people. He tried to *jolly them along*. And he hardly ever wore proper robes. He'd persuaded Mrs Whitlow, the University's dreaded housekeeper, to make him a sort of baggy trouser suit in garish blue and red; twice a day the wizards stood in bemusement and watched him jog purposefully around the University buildings, his pointy wizarding hat tied firmly on his head with string. He'd shout cheerfully up at them, because fundamental to the make-up of people like Mustrum Ridcully is an iron belief that everyone else would like it, too, if only they tried it.

*

Intellectually, Ridcully maintained his position for two reasons. One was that he never, ever, changed his mind about anything. The other was that it took him several minutes to understand any new idea put to him, and this is a very valuable trait in a leader, because anything anyone is still trying to explain to you after two minutes is probably important and anything they give up after a mere minute or so is almost certainly something they shouldn't have been bothering you with in the first place.

*

Although not common on the Discworld there are, indeed, such things as anti-crimes, in accordance with the fundamental law that everything in the multiverse has an opposite. They are, obviously, rare. Merely giving someone something is not the opposite of robbery; to be an anti-crime, it has to be done in such a way as to cause *outrage and/or humiliation to the victim*. So there is breaking-and-decorating, proffering-with-embarrassment (as in most retirement presentations) and whitemailing (as in threatening to reveal to his enemies a mobster's secret donations, for example, to charity). Anti-crimes have never really caught on.

*

For more than a century Windle Poons had lived inside the walls of Unseen University. In terms of accumulated years, he may have lived a long time. In terms of experience, he was about thirteen.

*

The Shades was the oldest part of the city. If you could do a sort of relief map of sinfulness, wickedness and all-round immorality, rather like those representations of the gravitational field around a Black Hole, then even in Ankh-Morpork The Shades would be represented by a shaft.

*

'If anyone's going to bury a wizard at a crossroads with a stake hammered through him, then wizards ought to do it. After all, we're his friends.'

*

Mustrum Ridcully, Archchancellor of Unseen University, was a shameless autocondimentor.†

*

'All right, you fellows,' Ridcully said. 'No magic at Table, you know the rules. Who's playing silly buggers?'

The other senior wizards stared at him.

'I, I, I don't think we can play it any more,' said the Bursar, 'I, I, I think we lost some of the pieces . . .'

*

The relationship between the University and the Patrician, absolute ruler and nearly benevolent dictator of Ankh-Morpork, was a complex and subtle one.

The wizards held that, as servants of a higher truth, they were not subject to the mundane laws of the city.

The Patrician said that, indeed, this was the case, but they would bloody well pay their taxes like everyone else.

The wizards said that, as followers of the light of wisdom, they owed allegiance to no mortal man.

The Patrician said that this may well be true but they also owed a city tax of two hundred dollars per head per annum, payable quarterly.

The wizards said that the University stood on magical ground and was therefore exempt from taxation and anyway you couldn't put a tax on knowledge.

The Patrician said you could. It was two hundred dollars per capita; if per capita was a problem, decapita could be arranged.

The wizards said that the University had never paid taxes to the civil authority.

The Patrician said he was not proposing to remain civil for long.

The wizards said, what about easy terms?

The Patrician said he was *talking* about easy terms. They wouldn't want to know about the hard terms.

†Someone who will put certainly salt and probably pepper on any meal you put in front of them *whatever it is and regardless of how much it's got on it already and regardless of how it tastes*. Behavioural psychiatrists working for fast-food outlets around the universe have saved billions of whatever the local currency is by noting the autocondimenting phenomenon and advising their employers to leave seasoning out in the first place. This is really true.

The wizards said that there was a ruler back in, oh, it would be the Century of the Dragonfly, who had tried to tell the University what to do. The Patrician could come and have a look at him if he liked.

The Patrician said that he would. He truly would.

In the end it was agreed that while the wizards of course paid no taxes, they would nevertheless make an entirely voluntary donation of, oh, let's say two hundred dollars per head, without prejudice, *mutatis mutandis*, no strings attached, to be used strictly for non-militaristic and environmentally acceptable purposes.

Thin, pale, and clad all in dusty black,

the Patrician always put Ridcully in mind of a predatory flamingo, if you could find a flamingo that was black and had the patience of a rock.

People get exactly the wrong idea about belief. They think it works back to front. They think the sequence is, first object, then belief. In fact, it works the other way.

Belief sloshes around in the firmament like lumps of clay spiralling into a potter's wheel. That's how gods get created, for example. They clearly must be created by their own believers, because a brief résumé of the lives of most gods suggests that their origins certainly couldn't be divine. They tend to do exactly the things people would do if only they could, especially when it comes to nymphs, golden showers, and the smiting of your enemies.

*

'And you're a vampire too, Countess Notfaroutoe?' Windle Poons enquired politely.

The Countess smiled. 'My vord, yes,' she said.

'By marriage,' said Arthur.

'Can you do that? I thought you had to be bitten,' said Windle.

'I don't see why I should have to go around biting my wife after thirty years of marriage, and that's flat,' said the Count.

*

'This vampiring's not all it's cracked up to be, you know. Can't go out in daylight, can't eat garlic, can't have a decent shave—'

'Why can't you have a—' Windle began.

'Can't use a *mirror*,' said Arthur.

*

'By the way, Sister Drull is a ghoul. If she offers you any of her meat patties, don't accept.'

'Oh, dear,' Windle said. 'You mean she makes them out of human flesh?'

'What? Oh. No. She just can't cook very well.'

*

SOMETIMES PEOPLE CHALLENGE ME TO A GAME. FOR THEIR LIVES, YOU KNOW, [said Death.]

'Do they ever win?'

NO. LAST YEAR SOMEONE GOT THREE STREETS AND ALL THE UTILITIES.

'What? What sort of game is that?'

I DON'T RECALL. 'EXCLUSIVE POSSESSION', I THINK. I WAS THE BOOT.

*

A compost heap comes to life and threatens a group of wizards:

The heap swivelled and lunged towards the Bursar.

The wizards backed away.

'It can't be intelligent, can it?' said the Bursar.

'All it's doing is moving around slowly and eating things,' said the Dean.

'Put a pointy hat on it and it'd be a faculty member,' said the Archchancellor.

*

Miss Flitworth had said that before they could start a graveyard in these parts they'd had to hit someone over the head with the shovel.

*

People have believed for hundreds of years that newts in a well mean that the water's fresh and drinkable, and *in all that time* never asked themselves whether the newts got out to go to the lavatory.

*

The ability of skinny old ladies to carry huge loads is phenomenal. Studies have shown that an ant can carry one hundred times its own weight, but there is no known limit to the lifting power of the average tiny eighty-year-old Spanish peasant grandmother.

'Why are you called One Man Bucket?'

in my tribe we're traditionally named after the first thing the mother sees when she looks out of the teepee after the birth. it's short for One-Man-Pouring-a-Bucket-of-Water-over-Two-Dogs.

'That's pretty unfortunate,' said Windle.

it's not too bad, said One-Man-Bucket. *it was my twin brother you had to feel sorry for. she looked out ten seconds before me to give him* his *name.*

'Don't tell me, let me guess,' Windle said. 'Two-Dogs-Fighting?'

*Two-Dogs-Fighting? Two-Dogs-*Fighting*?* said One-Man-Bucket. *wow, he'd have given his right arm to be called Two-Dogs-*Fighting.

In the Ramtop village where they dance the real Morris dance, for example, they believe that no one is finally dead until the ripples they cause in the world die away – until the clock he wound up winds down, until the wine she made has finished its ferment, until the crop they planted is harvested. The span of someone's life, they say, is only the core of their actual existence.

'Who's playing the maracas?'

Death grinned.

MARACAS? I DON'T NEED . . . MARACAS.

In the village in the Ramtops where they understand what the Morris dance is all about, they dance it just once, at dawn, on the first day of spring. They don't dance it after that, all through the summer. After all, what would be the point? What use would it be?

But on a certain day when the nights are drawing in, the dancers leave work early and take, from attics and cupboards, the *other* costume, the black one, and the *other* bells. And they go by separate ways to a valley among the leafless trees. They don't speak. There is no music. It's very hard to imagine what kind there could be.

The bells don't ring. They're made of octiron, a magic metal. But they're not, precisely, silent bells. Silence is merely the absence of noise. They make the opposite of noise, a sort of heavily textured silence.

And in the cold afternoon, as the light drains from the sky, among the frosty leaves and in the damp air, they dance the *other* Morris. Because of the balance of things.

You've got to dance both, they say. Otherwise you can't dance either.

WITCHES ABROAD

IT seemed an easy job ... After all, how difficult could it be to make sure that a servant girl doesn't marry a prince?

But for the witches Granny Weatherwax, Nanny Ogg and Magrat Garlick, travelling to the distant city of Genua, things are never that simple ...

Servant girls *have* to marry the Prince. That's what life is all about. You can't fight a Happy Ending.

At least, up until now ...

Just superstition. But a superstition doesn't have to be wrong.

*

Bad spelling can be lethal. For example, the greedy Seriph of Al-Ybi was once cursed by a badly educated deity and for some days everything he touched turned to Glod, which happened to be the name of a small dwarf from a mountain community hundreds of miles away who found himself magically dragged to the kingdom and relentlessly duplicated. Some two thousand Glods later the spell wore off. These days, the people of Al-Ybi are renowned for being unusually short and bad-tempered.

*

She had buried three husbands, and at least two of them had been already dead.

Never trust a dog with orange eyebrows.

Artists and writers have always had a rather exaggerated idea about what goes on at a witches' sabbat. This comes from spending too much time in small rooms with the curtains drawn, instead of getting out in the healthy fresh air.

For example, there's the dancing around naked. In the average temperate climate there are very few nights when anyone would dance around at midnight with no clothes on, quite apart from the question of stones, thistles, and sudden hedgehogs.

Then there's all that business with goat-headed gods. Most witches don't believe in gods. They know that the gods exist, of course. They even deal with them occasionally. But they don't believe in them. They know them too well. It would be like believing in the postman.

And there's the food and drink – the bits of reptile and so on. In fact, witches don't go for that sort of thing. The worst you can say about the eating habits of the older type of witch is that they tend to like ginger biscuits dipped in tea with so much sugar in it that the spoon won't move *and* will drink it out of the saucer if they think it's too hot. And do so with appreciative noises more generally associated with the cheaper type of plumbing system. Legs of toad and so on might be better than this.

Then there's the mystic ointments. By sheer luck, the artists and writers are on firmer ground here. Most witches are elderly, which is when ointments start to have an attraction, and at least two of those present tonight were wearing Granny Weatherwax's famous goose-grease-and-sage chest liniment. This didn't make you fly and see visions, but it *did* prevent colds, if only because the distressing smell that developed around about the second week kept everyone else so far away you couldn't catch anything from them.

And finally there's sabbats themselves. Your average witch is not, by nature, a social animal as far as other witches are concerned. There's a conflict of dominant personalities. There's a group of ringleaders without a ring. The natural size of a coven is one.

'I can't be having with foreign parts,' said Granny Weatherwax.

'You've been to Ankh-Morpork,' said Nanny mildly. 'That's foreign.'

'No it's not. It's just a long way off.'

Magrat would be the first to admit that she had an open mind. It was as open as a field, as open as the sky. No mind could be more open without special surgical implements. And she was always waiting for something to fill it up.

*

'I used to come over here quite often to look at Desiderata's books,' Magrat confessed. 'And . . . and she liked to cook foreign food and no one else round here would eat it, so I'd come up to keep her company.'

'Ah-*ha*! Curryin' favour!' snapped Granny.

*

Magrat has adopted trousers as practical wear for travelling by broomstick.

'I don't 'old with it,' said Granny. 'Everyone can see her legs.'

'No they can't,' said Nanny. 'The reason being, the material is in the way.'

'Yes, but they can see where her legs *are*,' said Granny Weatherwax.

'That's silly. That's like saying everyone's naked under their clothes,' said Magrat.

'Magrat Garlick, may you be forgiven,' said Granny Weatherwax.

'Well, it's true!'

'*I'm* not,' said Granny flatly, 'I got three vests on.'

*

To the rest of the world he was an enormous tomcat, a parcel of incredibly indestructible life forces in a skin that looked less like a fur than a piece of bread that had been left in a damp place for a fortnight. Ferocious dogs would whine and hide under the stairs when Greebo sauntered down the street. Foxes kept away from the village. Wolves made a detour.

'He's an old softie really,' said Nanny.

*

Above the noise of the river they could all hear, now, the steady slosh-slosh of another craft heading towards them.

'Someone's following us!' hissed Magrat.

Two pale glows appeared at the edge of the lamplight. Eventually they turned out to be the eyes of a small grey creature, vaguely froglike, paddling towards them on a log.

It reached the boat. Long clammy fingers grabbed the side, and a lugubrious face rose level with Nanny Ogg's.

' 'ullo,' it said. 'It'sss my birthday.'

All three of them stared at it for a while. Then Granny Weatherwax picked up an oar and hit it firmly over the head. There was a splash, and a distant cursing.

'Horrible little bugger,' said Granny, as they rowed on. 'Looked like a troublemaker to me.'

*

'Blessings be on this house,' Granny said, perfunctorily. It was always a good opening remark for a witch. It concentrated people's minds on what *other* things might be on this house.

*

Sometimes Magrat really wondered about the others' commitment to witchcraft. Half the time they didn't seem to *bother*.

Take medicine, for example . . . Granny just gave people a bottle of coloured water and told them they felt a lot better.

And what was so annoying was that they often did.

Where was the witchcraft in that?

*

Granny Weatherwax waking up was quite an impressive sight, and one not seen by many people.

Most people, on waking up, accelerate through a quick panicky pre-consciousness check-up: who am I, where am I, who is he/she, good god, why am I cuddling a policeman's helmet, *what happened last night*?

And this is because people are riddled by Doubt.

Granny Weatherwax went straight from fast asleep to instant operation on all six cylinders. She never needed to find herself because she always knew who was doing the looking.

Vampires have risen from the dead,

the grave and the crypt, but have never managed it from the cat.

Nanny Ogg sent a number of cards home to her family, not a single one of which got back before she did. This is traditional, and happens everywhere in the universe.

*

In a quiet little inn in a tiny country Granny Weatherwax sat and regarded the food with deep suspicion.

'Good simple home cooking,' said Granny. 'That's all I require. I just want simple food. Not all grease and stuff. It comes to something when you complain about something in your lettuce and it turns out to be what you ordered.'

Knowing how stories work is almost all the battle.

For example, when an obvious innocent sits down with three experienced card sharpers and says 'How do you play this game, then?', someone is about to be shaken down until their teeth fall out.

The dwarf bread was brought out for inspection. But it was miraculous, the dwarf bread. No one ever went hungry when they had some dwarf bread to avoid. You only had to look at it for a moment, and instantly you could think of dozens of things you'd rather eat. Your boots, for example. Mountains. Raw sheep. Your own foot.

*

There were only six suits of chain mail in the whole of Lancre, made on the basis of one-size-doesn't-quite-fit-all.

*

'When did *you* last have a bath, Esme?'

'What do you mean, *last*? Baths is unhygienic,' Granny declared. 'You know I've never agreed with baths. Sittin' around in your own dirt like that.'

'What do *you* do, then?' said Magrat.

'I just washes,' said Granny. 'All the bits. You know. As and when they becomes available.'

*

Granny Weatherwax had never turned anyone into a frog. The way she saw it, there was a technically less cruel but cheaper and much more satisfying thing you could do. You could leave them human and make them *think* they were a frog, which also provided much innocent entertainment for passers-by.

*

'I don't mind criticism,' said Granny. 'You know me. I've never been one to take offence at criticism. No one could say I'm the sort to take offence at criticism—'

'Not twice, anyway,' said Nanny.

*

People like Nanny Ogg turn up everywhere. It's as if there's some special morphic generator dedicated to the production of old women who like a laugh and aren't averse to the odd pint, especially of some drink normally sold in very small glasses. You find them all over the place, often in pairs.†

*

Nanny Ogg quite liked cooking, provided there were other people around to do things like chop up the vegetables and wash the dishes afterwards.

*

'That's the trouble with second sight,' Desiderata said. 'You can *see* what's happenin', but you don't know what it *means*. I've seen the future. There's a coach made out of a pumpkin. And that's impossible. And there's coachmen made out of mice, which is unlikely. And there's a clock striking midnight, and something about a glass slipper. And it's all going to happen. Because that's how stories have to work.'

*

But then Granny and Nanny have to try to stop the story from happening.

'It's no good, you know [said Lily Weatherwax]. You can't stop this sort of thing. It has the momentum of inevitability. You can't spoil a good story. I should know.'

She handed the slipper to the Prince, but without taking her eyes off Granny.

'It'll fit her,' she said.

Two of the courtiers held Magrat's leg as the Prince wrestled the slipper past her protesting toes.

'There,' said Lily, still without looking down. 'And do stop trying that hedge-witch hypnotism on me, Esme.'

'It fits,' said the Prince, but in a doubtful tone of voice.

'Yes, anything would fit,' said a cheerful voice from somewhere towards the back of the crowd, 'if you were allowed to put two pairs of hairy socks on first.'

Lily looked down. Then she looked at Magrat's mask. She reached out and pulled it off.

'Wrong girl,' said Lily. 'But it still doesn't matter, Esme, because it is the right slipper. So all we have to do is find the girl whose foot it fits—'

There was a commotion at the back of the crowd. Courtiers parted, revealing Nanny Ogg.

'If it's a five-and-a-half narrow fit, I'm your man,' she said. 'Just let me get these boots off . . .'

'I wasn't referring to you, old woman,' said Lily coldly.

'Oh, yes you was,' said Nanny. 'We know how this bit goes, see. The Prince goes all round the city with the slipper, trying to find the girl whose foot fits. That's what you was

† Always in front of you in any queue, for a start.

plannin'. So I can save you a bit of trouble, how about it?'

There was a flicker of uncertainty in Lily's expression.

'A *girl*,' she said, 'of *marriageable* age.'

'No problem there,' said Nanny cheerfully . . .

Nanny grabbed the slipper out of the Prince's hands and, before anyone else could move, slid it on to her foot.

Then she waggled the foot in the air.

It was a perfect fit.

'There!' she said. 'See? You could have wasted the whole day.'

'Especially because there must be hundreds of five-and-a-half—'

'– narrow fit –'

'—narrow fit wearers in a city this size,' Granny went on. 'Unless, of course, you happened to sort of go to the right house right at the start. If you had, you know, a lucky guess?'

'But that'd be *cheatin'*,' said Nanny.

She nudged the Prince.

'I'd just like to add,' she said, 'that I don't mind doin' all the waving and opening things and other royal stuff, but I draw the line at sleepin' in the same bed as sunny jim here.'

'Because he doesn't sleep in a bed,' said Granny.

'No, he sleeps in a pond,' said Nanny.

'Because he's a frog,' said Granny.

'This is Greebo. Between you and me, he's a fiend from hell.'

'Well, he's a cat,' said Mrs Gogol. 'It's only to be expected.'

No one knew better than Granny Weatherwax that hats were important. They weren't just clothing. Hats defined the head. They defined who you *were*. No one had ever heard of a wizard without a pointy hat – at least, no wizard worth speaking of. And you certainly never heard of a witch without one . . . It wasn't the wearing of the hats that counted so much as having one to wear. Every trade, every craft had its hat. That's why kings had hats. Take the crown off a king and all you had was someone good at having a weak chin and waving to people. Hats had power. Hats were important.

*

'You always used to say *I* was wanton, when we was younger,' said Nanny.

'You was, of course,' said Granny. 'But you never used magic for it, did you?'

'Din't have to,' said Nanny happily.

'An off-the-shoulder dress did the trick most of the time.'

'Right off the shoulder and on to the grass, as I recall,' said Granny.

*

Every established kitchen has one ancient knife, its handle worn thin, its blade curved like a banana, and so inexplicably sharp that reaching into the drawer at night is like bobbing for apples in a piranha tank.

*

'Look at the three of you,' Lily said. 'The maiden, the mother and the crone.'

'Who are you calling a maiden?' said Nanny Ogg.

'Who are you calling a mother?' said Magrat.

Granny Weatherwax glowered briefly like the person who has discovered that there is only one straw left and everyone else has drawn a long one.

*

'Don't you talk to me about progress. Progress just means bad things happen faster.'

*

'How come you're in the palace guard, Casanunda? All the rest of 'em are six foot tall and you're – of the shorter persuasion.'

'I lied about my height, Mrs Ogg.'

*

'I don't want to hurt you, Mistress Weatherwax,' said Mrs Gogol.

'That's good,' said Granny. 'I don't want you to hurt me either.'

SMALL GODS

IN the beginning was the Word. And the Word was: 'Hey, you!'

For Brutha the novice is the Chosen One. He wants peace and justice and brotherly love.

He also wants the Inquisition to stop torturing him now, please . . .

Brother Preptil, the master of the music, had described Brutha's voice as putting him in mind of a disappointed vulture arriving too late at the dead donkey.

*

There was something creepy about that boy [Brutha], Nhumrod thought. It was the way he looked at you when you were talking, as if he was *listening*.

*

'It's a big bull,' said the tortoise.

'The very likeness of the Great God Om in one of his worldly incarnations!' said Brutha proudly. 'And you say you're *him*?'

'I haven't been well lately,' said the tortoise.

*

'How should I know? I don't know!' lied the tortoise.

'But you . . . you're omnicognizant,' said Brutha.

'That doesn't mean I know everything.'

Brutha bit his lip. 'Um. Yes. It does.'

*

Everyone in the city knew Cut-Me-Own-Hand-Off Dhblah, purveyor of suspiciously new holy relics, suspiciously old rancid sweetmeats on a stick, gritty figs, and long-past-their--sell-by dates.

*

'I – I do not know how to ride, my lord,' said Brutha.

'Any man can get on a mule,' said Vorbis. 'Often many times in a short distance.'

*

It was a small mule and Brutha had long legs; if he'd made the effort he could have remained standing and let the mule trot out from underneath.

'My grandmother used to give me a thrashing every morning because I would certainly do something to deserve it during the day,' said Brutha.

If you spend your whole time thinking about the universe, you tend to forget the less important bits of it. Like your pants.

*

People think that professional soldiers think a lot about fighting, but *serious* professional soldiers think a lot more about food and a warm place to sleep, because these are two things that are generally hard to get, whereas fighting tends to turn up all the time.

*

Humans! They lived in a world where the grass continued to be green and the sun rose every day and flowers regularly turned into fruit, and what impressed them? Weeping statues. And wine made out of water! A mere quantum-mechanistic tunnel effect, that'd happen anyway if you were prepared to wait zillions of years. As if the turning of sunlight into wine, by means of vines and grapes and time and enzymes, wasn't a thousand times more impressive and happened all the time . . .

*

No other library anywhere, for example, has a whole gallery of unwritten books – books that *would* have been written if the author hadn't been eaten by an alligator around chapter 1, and so on. Atlases of imaginary places. Dictionaries of illusory words. Spotters' guides to invisible things. Wild thesauri in the Lost Reading Room. A library so big that it distorts reality and has opened gateways to all other libraries, everywhere and everywhen . . .

*

'Prince Lasgere of Tsort asked me how he could become learned, especially since he hadn't got any time for this reading business. I said to him, "There is no royal road to learning, sire," and he said to me, "Bloody well build one or I shall have your legs chopped off. Use as many slaves as you like." A refreshingly direct approach, I always thought. Not a man to mince words. People, yes. But not words.'

*

Gods are not very introspective. It has never been a survival trait. The ability to cajole, threaten and terrify has always worked well enough. When you can flatten entire cities at a whim, a tendency towards quiet reflection and seeing-things-from-the-other-fellow's-point-of-view is seldom necessary.

Which had led, across the multiverse, to men and women of tremendous brilliance and empathy devoting their entire lives to the service of deities who couldn't beat them at a quiet game of dominoes. For example, Sister Sestina of Quirm defied the wrath of a local king and walked unharmed across a bed of coals and propounded a philosophy of sensible ethics on behalf of a goddess whose only real interest was in hairstyles, and Brother Zephilite of Klatch left his vast estates and his family and spent his life ministering to the sick and poor on behalf of the invisible god F'rum, generally considered unable, should he have a backside, to find it with both hands, should he have hands. Gods never need to be very bright when there are humans around to be it for them.

*

Mountains rise and fall, and under them the Turtle swims onward. Men live and die, and the Turtle Moves. Empires grow and crumble, and the Turtle Moves. Gods come and go, and still the Turtle Moves. The Turtle Moves.

*

Words are the litmus paper of the mind. If you find yourself in the power of someone who will use the word 'commence' in cold blood, go somewhere else very quickly. But if they say 'Enter,' don't stop to pack.

LORDS AND LADIES

THE Fairies are back – but this time they don't just want your teeth . . .

Granny Weatherwax and her tiny coven are up against real elves.

It's Midsummer Night.

No time for dreaming . . .

With full supporting cast of dwarfs, wizards, trolls, Morris dancers and one orang-utan. And lots of hey-nonny-nonny and blood all over the place.

Nanny Ogg never did any housework herself, but she was the cause of housework in other people.

*

Lancre was so small that you couldn't lie down without a passport.

*

WILLIAM SCROPE.

'Yes?'

IF YOU WOULD PLEASE STEP THIS WAY.

'Are you a hunter?'

I LIKE TO THINK I AM A PICKER-UP OF UNCONSIDERED TRIFLES.

Death grinned hopefully. Scrope's post-physical brow furrowed.

'What? Like . . . sherry, custard . . . that sort of thing?'

*

'Someone got killed up here.'

'Oh, no,' moaned Nanny Ogg.

'A tall man. He had one leg longer'n the other. And a beard. He was probably a hunter.'

'How'd you know all that?'

'I just trod on 'im.'

*

'Hope Magrat does all right as queen,' said Nanny.

'We taught her everything she knows,' said Granny Weatherwax.

'Yeah,' said Nanny Ogg. 'D'you think . . . maybe . . .?'

'What?'

'D'you think maybe we ought to have taught her everything *we* know?'

*

The thing about the Librarian was that no one *noticed* he was an orang-utan any more, unless a visitor to the University happened to point it out. In which case someone would say, 'Oh, yes. Some kind of magical accident, wasn't it? Pretty sure it was something like that. One minute human, next minute an ape. Funny thing, really . . . can't remember what he looked like before. I mean, he *must* have been human, I suppose. Always thought of him as an ape, really. It's more *him*.'

*

Magrat normally wore a simple dress with not much underneath it except Magrat.

*

Nanny subtly breaks the news of a death:

'Well, now,' said Nanny, 'you know the widow Scrope, lives over in Slice?'

Quarney's mouth opened.

'She's not a widow,' he said. 'She—'

'Bet you half a dollar?' said Nanny.

*

Esme's skill at Borrowing unnerved Nanny Ogg. It was all very well entering the minds of animals and such, but too many witches had never come back. For several years Nanny had put out lumps of fat and bacon rind for a bluetit that she was sure was old Granny Postalute, who'd gone out Borrowing one day and never came back.

*

Granny Weatherwax had a feeling she was going to die. This was beginning to get on her nerves.

*

'I do apologize for this,' said the very small highwayman. 'I find myself a little short.'

*

The dwarf bowed and produced a slip of pasteboard from one grubby but lace-clad sleeve.

'My card,' he said.

It read:

GIAMO CASANUNDA
World's Second Greatest Lover
'WE NEVER SLEEP'
FINEST SWORDSMAN · SOLDIER OF FORTUNE
OUTRAGEOUS LIAR · STEPLADDERS REPAIRED

'Are you really an outrageous liar?'

'No.'

'Why are you trying to rob coaches, then?'

'I am afraid I was waylaid by bandits.'

'But it says here,' said Ridcully, 'that you are a finest swordsman.'

'I was outnumbered.'

'How many of them were there?'

'Three million.'

*

'You know,' said Ponder, 'this reminds me of that famous logical puzzle . . . There was this man, right, who had to choose between going through two doors, apparently, and the guard on one door always told the truth and the guard on the other door always told a lie, and the thing *was*, behind one door was certain death, and behind the other door was freedom, and he didn't know which guard was which, and he could only ask them one question and so: what did he ask?'

'Hang on,' said Casanunda, 'I think I've worked it out. One question, right?'

'Yes,' said Ponder, relieved.

'And he can ask either guard?'

'*Yes.*'

'Oh, right. Well, in that case he goes up to the smallest guard and says, "Tell me which is the door to freedom if you don't want to see the colour of your kidneys and incidentally I'm walking through it *behind* you, so if you're trying for the Mr Clever Award just remember who's going through it *first*." '

'No, no, no!'

'Sounds logical to me,' said Ridcully. 'Very good thinking.'

'But you haven't got a weapon!'

'Yes I have. I wrested it from the guard while he was considering the question,' said Casanunda.

*

Ponder Stibbons tries to explain parallel universes to Ridcully:

'*Parallel* universes, I said. Universes where things didn't happen like—' He hesitated. 'Well, you know that girl?'

'What girl?'

'The girl you wanted to marry?'

'How'd you know that?'

'You were talking about her just after lunch.'

'Was I? More fool me. Well, what about her?'

'Well . . . in a way, you *did* marry her,' said Ponder.

Ridcully shook his head. 'Nope. Pretty certain I didn't. You remember that sort of thing.'

'Ah, but not in *this* universe—'

'You suggestin' I nipped into some other universe to get married?' said Ridcully.

'No! I mean, you got married in that universe and not in this universe,' said Ponder.

'Did I? What? A proper ceremony and everything?'

'Yes!'

'Hmm.' Ridcully stroked his beard. 'You sure?'

'Certain, Archchancellor.'

'My word! I never knew that.'

Ponder felt he was getting somewhere.

'So—'

'Yes?'

'Why don't I remember it?'

Ponder had been ready for this.

'Because the you in the other universe is different from the you here,' he said. 'It was a different you that got married. He's probably settled down somewhere. He's probably a great-grandad by now.'

'He never writes, I know that,' said Ridcully. 'And the bastard never invited me to the wedding.'

'Who?'

'Him.'

'But he's you!'

'Is he? Huh! You'd think *I'd* think of *me*, wouldn't you? What a bastard!'

It wasn't that Ridcully was stupid.

Truly stupid wizards have the life expectancy of a glass hammer. He had quite a powerful intellect, but it was powerful like a locomotive, and ran on rails and was therefore almost impossible to steer.

Shawn took a deep breath and leaned over the battlements.

'Halt! Who Goes There?' he said.

'It's me, Shawn. Your mum.'

'Oh, hello, Mum. Hello, Mistress Weatherwax.'

'Let us in, there's a good boy.'

'Friend or Foe?'

'What?'

'It's what I've got to say, Mum. It's official. And then you've got to say Friend.'

'I'm your *mum*.'

'You've got to do it properly, Mum,' said Shawn, 'otherwise what's the point?'

'It's going to be Foe in a minute, my lad.'

'Oooaaaww, *Mum*!'

'Oh, all right. Friend, then.'

'Yes, but you could just be saying that—'

*

A witch's cottage is a very specific architectural item. It is not exactly built, but put together over the years as the areas of repair join up, like a sock made entirely of darns. The chimney twists like a corkscrew. The roof is thatch so old that small but flourishing trees are growing in it, the floors are switchbacks, it creaks at night like a tea clipper in a gale. If at least two walls aren't shored up with balks of timber then it's not a true witch's cottage at all, but merely the home of some daft old bat who reads tea leaves and talks to her cat.

*

The bandit chief knocked on the coach door. The window slid down.

'I wouldn't like you to think of this as a robbery,' he said. 'I'd like you to think of it more as a colourful anecdote you might enjoy telling your grandchildren about.'

A wizard's staff poked out. The chieftain saw the knob on the end.

'Now, then,' he said, pleasantly. 'I know the rules. Wizards aren't allowed to use magic against civilians except in genuine life-threatening situa—'

There was a burst of octarine light.

'Actually, it's not a rule,' said Ridcully. 'It's more a guideline.'

*

'I thought that sort of thing was, you know,' the king grinned sickly, 'folklore?'

'Of course it's folklore, you stupid man!'

'I *do* happen to be king, you know,' said Verence reproachfully.

'You stupid king, your majesty.'

'Thank you.'

'Elves are beautiful. They've got *style*. Beauty. Grace.

That's what matters. If cats looked like frogs we'd realize what nasty, cruel little bastards they are. Style. That's what people remember.'

'Nanny, would you like to be a bridesmaid?'

'Not really, dear. Bit old for that sort of thing.' Nanny hovered. 'There isn't anything you need to ask me, though, is there?'

'What do you mean?'

'What with your mum being dead and you having no female relatives and everything . . .'

Magrat still looked puzzled.

'After the wedding, is what I'm hinting about,' said Nanny.

'Oh, *that*. No, most of that's being done by a caterer.'

*

It wasn't that Nanny Ogg sang badly. It was just that she could hit notes which, when amplified by a tin bath half full of water, ceased to be sound and became some sort of invasive presence.

There had been plenty of singers whose high notes could smash a glass, but Nanny's high C could clean it.

*

'Swish city bastards.'

'They don't know what it's like to be up to the armpit in a cow's backside on a snowy night. Hah!'

'And there ain't one of 'em that—what're you talking about? You ain't got a cow.'

'No, but I know what it's like.'

*

'What do we do with the mail?' said Ridcully.

'I take the palace stuff, and we generally leave the sack hanging up on a nail outside the tavern so that people can help themselves,' said Shawn.

'Isn't that dangerous?' said Ponder.

'Don't think so. It's a strong nail,' said Shawn.

*

'I remember years ago my granny telling me about Queen Amonia, well, I say queen, but she never was queen except for about three hours because of what I'm about to unfold, on account of them playing hide-and-seek at the wedding party and her hiding in a big heavy old chest in some attic and the lid slamming shut and no one finding her for seven months, by which time you could definitely say the wedding cake was getting a bit stale.'

'That's the thing about witchcraft,' she said. 'It doesn't exactly keep you young, but you do stay old for longer.'

Nanny said, 'Funny to think of our Magrat being married and everything.'

'What do you mean, everything?'

'Well, *you* know – *married*,' said Nanny. 'I gave her a few tips. Always wear something in bed. Keeps a man interested.'

'You always wore your hat.'

'Right.'

*

'What was that dance your Jason and his men did when they'd got drunk?' said Granny.

'It's the Lancre Stick and Bucket Dance, Esme.'

'It's legal, is it?'

'Technically they shouldn't do it when there's women present,' said Nanny. 'Otherwise it's sexual morrisment.'

*

The Monks of Cool, whose tiny and exclusive monastery is hidden in a really cool and laid-back valley in the lower Ramtops, have a passing-out test for a novice. He is taken into a room full of all types of clothing and asked: Yo, my son, which of these is the most stylish thing to wear? And the correct answer is: Hey, whatever I select.

MEN AT ARMS

'BE a MAN in the City Watch! The City Watch needs MEN!'

But what it's *got* includes Corporal Carrot (technically a dwarf), Lance-Constable Detritus (a troll), Lance-Constable Angua (a woman ... most of the time) and Corporal Nobbs (disqualified from the human race for shoving).

And they need all the help they can get. Because they've only got twenty-four hours to clean up the town and this is Ankh-Morpork we're talking about...

'Sergeant Colon,' said Angua. 'He was the fat one, yes?'

'That's right.'

'Why has he got a pet monkey?'

'Ah,' said Carrot. 'I think it is Corporal Nobbs to whom you refer . . .'

*

'Who was that man with the granite face I saw in the Watch House?' said Angua.

'That was Detritus the troll,' said Carrot.

'No, that *man*,' said Angua, learning as had so many others that Carrot tended to have a bit of trouble with metaphors. 'Face like thu— face like someone very disgruntled.'

'Oh, that was Captain Vimes. But he's never *been* gruntled, I think.'

*

Vimes's meeting with the Patrician ended as all such meetings did, with the guest going away in possession of an unfocused yet nagging suspicion that he'd only just escaped with his life.

*

Sybil Ramkin lived in the kind of poverty that was only available to the very rich, a poverty approached from the other side. Women who were merely well-off saved up and bought dresses made of silk edged with lace and pearls, but Lady Ramkin was so rich she could afford to stomp around the place in rubber boots and a tweed skirt that had belonged to her mother. She was so rich she could afford to live on biscuits and cheese sandwiches. She was so rich she lived in three rooms in a thirty-four-roomed mansion; the rest of them were full of very expensive and very *old* furniture, covered in dust sheets.

*

The reason that the rich were so rich, Vimes reasoned, was because they managed to spend less money.

Take boots, for example. He earned thirty-eight dollars a month plus allowances. A really good pair of leather boots cost fifty dollars. But an *affordable* pair of boots, which were sort of okay for a season or two and then leaked like hell when the cardboard gave out, cost about ten dollars. Those were the kind of boots Vimes always bought, and wore until the soles were so thin that he could tell where he was in Ankh-Morpork on a foggy night by the feel of the cobbles.

But the thing was that *good* boots lasted for years and years. A man who could afford fifty dollars had a pair of boots that'd still be keeping his feet dry in ten years' time, while a poor man who could only afford cheap boots would have spent a hundred dollars on boots in the same time and *would still have wet feet.*

This was the Captain Samuel Vimes 'Boots' theory of socio-economic unfairness.

*

The natural condition of the common swamp dragon is to be chronically ill, and the natural state of an unhealthy dragon is to be laminated across the walls, floor and ceiling of whatever room it is in. A swamp dragon is a badly run, dangerously unstable chemical factory one step from disaster. One quite small step.

It has been speculated that its habit of exploding violently when angry, excited, frightened or merely plain bored is a developed survival trait† to discourage predators. Eat dragons, it proclaims, and you'll have a case of indigestion to which the term 'blast radius' will be appropriate.

*

To understand why dwarfs and trolls don't like each other you have to go back a long way.

They get along like chalk and cheese. Very like chalk and cheese, really. One is organic, the other isn't, and also smells a bit cheesy. Dwarfs make a living by smashing up rocks with valuable minerals in them and the silicon-based lifeform known as trolls are, basically, rocks with valuable minerals in them.

*

Carrot often struck people as simple. And he was.

Where people went wrong was thinking that simple meant the same thing as stupid.

Carrot was not stupid. He was direct, and honest, and good-natured and honourable in all his dealings. In Ankh-Morpork this would normally have added up to 'stupid' in any case and would have given him the survival quotient of a jellyfish in a blast furnace, but there were a couple of other factors. One was a punch that even trolls had learned to respect. The other was that Carrot was genuinely, almost supernaturally, likeable. He got on well with people, even while arresting them. He had an exceptional memory for names.

Vimes would be the first to admit that he wasn't a good copper,

but he'd probably be spared the chore because lots of other people would happily admit it for him.

There were such things as dwarf gods. Dwarfs were not a naturally religious species, but in a world where pit props could crack without warning and pockets of fire damp could suddenly explode they'd seen

† From the point of view of the species as a whole. Not from the point of view of the dragon now landing in small pieces around the landscape.

the need for gods as the sort of supernatural equivalent of a hard hat. Besides, when you hit your thumb with an eight-pound hammer it's nice to be able to blaspheme. It takes a very special and strong-minded kind of atheist to jump up and down with their hand clasped under their other armpit and shout, 'Oh, random-fluctuations-in-the-space-time-continuum!' or 'Aaargh, primitive-and-outmoded-concept on a crutch!'

No clowns were funny.

That was the whole purpose of a clown. People laughed at clowns, but only out of nervousness. The point of clowns was that, after watching them, anything else that happened seemed enjoyable. It was nice to know there was someone worse off than you.

Three and a half minutes after waking up, Captain Samuel Vimes, Night Watch, staggered up the last few steps on to the roof of the city's opera house, gasped for breath and threw up *allegro ma non troppo*.

*

He didn't know much about gargoyles. Carrot had said something once about how marvellous it was, an urban troll species that had evolved a symbiotic relationship with gutters, and he had admired the way they funnelled run-off water into their ears and out through fine sieves in their mouths. You didn't get many birds nesting on buildings colonized by gargoyles.

*

Vimes snorted. I grew up here, he thought, and when I walk down the street everyone says, 'Who's that glum bugger?' Carrot's been here a few months and *everyone* knows him. And he knows everyone. *Everyone* likes him. I'd be annoyed about that, if only he wasn't so likeable.

*

'I'd like a couple of eggs,' said Vimes, 'with the yolks real hard but the whites so runny that they drip like treacle. And I want bacon, that special bacon all covered with bony nodules and dangling bits of fat. And a slice of fried bread. The kind that makes your arteries go clang just by looking at it.'

'Tough order,' said Harga.

'You managed it yesterday.'

*

Probably no other world in the multiverse has warehouses for things which only exist *in potentia*, but the pork futures warehouse in Ankh-Morpork is a product of the Patrician's rules about baseless metaphors, the literal-mindedness of citizens who assume that everything must exist somewhere, and the general thinness of the fabric of reality around Ankh, which is so thin that it's as thin as a very thin thing. The net result is that trading in pork futures – in pork *that doesn't exist yet* – led to the building of the warehouse to store it in until it does.

*

C. M. O. T. Dibbler had a number of bad points, but species prejudice was not one of them. He liked anyone who had money, regardless of the colour and shape of the hand that was proffering it. For Dibbler believed in a world where a sapient creature could walk tall, breathe free, pursue life, liberty and happiness, and step out towards the bright new dawn. If they could be persuaded to gobble something off Dibbler's hot-food tray at the same time, this was all to the good.

*

Leonard of Quirm was not all that old. He was one of those people who started looking venerable around the age of thirty, and would probably still look about the same at the age of ninety. He wasn't exactly bald, either. His head had just grown up through his hair, rising like a mighty rock dome through heavy forest.

*

'This city is full of clever men,' said the Patrician . . .'They never *think*. They do things like open the Three Jolly Luck Take-Away Fish Bar on the site of the old temple in Dagon Street on the night of the winter solstice when it also happens to be a full moon.'

*

'Captain Vimes?' said Carrot, waving a hand in front of his eyes. There was no response.

'How much has he had?'

'Two nips of whiskey, that's all.'

'That shouldn't do this to him, even on an empty stomach,' said Carrot.

Angua pointed at the neck of a bottle protruding from Vimes's pocket.

'I don't think he's been drinking on an empty stomach,' she said. 'I think he put some alcohol in it first.'

*

'Oh, no,' said Sergeant Colon. 'He's had a whole bottle!'

Angua picked out the bottle and looked at the label.

'C. M. O. T. Dibbler's Genuine Authentic Soggy Mountain Dew,' she read. 'He's going to die! It says, "One hundred and fifty per cent proof"!'

'Nah, that's just old Dibbler's advertising,' said Nobby. 'It ain't got no *proof*. Just circumstantial evidence.'

*

'He only drinks when he gets depressed,' said Carrot.

'Why does he get depressed?'

'Sometimes it's because he hasn't had a drink.'

*

'I appear . . . to be losing a lot of blood,' said Lord Vetinari.

'Who would have thought you had it in you,' said Vimes, with the frankness of those probably about to die.

'Captain *Quirke*?' said Carrot. 'But he's . . . not a good choice.'

'Mayonnaise Quirke, we used to call him,' said Colon. 'He's a pillock.'

'Don't tell me,' said Angua. 'He's rich, thick and oily, yes?'

'And smells faintly of eggs,' said Carrot.

It's generally very quiet in the Unseen University library. There's perhaps the shuffling of feet as wizards wander between the shelves, the occasional hacking cough to disturb the academic silence, and every once in a while a dying scream as an unwary student fails to treat an old magical book with the caution it deserves.

*

Carrot could lead armies, Angua thought. Some people have inspired whole countries to great deeds because of the power of their vision. And so could he. Not because he dreams about marching hordes, or world domination, or an empire of a thousand years. Just because he thinks that everyone's really decent underneath and would get along just fine if only they made the effort, and he believes that so strongly it burns like a flame which is bigger than he is. He's got a dream and we're all part of it, so that it shapes the world around him. And the weird thing is that no one wants to disappoint him. It'd be like kicking the biggest puppy in the universe. It's a kind of magic.

*

'Captain Vimes always told me, sir, that there's big crimes and little crimes. Sometimes the little crimes look big and the big crimes you can hardly see, but the crucial thing is to decide which is which.'

*

Foul Ole Ron was a Beggars' Guild member in good standing. He was a Mutterer, and a good one. He would walk behind people muttering in his own private language until they gave him money not to. People thought he was mad, but this was not, technically, the case. It was just that he was in touch with reality on the cosmic level, and had a bit of trouble focusing on things smaller, like other people, walls and soap (although on very small things, such as coins, his eyesight was Grade A).

'You can really talk?' said Carrot. Gaspode rolled his eyes. ' 'Course not,' he said.

'Who are you?' said the Patrician.

'Corporal Nobbs, sir!' said Nobby, saluting.

'Do we employ you?'

'Yessir!'

'Ah. You're the dwarf, are you?'

'Nosir. That was the late Cuddy, sir! I'm one of the human beings, sir!'

'You're not employed as the result of any . . . special hiring procedures?'

'Nosir,' said Nobby, proudly.

'My word.'

*

The Patrician steepled his fingers and looked at Carrot over the top of them. It was a mannerism that had unnerved many.

SOUL MUSIC

OTHER children got given xylophones. Susan just had to ask her grandfather to take his vest off.

Yes. There's a Death in the family.

It's hard to grow up normally when Grandfather rides a white horse and wields a scythe – especially when you have to take over the family business, and everyone mistakes you for the Tooth Fairy. And *especially* when you have to face the new and addictive music that has entered the Discworld.

It's lawless. It changes people.

It's called *Music With Rocks In.*

It's got a beat and you can dance to it, but . . .

It's *alive.*

And it won't fade away.

It was raining in the small, mountainous country of Llamedos. It was always raining in Llamedos. Rain was the country's main export. It had rain mines.

People came to Ankh-Morpork to seek their fortune.

Unfortunately, other people sought it too.

Lord Vetinari had encouraged the growth of the Guilds. They were the big wheels on which the clockwork of a well-regulated city ran. A drop of oil here . . . a spoke inserted there, of course . . . and by and large it all *worked*.

*

It looked the kind of musical instrument emporium which doubles as a pawnshop, since every musician has at some time in his life to hand over his instrument if he wants to eat and sleep indoors.

*

'We haven't even practised together properly,' said Imp.

'We'll practise as we go along,' said Glod. 'Welcome to the world of professional musicianship.'

*

The raven had grown up in the forever-crumbling, ivy-clad Tower of Art, overlooking Unseen University in far Ankh-Morpork . . .

The wizard who thought he owned him called him Quoth.

*

There is a type of girl who, while incapable of cleaning her bedroom even at knifepoint, will fight for the privilege of being allowed to spend the day shovelling manure in a stable.

*

Quirm wasn't a night town. People who came to Quirm looking for a good time went somewhere else. Quirm was so respectable that even dogs asked permission before going to the lavatory.

*

'Ride the horse.'

'Where to?'

'That's for me not to know and you to find out.'

*

CURRY GARDENS

Curry with Vegetable 8p
Curry with Meat 10p
Curry with Named Meat 15p

*

Albert was bent over the stove. 'Morning,' he said. 'You want fried bread with your sausages?'

Susan looked at the mess sizzling in the huge frying pan. It wasn't a sight to be seen on an empty stomach, although it could probably cause one. Albert could make an egg wish it had never been laid.

*

The Mended Drum had traditionally gone in for, well, traditional pub games, such as dominoes, darts and Stabbing People In The Back And Taking All Their Money.

*

'Why'd you want to come here?' she said.

'This is a battlefield, isn't it?' said the raven patiently. 'You've got to have ravens afterwards.' Its free-wheeling eyes swivelled in its head. 'Carrion regardless, as you might say.'

*

Death decides to join the Klatchian Foreign Legion. He arrives at one of their forts and knocks:

IS THIS THE KLATCHIAN FOREIGN LEGION?

The face of the little man on the other side of the door went blank.

'Ah,' he said, 'you've got me there. Hang on a moment.' The hatch shut. There was a whispered discussion on the other side of the door. The hatch opened.

'Yes, it appears we are the . . . the . . . what was that again? Right, got it . . . the Klatchian Foreign Legion. Yes. What was it you were wanting?'

I WISH TO JOIN.

'Join? Join what?'

THE KLATCHIAN FOREIGN LEGION.

'Where's that?'

There was some more whispering.

'Oh. Right. Sorry. Yes. That's us.'

The doors swung open. The visitor strode in. A legionary with corporal's stripes on his arm walked up to him.

'You'll have to report to . . .' his eyes glazed a little, '. . . you know . . . big man, three stripes . . . on the tip of my tongue a moment ago . . .'

SERGEANT?

'Right,' said the corporal, with relief. 'What's your name, soldier?'

ER . . .

'You don't have to say, actually. That's what the . . . the . . .'

KLATCHIAN FOREIGN LEGION?

'. . . what it's all about. People join to . . . to . . . with your mind, you know, when you can't . . . things that happened . . .'

FORGET?

'Right. I'm . . .' The man's face went blank. 'Wait a minute, would you?'

He looked down at his sleeve. 'Corporal . . .' he said. He hesitated, looking worried. Then an idea struck him and he pulled at the collar of his vest and twisted his neck until he could squint, with considerable difficulty, at the label thus revealed.

'Corporal . . . Medium? Does that sound right?'

I DON'T THINK SO.

'Corporal . . . Hand Wash Only?'

PROBABLY NOT.

'Corporal . . . Cotton?'

IT'S A POSSIBILITY.

'Right. Well, welcome to the . . . er . . .'

KLATCHIAN FOREIGN LEGION . . .

'Right. The pay is three dollars a week and all the sand you can eat.'

*

The tradition of promotion in the University by filling dead men's shoes, sometimes by firstly ensuring the death of the man in those shoes, had lately ceased. This was largely because of Ridcully himself, who was big and kept himself in trim and, as three late-night aspirants to the Archchancellorship had found, also had very good hearing. They had been variously hung out of the window by their ankles, knocked unconscious with a shovel, and had their arm broken in two places. Besides, Ridcully was known to sleep with two loaded crossbows by his bed. He was a kind man and probably wouldn't shoot you in *both* ears.

*

There was an Ankh-Morpork legend about some old drum in the Palace that was supposed to bang itself if an enemy fleet was seen sailing up the Ankh. The legend had died out in recent centuries, partly because this was the Age of Reason and also because no enemy fleet could sail up the Ankh without a gang of men with shovels going in front.

*

Unseen University was used to eccentricity among the faculty. After all, humans derive their notions of what it means to *be* a normal human being by constant reference to the humans around them, and when those humans are other wizards the spiral can only wiggle downwards. The Librarian was an orang-utan, and no one thought that was at all odd. The Reader in Esoteric Studies spent so much time reading in what the Bursar referred to as 'the smallest room' that he was generally referred to as the Reader in The Lavatory, even on official documents.† The Bursar himself in any normal society would have been considered more unglued than a used stamp in a downpour. The Archchancellor, who regularly used the long gallery above the Great Hall for archery practice and had accidentally shot the Bursar twice, thought the whole faculty was as crazy as loons, whatever a loon was. 'Not enough fresh air,' he'd say. 'Too much sittin' around indoors. Rots the brain.' More often he'd say, 'Duck!'

*

Leonard of Quirm: skilled artist and certified genius with a mind that wandered so much it came back with souvenirs.

Leonard's books were full of sketches – of kittens, of the way water flows, of the wives of influential Ankh-Morporkian merchants whose

---

† The Reader had a theory that all the really good books in any building – at least, all the really funny ones‡ – gravitate to a pile in the privy but no one ever has time to read all of them, *or even knows how they came to be there.*

‡ The ones with cartoons about cows and dogs. And captions like: 'As soon as he saw the duck, Elmer knew it was going to be a bad day.'

portraits had provided his means of making a living. But Leonard had been a genius and was deeply sensitive to the wonders of the world, so the margins were full of detailed doodles of whatever was on his mind at that moment – vast water-powered engines for bringing down city walls on the heads of the enemy, new types of siege guns for pumping flaming oil over the enemy, gunpowder rockets that showered the enemy with burning phosphorus, and other manufactures of the Age of Reason.

*

'Proper footwear for a wizard is pointy shoes or good stout boots,' said Ridcully. 'When one's footwear turns creepy, something's amiss.'

'It's crêpe,' said the Dean. 'It's got a little pointy thingy over the—'

Ridcully breathed heavily. '*When your boots change by themselves—*' he growled.

'There's magic afoot?'

*

Susan . . . it wasn't a good name, was it? It wasn't a truly *bad* name, it wasn't like poor Iodine in the fourth form, or Nigella, a name which means 'oops, we wanted a boy'. But it was *dull*. Susan. Sue. Good old Sue. It was a name that made sandwiches, kept its head in difficult circumstances and could reliably look after other people's children.

It was a name used by no queens or goddesses anywhere.

And you couldn't do much even with the spelling. You could turn it into Suzi, and it sounded as though you danced on tables for a living. You could put in a Z and a couple of Ns and an E, but it still looked like a name with extensions built on. It was as bad as Sara, a name that cried out for a prosthetic H.

Dwarfs respected learning, provided they didn't have to experience it.

The Patrician leaned back in an attitude that suggested attentive listening. He was extremely good at listening. He created a kind of mental suction. People told him things just to avoid the silence.

*

'mumblemumblemumble,' said the Dean defiantly, a rebel without a pause.

*

Chrysoprase had been a very quick learner when he arrived in Ankh-Morpork. He began with an important lesson: hitting people was thuggery. Paying other people to do the hitting on your behalf was good business.

*

There is something very sad about an empty dressing room. It's like a discarded pair of underpants, which it resembles in a number of respects. It's seen a lot of activity. It may even have witnessed excitement and a whole gamut of human passions. And now there's nothing much left but a faint smell.

*

Foul Ole Ron was a physical schizophrenic. There was Foul Ole Ron, and there was the *smell* of Foul Ole Ron, which had obviously developed over the years to such an extent that it had a distinct personality. Anyone could have a smell that lingered long after they'd gone somewhere else, but the smell of Foul Ole Ron could actually arrive somewhere several minutes *before* he did, in order to spread out and get comfortable before he arrived. It had evolved into something so striking that it was no longer perceived with the nose, which shut down instantly in self-defence; people could tell that Foul Ole Ron was approaching by the way their ear wax started to melt.

*

'Ah, Drumknott,' said Lord Vetinari, 'just go and tell the head of the Musicians' Guild he wants a word with me, will you?'

*

Glod the dwarf looked up at a blank wall.

'I knew it!' he said. 'Didn't I say? Magic! How many times have we heard this story? There's a mysterious shop no one's ever seen before, and someone goes in and buys some rusty old curio, and it turns out to—'

'Glod—'

'—be some kind of talisman or a bottle full of genie, and then when there's trouble they go back and the shop—'

'Glod—?'

'—has *mysteriously disappeared* and gone back to whatever dimension it came from— yes, what is it?'

'You're on the wrong side of the road. It's over here.'

*

Senior wizards developed a distinctive 50″ waist, 25″ leg shape that suggested someone who sat on a wall and required royal assistance to be put together again.

*

The Patrician was a pragmatist. He never tried to fix things that worked. Things that didn't work, however, got broken.

*

The question seldom addressed is *where* Medusa had snakes. Underarm hair is an even more embarrassing problem when it keeps biting the top of the deodorant bottle.

*

According to rural legend – at least in those areas where pigs are a vital part of the household economy – the

Hogfather is a winter myth figure who, on Hogswatchnight, gallops from house to house on a crude sledge drawn by four tusked wild boars to deliver presents of sausages, black puddings, pork scratchings and ham to all children who have been good. He says 'Ho ho ho' a lot. Children who have been bad get a bag full of bloody bones (it's these little details which tell you it's a tale for the little folk). There is a song about him. It begins: *You'd Better Watch Out . . .*

The Hogfather is said to have originated in the legend of a local king who, one winter's night, happened to be passing, or so he said, the home of three young women and heard them sobbing because they had no food to celebrate the midwinter feast. He took pity on them and threw a packet of sausages through the window.†

*

Rats had featured largely in the history of Ankh-Morpork. Shortly before the Patrician came to power there was a terrible plague of rats. The city council countered it by offering twenty pence for every rat tail. This did, for a week or two, reduce the number of rats – and then people were suddenly queuing up with tails, the city treasury was being drained, and no one seemed to be doing much work. And there *still* seemed to be a lot of rats around. Lord Vetinari had listened carefully while the problem was explained, and had solved the thing with one memorable phrase which said a lot about him, about the folly of bounty offers, and about the natural instinct of Ankh-Morporkians in any situation involving money: 'Tax the rat farms.'

Old shoes always turn up in the bottom of every wardrobe.

If a mermaid had a wardrobe old shoes would turn up in the bottom of it.

† Badly concussing one of them, but there's no point in spoiling a good legend.

INTERESTING TIMES

MIGHTY battles! Revolution! Death! War! (and his sons Terror and Panic, and daughter Clancy).

The oldest and most inscrutable empire on the Discworld is in turmoil, brought about by the revolutionary treatise *What I Did On My Holidays*. Workers are uniting, with nothing to lose but their water buffaloes. War (and Clancy) are spreading throughout the ancient cities.

And all that stands in the way of terrible doom for everyone is:

Rincewind the Wizzard, who can't even spell the word 'wizard'...

Cohen the barbarian hero, five foot tall in his surgical sandals, who has a lifetime's experience of not dying ...

... and a very *special* butterfly.

It was, as always, a matter of protocol . . .

Lord Vetinari, as supreme ruler of Ankh-Morpork, could in theory summon the Archchancellor of Unseen University to his presence and, indeed, have him executed if he failed to obey.

On the other hand Mustrum Ridcully, as head of the college of wizards, had made it clear in polite but firm ways that he could turn him into a small amphibian and, indeed, start jumping around the room on a pogo stick.

Alcohol bridged the diplomatic gap nicely. Sometimes Lord Vetinari invited the Archchancellor to the Palace for a convivial drink. And of course the Archchancellor went, because it would be *bad manners* not to. And everyone understood the position, and everyone was on their best behaviour, and thus civil unrest and slime on the carpet were averted.

*

Many things went on at Unseen University and, regrettably, teaching had to be one of them. The faculty had long ago confronted this fact and had perfected various devices for avoiding it. But this was perfectly all right because, to be fair, so had the students.

The system worked quite well and, as happens in such cases, had taken on the status of a tradition. Lectures clearly took place, because they were down there on the timetable in black and white. The fact that no one attended was an irrelevant detail. It was occasionally maintained that this meant that the lectures did not in fact happen at all, but no one ever attended them to find out if this was true. Anyway, it was argued that lectures had taken place *in essence*, so that was all right, too.

And therefore education at the University mostly worked by the age-old method of putting a lot of young people in the vicinity of a lot of books and hoping that something would pass from one to the other, while the actual young people put themselves in the vicinity of inns and taverns for exactly the same reason.

*

'Round everyone up. My study. Ten minutes,' said Ridcully. He was a great believer in this approach. A less direct Archchancellor would have wandered around looking for everyone. His policy was to find one person and make their life difficult until everything happened the way he wanted it to.

*

'Oh, no,' said the Lecturer in Recent Runes, pushing his chair back. 'Not that. That's meddling with things you don't understand.'

'Well we *are* wizards,' said Ridcully. 'We're supposed to meddle with things we don't understand. If we hung around waitin' till we understood things we'd never get anything done.'

*

Lord Hong had risen to the leadership of one of the most influential families in the Empire by relentless application, total focusing of his mental powers, and six well-executed deaths. The last one had been that of his father, who'd died happy in the knowledge that his son was maintaining an old family tradition. The senior families venerated their ancestors, and saw no harm in prematurely adding to their number.

*

'Comrades, we must strike at the very heart of the rottenness. We must storm the Winter Palace!'

'Excuse me, but it is June.'

'Then we can storm the Summer Palace!'

*

Lord Hong was playing chess, against himself. It was the only way he could find an opponent of his calibre but, currently, things were stalemated because both sides were adopting a defensive strategy which was, admittedly, brilliant.

*

There was this to be said about Cohen. If there was no reason for him to kill you, such as you having any large amount of treasure or being between him and somewhere he wanted to get to, then he was good company.

*

'You know their big dish down on the coast?' [said Cohen.]

'No.'

'Pig's ear soup. Now, what's that tell you about a place, eh?'

Rincewind shrugged. 'Very provident people?'

'Some other bugger pinches the pig . . . There's men here who can push a wheelbarrow for thirty miles on a bowl of millet with a bit of scum in it. What does that tell you? It tells *me* someone's porking all the beef.'

*

Self-doubt was not something regularly entertained within the Cohen cranium. When you're trying to carry a struggling temple maiden and a sack of looted temple goods in one hand and fight off half a dozen angry priests with the other there is little time for reflection. Natural selection saw to it that professional heroes who at a crucial moment tended to ask themselves questions like 'What is my purpose in life?' very quickly lacked both.

*

Cohen's father had taken him to a mountain top, when he was no more than a lad, and explained to him the hero's creed and told him that there was no greater joy than to die in battle.

Cohen had seen the flaw in this straight away, and a lifetime's experience had reinforced his belief that in fact a greater joy was to kill the *other* bugger in battle and end up sitting on a heap of gold higher than your horse.

*

'We are a travelling theatre,' she said. 'It is convenient. Noh actors are allowed to move around.'

'Aren't they?' said Rincewind.

'You do not understand. We *are* Noh actors.'

'Oh, you weren't too bad.'

*

Merchants always had money. But it seemed wrong to think of it as *belonging* to them; it *belonged* to whoever took it off them. Merchants didn't actually *own* it, they were just looking after it until it was needed.

*

The Silver Horde were honest (from their specialized point of view) and decent (from their specialized point of view) and saw the world as hugely simple. They stole from rich merchants and temples and kings. They didn't steal from poor people; this was not because there was anything virtuous about poor people, it was simply because poor people had no money.

And although they didn't set out to give the money *away* to the poor, that was nevertheless what they did (if you accepted that the poor consisted of innkeepers, ladies of negotiable virtue, pickpockets, gamblers and general hangers-on), because although they would go to great lengths to steal money they then had as much control over it as a man trying to herd cats. It was there to be spent and lost. So they kept the money in circulation, always a praiseworthy thing in any society.

*

Eventually an officious voice said, 'What do you have to say for yourself, miserable louse?'

'Well, I—'

'Silence!'

Ah. So it was going to be *that* kind of interview.

*

Six Beneficent Winds had the same sense of humour as a chicken casserole. True, he played the accordion for amusement, and disliked cats intensely, and had a habit of dabbing his upper lip with his napkin after his tea ceremony in a way that had made Mrs Beneficent Winds commit murder in her mind on a regular basis over the years. And he kept his money in a small leather shovel purse, and counted it out very thoroughly whenever he made a purchase, especially if there was a queue behind him.

*

Rincewind and Twoflower lay in their separate cells and talked about the good old days. At least, Twoflower talked about the good old days. Rincewind worked at a crack in the stone with a piece of straw, it being all he had to hand. It would take several thousand years to make any kind of impression, but that was no reason to give up . . .

A little piece of mortar fell away.

Not bad for ten minutes' work, thought Rincewind. Come the next Ice Age, we're out of here . . .

*

'But there are causes worth dying for,' said Butterfly.

'No, there aren't! Because you've only got one life but you can pick up another five causes on any street corner!'

'Good grief, how can you *live* with a philosophy like that?'

Rincewind took a deep breath.

'Continuously!'

'Luck is my middle name,' said Rincewind, indistinctly. 'Mind you, my first name is Bad.'

It was something about Cohen. Maybe it was what they called charisma. It overpowered even his normal smell of a goat that had just eaten curried asparagus.

*

There was muttering from the Horde.

'Bruce the Hoon never went in the back way.'

'Shut up.'

'Never one for back gates, Bruce the Hoon.'

'Shut up.'

'When Bruce the Hoon attacked Al Khali, he did it right at the main guard tower, with a thousand screaming men on very small horses.'

'Yeah, but . . . last I saw of Bruce the Hoon, his head was on a spike.'

'All right, I'll grant you that. But at least it was over the main gate. I mean, at least he got in.'

'His head did.'

*

'Who're you?' said Cohen. He drew his sword. 'I need to know so's it can be put on your gravestone—'

*

'They want to parley,' said Six Beneficent Winds.

'Why don't we just invite them to dinner and massacre them all when they're drunk?'

'You heard the man. There's seven hundred thousand of them.'

'Ah? So it'd have to be something simple with pasta, then.'

*

The Four Horsemen whose Ride presages the end of the world are known to be Death, War, Famine and Pestilence. But even less significant events have their own Horsemen. For example, the Four Horsemen of the Common Cold are Sniffles, Chesty, Nostril and Lack of Tissues; the Four Horsemen whose appearance foreshadows any public holiday are Storm, Gales, Sleet and Contra-flow.

*

Lord Hong looked at himself in the mirror.

He'd gone to great lengths to achieve this. He had used several agents, none of whom knew the whole plan. But the Ankh-Morpork tailor had been good at his work and the measurements had been followed exactly. From pointy boots to hose to doublet, cloak and hat with a feather in it, Lord Hong knew he was a perfect Ankh-Morpork gentleman. The cloak was lined with silk.

He'd walk through the city on that first great day and the people would be silent when they saw their natural leader.

It never crossed his mind that anyone would say, ''Ere, wot a toff! 'Eave 'arf a brick at 'im!'

*

'You sound a very educated man for a barbarian,' said Rincewind.

'I didn't start out a barbarian. I used to be a school teacher. But I decided to give it up and make a living by the sword.'

'After being a teacher all your life?'

'It did mean a change of perspective, yes.'

'But . . . well . . . surely . . . the privation, the terrible hazards, the daily risk of death . . .'

Mr Saveloy brightened up. 'Oh, you've *been* a teacher, have you?'

*

'There's a lot of waiting in warfare,' said Boy Willie.

'Ah, yes,' said Mr Saveloy. 'I've heard people say that. They say there's long periods of boredom followed by short periods of excitement.'

'Not really,' said Cohen. 'It's more like short periods of waiting followed by long periods of being dead.'

*

There were a large number of ranks in the armies of the Empire, and many of them were untranslatable. Three Pink Pig and Five White Fang were, loosely speaking, privates, and not just because they were pale, vulnerable and inclined to curl up and hide when danger threatened.

*

Pushing their way angrily through the soldiers came an altogether different breed of warrior. They were taller, and heavier armoured, with splendid helmets and moustaches that looked like a declaration of war in themselves.

'Wassat?' said Cohen.

'He's a samurai,' said Mr Saveloy.

One samurai glared at Cohen. He pulled a scrap of silk out of his armour and tossed it into the air. His other hand grabbed the hilt of his long, thin sword . . .

There was hardly even a hiss, but three shreds of silk tumbled gently to the ground.

'Get back, Teach,' said Cohen slowly. 'I reckon this one's mine. Got another hanky? Thanks.'

The samurai looked at Cohen's sword. It was long, heavy and had so many notches it could have been used as a saw.

'You'll never do it,' he said. 'With that sword? Never.'

Cohen blew his nose noisily.

'You say?' he said. 'Watch this.'

The handkerchief soared into the air. Cohen gripped his sword . . .

He'd beheaded three upward-staring samurai before the handkerchief started to tumble.

'And the message is,' said Cohen, 'either fight or muck about, it's up to you.'

*

Golem . . . They were usually just figures made out of clay and animated with some suitable spell or prayer. They pottered about doing simple odd jobs. The problem was not putting them to work but stopping them from working; if you set a golem to digging the garden and then forgot about it, you'd come back to find it'd planted a row of beans 1500 miles long.

Woolly Thinking. Which is like Fuzzy Logic, only less so.

MASKERADE

THE Opera House, Ankh-Morpork . . .

. . . a huge, rambling building, where masked figures and hooded shadows do wicked deeds in the wings . . . where dying the death on stage is a little bit more than just a metaphor . . . where innocent young sopranos are lured to their destiny by an evil mastermind in a hideously deformed evening dress . . .

Where . . .

. . . there's a couple of old ladies in pointy hats eating peanuts in the gods and looking up at the big chandelier and saying things like: 'There's an accident waiting to happen if ever I saw one.'

Yes . . . Granny Weatherwax and Nanny Ogg, the Discworld's greatest witches, are back for an innocent night out at the opera.

So there's going to be trouble (but nevertheless a good evening's entertainment with murders you can really *hum* . . .)

Black Aliss; pushed into her own stove by a couple of kids, and everyone said it was a damn' good thing, even if it took a whole week to clean the oven.

They said weapons couldn't pierce her. Swords bounced off her skin. And she turned people into gingerbread and had a house made of frogs.

*

She stopped. At least, *most* of Agnes stopped. There was a lot of Agnes. It took some time for outlying regions to come to rest.

*

Agnes had woken up one morning with the horrible realization that she'd been saddled with a lovely personality. It was the lack of choice that rankled. No one had asked her, before she was born, whether she wanted a lovely personality or whether she'd prefer, say, a miserable personality but a body that could take size 9 in dresses. Instead, people would take pains to tell her that beauty was only skin-deep, as if a man ever fell for an attractive pair of kidneys.

*

People were generally glad to see Nanny Ogg. She was good at making them feel at home in their own home.

*

Lancre had always bred strong, capable women. A Lancre farmer needed a wife who'd think nothing of beating a wolf to death with her apron when she went out to get some firewood. And, while kissing initially seemed to have more charms than cookery, a stolid Lancre lad looking for a bride would bear in mind his father's advice that kisses eventually lost their fire but cookery tended to get even better over the years, and direct his courting to those families that clearly showed a tradition of enjoying their food.

*

Granny is always there for the difficult times.

'Maybe you could . . . help us?'

'What's wrong?'

'It's my boy . . .'

Granny opened the door further and saw the woman standing behind Mr Slot. One look at her face was enough. There was a bundle in her arms.

Granny stepped back. 'Bring him in and let me have a look at him.'

She took the baby from the woman, sat down on the room's one chair, and pulled back the blanket.

'Hmm,' said Granny, after a while.

'There's a curse on this house, that's what it is,' said Slot. 'My best cow's been taken mortally sick, too.'

'Oh? You have a cowshed?' said Granny. 'Very good place for a sickroom, a cowshed. It's the warmth. You better show me where it is.'

'You want to take the boy down there?'

'Right now.'

The man looked at his wife, and shrugged. 'Well, I'm sure you know your business best,' he said. 'It's this way.'

He led the witches down some back stairs and across a yard and into the fetid sweet air of the byre. A cow was stretched out on the straw. It rolled an eye madly as they entered, and tried to moo.

Granny took in the scene and stood looking thoughtful for a moment.

Then she said, 'This will do.'

'What do you need?' said Slot.

'All I shall require is a candle,' said Granny. 'A new one, for preference.'

'That's all?'

'And some matches,' said Granny. 'A pack of cards might be useful, too.'

The child was brought down in a blanket and made as comfortable as possible.

'You just leave me in here tonight. And no one is to come in, right? No matter what.'

The mother gave a worried curtsey. 'But I thought I might look in about midn—'

'No one. Now, off you go.'

Granny closed the door.

She spent some time arranging boxes and barrels so that she had a crude table and something to sit on. The air was warm and smelled of bovine flatulence. Periodically she checked the health of both patients, although there was little enough to check.

She waited a little longer and then lit the candle. Its cheery flame gave the place a warm and comforting glow.

After some immeasurable piece of time the flame flickered. It would have passed unnoticed by anyone who hadn't been concentrating on it for some while.

She took a deep breath and—

'Good morning,' said Granny Weatherwax.

GOOD MORNING, said a voice by her ear.

Granny breathed out, slowly.

'Come and sit where I can see you. That's good manners. And let me tell you right now that I ain't at all afraid of you.'

The tall, black-robed figure walked across the floor and sat down on a handy barrel, leaning its scythe against the wall. Then it pushed back its hood. Granny folded her arms and stared calmly at the visitor, meeting his gaze eye-to-socket.

Death leaned forward. The candlelight raised new shadows on his skull.

COURAGE IS EASY BY CANDLELIGHT. YOUR FAITH, I SUSPECT, IS IN THE FLAME.

Granny leaned forward, and blew out the candle. Then she folded her arms again and stared fiercely ahead of her.

After some length of time a voice said, ALL RIGHT, YOU'VE MADE YOUR POINT.

Granny lit a match. Its flare illuminated the skull opposite, which hadn't moved.

'Fair enough,' she said, as she relit the candle. 'We don't want to be sitting here all night, do we? How many have you come for?'

ONE.

'The cow?'

Death shook his head.

'It could *be* the cow.'

NO. THAT WOULD BE CHANGING HISTORY.

'History is about things changing.'

NO.

Granny sat back.

'Then I challenge you to a game. That's traditional. That's *allowed*.'

Death was silent for a moment.

THIS IS TRUE.

'Good.'

HOWEVER . . . YOU UNDERSTAND THAT TO WIN ALL YOU MUST GAMBLE ALL?

'Double or quits? Yes, I know.'

BUT NOT CHESS.

'Can't abide chess.'

OR CRIPPLE MR ONION. I'VE NEVER BEEN ABLE TO UNDERSTAND THE RULES.

'Very well. How about one hand of poker? Five cards each, no draws? Sudden death, as they say.'

Death thought about this, too.

YOU KNOW THIS FAMILY?

No.

THEN WHY?

'Are we talking or are we playing?'

OH, VERY WELL.

Granny picked up the pack of cards and shuffled it, not looking at her hands, and smiling at Death all the time. She dealt five cards each.

Granny looked at her cards, and threw them down.

FOUR QUEENS. HMM. THAT *IS* VERY HIGH.

Death looked down at his cards, and then up into Granny's steady, blue-eyed gaze.

Neither moved for some time.

Then Death laid the hand on the table.

I LOSE, he said. ALL I HAVE IS FOUR ONES.

He looked back into Granny's eyes for a moment. There was a blue glow in the depth of his eye-sockets. Maybe, for the merest fraction of a second, barely noticeable even to the closest observation, one winked off.

Granny nodded, and extended a hand.

She prided herself on the ability to judge people by their gaze and their handshake, which in this case was a rather chilly one.

'Take the cow,' she said.

IT IS A VALUABLE CREATURE.

'Who knows what the child will become?'

Death stood up, and reached for his scythe.

He said, OW.

'Ah, yes. I couldn't help noticing,' said Granny Weatherwax, as the tension drained out of the atmosphere, 'that you seem to be sparing that arm.'

OH, YOU KNOW HOW IT IS. REPETITIVE ACTIONS AND SO ON . . .

'It could get serious if you left it.'

HOW SERIOUS?

'Want me to have a look?'

WOULD YOU MIND? IT CERTAINLY ACHES ON COLD NIGHTS.

Granny's hands touched smooth bone. She felt, thought, gripped, twisted . . .

There was a click.

Ow.

'Now try it above the shoulder.'

ER. HMM. YES. IT DOES SEEM CONSIDERABLY MORE FREE. YES, INDEED. MY WORD, YES. THANK YOU VERY MUCH.

Death walked away. A moment later there was a faint gasp from the cow. That and a slight sagging of the skin were all that apparently marked the transition from living animal to cooling meat.

Granny picked up the baby and laid a hand on its forehead.

'Fever's gone,' she said.

MISTRESS WEATHERWAX? said Death from the doorway.

'Yes, sir?'

I HAVE TO KNOW. WHAT WOULD HAVE HAPPENED IF I HAD NOT . . . LOST?

'At the cards, you mean?'

YES. WHAT WOULD YOU HAVE DONE?

Granny laid the baby down carefully on the straw, and smiled.

'Well,' she said, 'for a start . . . I'd have broken your bloody arm.'

*

'So you'll go and see Mr Goatberger and have this stopped, right?'

'Yes, Esme.'

'And I'll come with you to make sure you do.'

'Yes, Esme.'

'And we'll talk to the man about your money.'

'Yes, Esme.'

'And we might just drop in on young Agnes to make sure she's all right.'

'Yes, Esme.'

'But we'll do it diplomatic like. We don't want people thinkin' we're pokin' our noses in.'

'Yes, Esme.'

'No one could say I interfere where I'm not wanted. You won't find anyone callin' *me* a busybody.'

'Yes, Esme.'

'That was, "Yes, Esme, you won't find anyone callin' *you* a busybody", was it?'

'Oh, yes, Esme.'

'You sure about that?'

'Yes, Esme.'

'Good.'

'It's too draughty on broomsticks this time of year, Esme. The breeze gets into places I wouldn't dream of talking about.'

'Really? Can't imagine where those'd be, then.'

She looked around with a wide, friendly grin at the occupants of the coach.

'Morning,' she said, delving into the sack. 'I'm Gytha Ogg, I've got fifteen children, this is my friend Esme Weatherwax, we're going to Ankh-Morpork, would anyone like an egg sandwich? I've brung plenty. The cat's been sleepin' on them but they're fine, look, they bend back all right. No? Please yourself, I'm sure. Let's see what else we've got . . . ah, has anybody got an opener for a bottle of beer?'

A man in the corner indicated that he might have such a thing.

'Fine,' said Nanny Ogg. 'Anyone got something to drink a bottle of beer out of?'

Another man nodded hopefully.

'Good,' said Nanny Ogg. 'Now, has anybody got a bottle of beer?'

Ahahahahaha! Ahahahaha! Aahahaha! BEWARE!!!!! Yrs sincerely, The Opera Ghost

'What sort of person,' said Salzella, 'sits down and *writes* a maniacal laugh? And all those exclamation marks, you notice? Five? A sure sign of someone who wears his underpants on his head. Opera can do that to a man.'

Most people in Lancre, as the saying goes, went to bed with the chickens and got up with the cows.†

*

'I grew up in Rookery Yard in The Shades. They're in Ankh-Morpork,' said Henry. 'It was a terrible rough place. There were only three ways out. You could sing your way out or you could fight your way out.'

'What was the third way?' said Nanny.

'Oh, you could go down that little alleyway into Shamlegger Street and then cut down into Treacle Mine Road,' said Henry. 'But no one ever amounted to anything who went *that* way.'

*

'You . . . you do *know* what *kind* of place this is, do you, Esme?' said Nanny Ogg.

'Oh, yes,' said Granny, calmly.

Nanny's patience gave out. 'It's a house of ill repute, is what it is!'

'On the contrary,' said Granny. 'I believe people speak very highly of it.'

*

'I'm Mrs Ogg,' said Nanny Ogg.

The man looked her up and down.

'Oh yes? Can you identify yourself?'

'Certainly. I'd know me anywhere.'

† Er. That is to say, they went to bed at the same time as the chickens went to bed, and got up at the same time as the cows got up. Loosely worded sayings can really cause misunderstandings.

*

'Honestly, Salzella . . . what *is* the difference between opera and madness?'

'Is this a trick question?'

*

The Opera House was that most efficiently multifunctional of building designs. It was a cube. But the architect had suddenly realized late in the day that there ought to be *some* sort of decoration, and had shoved it on hurriedly, in a riot of friezes, pillars, corybants and curly bits. Gargoyles had colonized the higher reaches. The effect, seen from the front, was of a huge wall of tortured stone.

Round the back, of course, there was the usual drab mess of windows, pipes and damp stone walls. One of the rules of a certain type of public architecture is that it only happens at the front.

*

'Well, basically there are two sorts of opera,' said Nanny, who also had the true witch's ability to be confidently expert on the basis of no experience whatsoever. 'There's your heavy opera, where basically people sing foreign and it goes like "Oh oh oh, I am dyin', oh, I am dyin', oh, oh, oh, that's what I'm doin' ", and there's your light opera, where they sing in foreign and it basically goes "Beer! Beer! Beer! Beer! I like to drink lots of beer!", although sometimes they drink champagne instead. That's basically all of opera, reely.'

*

Someone tapped Granny Weatherwax on her shoulder. 'Madam, kindly remove your hat.'

Nanny Ogg choked on her peppermint.

Granny Weatherwax turned to the red-faced gentleman behind her. 'You do know what a woman in a pointy hat is, don't you?' she said.

'*Yes*, madam. A woman in a pointy hat is sitting in front of me.'

*

People didn't take any notice of little old ladies who looked as though they fitted in, and Nanny Ogg could fit in faster than a dead chicken in a maggot factory.

Nanny had a mind like a buzzsaw behind a face like an elderly apple.

This was Ankh-Morpork's most prestigious dress shop, and one way of telling was the apparent absence of anything so crass as merchandise. The occasional carefully placed piece of expensive material merely hinted at the possibilities available.

This was not a shop where things were bought. This was an emporium where you had a cup of coffee and a chat. Possibly, as a result of that muted conversation, four or five yards of exquisite fabric would change ownership in some ethereal way, and yet nothing so crass as *trade* would have taken place.

There was a crash from the direction of the kitchen,

although it was really more of a crashendo—the long-drawn-out clatter that begins when a pile of plates begins to slip, continues when someone tries to grab at them, develops a desperate counter-theme when the person realizes they don't have three hands, and ends with the *roinroinroin* of the one miraculously intact plate spinning round and round on the floor.

'Everyone acts as if it's only the music that matters! The plots don't make sense! Half the stories rely on people not recognizing their servants or wives because they've got a tiny mask on! Large ladies play the part of consumptive girls! No one can act properly! There should be a sign on the door saying "Leave your common sense here"! If it wasn't for the music the whole thing would be ridiculous!'

*

'Madam has *marvellous* hair,' said the hairdresser. 'What is the secret?'

'You've got to make sure there's no newts in the water,' said Granny.

*

The hulking figure seated at the organ turned around and gave her a friendly grin, which was much wider than the average grin. Its owner was covered in red hair and, while short-changed in the leg department, had obviously been first in the queue when the arm counter opened. And had also been given a special free offer of lip.

*

Nanny didn't so much enter places as insinuate herself; she had unconsciously taken a natural talent for liking people and developed it into an occult science.

*

'And what can I get you, officers?' she said.

'Officers? Us? What makes you think we're watchmen?'

'He's got a helmet on,' Nanny pointed out.

'Milit'ry chic,' Nobby said. 'It's just a fashion accessory. Actually, we are gentlemen of means and have nothing to do with the City Watch whatsoever.'

'Well, *gentlemen*, would you like some wine?'

'Not while we on duty, t'anks,' said the troll.

*

Granny Weatherwax could be nasty, but then nastiness was always in the window: you were aware that it might turn up on the menu. Sharpness from Nanny Ogg, though, was like being bitten by a big friendly dog. It was all the worse for being unexpected.

'What about the show? We can't just stop! You *never* stop the show, not even if someone dies!'

'Oh, we have stopped when people died . . .'

'Yes, but only as long as it took to get the body off-stage!'

*

'Corporal Nobbs has got some papers to prove he's a human being.'

'Forged?'

'I don't think so.'

FEET OF CLAY

THERE'S a werewolf with Pre-Lunar Tension in Ankh-Morpork.

And a dwarf with attitude and a golem who's begun to think for itself.

But for Commander Vimes, Head of Ankh-Morpork City Watch, that's only the start . . .

There's treason in the air.

A crime has happened.

He's not only got to find out whodunit, but howdunit too. He's not even sure what they dun.

But as soon as he knows what the questions are, he's going to want some answers.

'Your sedan chair is outside, sir.'

It had been a wedding present from the Patrician. Lord Vetinari knew that Vimes loved walking the streets of the city, and so it was very typical of the man that he presented him with something that did not allow him to do so.

It was waiting outside. The two bearers straightened up expectantly.

Vimes looked at the front man and motioned with a thumb to the chair's door. 'Get in,' he commanded.

'But sir—'

'It's a nice morning,' said Vimes, taking off his coat. 'I'll drive myself.'

*

Through werewolf eyes the world was *different*.

For one thing, it was in black-and-white. At least, that small part of it which as a human she'd thought of as 'vision' was monochrome – but who cared that vision had to take a back seat when smell drove instead, laughing and sticking its arm out of the window and making rude gestures at all the other senses?

*

She kept telling herself she had it under control and she did, in a way. She prowled the city on moonlit nights and, okay, there was the occasional chicken, but she always remembered where she'd been and went round next day to shove some money under the door.

It was hard to be a vegetarian who had to pick bits of meat out of her teeth in the morning.

It was easy to be a vegetarian by day. It was preventing yourself from becoming a humanitarian at night that took the real effort.

*

Vimes has some problems with his imp-driven personal organizer:

'Memo: See Corporal Nobbs re timekeeping; also re Earldom.'

'Got it,' said the imp. 'Would you like to be reminded of this at any particular time?'

'I think I'll write it in my notebook, if you don't mind,' said Vimes.

'Oh, well, if you prefer, I can recognize handwriting,' said the imp proudly. 'I'm quite advanced.'

Vimes pulled out his notebook and held it up. 'Like this?' he said.

The imp squinted for a moment. 'Yep,' it said. 'That's handwriting, sure enough. Curly bits, spiky bits, all joined together. Yep. Handwriting. I'd recognize it anywhere.'

*

Mr Raddley drew himself up.

'We want to take Father Tubelcek away to bury him,' he said.

Detritus turned to Cheery Littlebottom. 'You done everyt'ing you need?'

'I suppose so . . .'

'He dead?'

'Oh, yes.'

'He gonna get any better?'

'Better than dead? I doubt it.'

'Okay, den you people can take him away.'

The Patrician is taken unwell and receives a visit from horse doctor Doughnut Jimmy.

'Commander Vimes is right. It *could* be arsenic,' Cheery said. 'It looks like arsenic poisoning to me. Look at his colour.'

'Nasty stuff,' said Doughnut Jimmy. 'Has he been eating his bedding?'

'All the sheets seem to be here, so I suppose the answer is no.'

'How's he pissing?'

'Er. The usual way, I assume.'

'Walk him round a bit on the loose rein,' Doughnut said.

The Patrician opened his eyes. 'You *are* a doctor, aren't you?' he said.

'Well, yeah . . . I have a lot of patients,' he said.

'Indeed? I have very little,' said the Patrician.

'Do you remember your father, Nobby?'

'Old Sconner, sir? Not much, sir. Never used to see him much except when the milit'ry police used to come for to drag him outa the attic.'

Vimes waved a hand vaguely. 'He didn't . . . leave you anything? Or anything?'

'Coupla scars, sir. And this trick elbow of mine. It aches sometimes, when the weather changes. And this, o' course . . .' The corporal pulled out a leather thong that hung around his neck. There was a gold ring on it.

'He left it to me when he was on his deathbed,' said Nobby. 'Well, when I say "left it" . . .'

'Did he say anything?'

'Well, yeah, he did say "Give it back, you little bugger!", sir.'

*

Cheery is new to the Watch and has gone out on an official visit with Angua.

'You can knock.'

'Me? They won't take any notice of me!' said Cheery.

'You show them your badge and tell them you're the Watch.'

'They'll ignore me! They'll laugh at me!'

'You're going to have to do it sooner or later. Go on.'

The door was opened by a stout man . . . A dwarf voice in the region of his navel said, 'We're the Watch, right? Oh, yes! And if you don't let us in we'll have your guts for starters!'

'Good try,' murmured Angua.

*

'I've got a lot to learn, I can see,' said Cheery. 'I never thought you had to carry bits of blanket, for a start!'

'It's special equipment if you're dealing with the undead.'

'Well, I knew about garlic and vampires. Anything holy works on vampires. What else works on werewolves?'

'A gin and tonic's always welcome,' said Angua distantly.

*

The tincture of night began to suffuse the soup of the afternoon.

Lord Vetinari considered the sentence, and found it good. He liked 'tincture' particularly. Tincture. *Tinc*ture. It was a distinguished word, and pleasantly countered by the flatness of 'soup'. The soup of the afternoon. Yes. In which may well be found the croutons of teatime.

*

'I have to admit,' said Mrs Palm, 'that under Vetinari it has certainly been safer to walk the streets—'

'You should know, madam,' said Mr Sock. Mrs Palm gave him an icy look. There were a few sniggers.

'I *meant* that a modest payment to the Thieves' Guild is all that is required for perfect safety,' she finished.

'And, indeed, a man may visit a house of ill—'

'Negotiable hospitality,' said Mrs Palm quickly.

'Indeed, and be quite confident of not waking up stripped stark naked and beaten black and blue,' said Sock.

'Unless his tastes run that way,' said Mrs Palm. 'We aim to give satisfaction. Very accurately, if required.'

'Life has certainly been more reliable under Vetinari,' said Mr Potts of the Bakers' Guild.

'He does have all street-theatre players and mime artists thrown into the scorpion pit,' said Mr Boggis of the Thieves' Guild.

'True. But let's not forget that he has his bad points too.'

'What's this?'

'A Klatchian Hots without anchovies,' said Vimes, lifting the cover. 'We got it from Ron's Pizza Hovel round the corner.'

'Has someone *already* eaten this, Vimes?'

'No, sir. That's just how they chop up the food.'

'Oh, I *see*. I thought perhaps the food-tasters were getting over-enthusiastic,' said the Patrician. 'My word. What a treat I have to look forward to.'

'I think he's got a sort of soft spot for the Patrician, in his way. He once said that if anyone was going to kill Vetinari he'd like it to be him.'

*

'I've been running around looking for damn Clues instead of just thinking for five minutes!' said Vimes.

'What is it I'm always telling you?'
'Never trust anybody, sir?'
'No, not that.'
'Everyone's guilty of something, sir?'
'Not that, either.'
'Just because someone's a member of an ethnic minority doesn't mean they're not a nasty small-minded little jerk, sir?'
'N— When did I say that?'
'Last week, sir. After we'd had that visit from the Campaign for Equal Heights, sir.'

*

Angua thinks Carrot is about to propose.

'Hello, Angua!' said Carrot cheerfully. 'I was just coming to see you.'
He took off his helmet, and smoothed back his hair. 'Er . . .' he began.
'I know what you're going to ask,' said Angua.
'You do?'
'I know you've been thinking about it. You knew I was wondering about going.'
'It was obvious, was it?'
'And the answer's no. I wish it could be yes.'
Carrot looked astonished. 'It never occurred to me that you'd say no,' he said. 'I mean, why should you?'
'Good grief, you amaze me,' she said. 'You really do.'
'I thought it'd be something you'd want to do,' said Carrot. He sighed. 'Oh, well . . . it doesn't matter, really.'
Angua felt that a leg had been kicked away. 'It doesn't *matter*?' she said.
'I mean, yes, it'd have been nice, but I won't lose any sleep over it.'
'You won't?'
'Well, no. Obviously not. You've got other things you want to do. That's fine. I just thought you might enjoy it. I'll do it by myself.'
'What? How can . . .?' Angua stopped. 'What are you *talking* about, Carrot?'
'The Dwarf Bread Museum. I promised Mr Hopkinson's sister that I'd tidy it up. I just thought it might cheer you up, but I appreciate that bread isn't everyone's cup of tea.'

Detritus was particularly good when it came to asking questions. He had three basic ones. They were the direct ('Did you do it?'), the persistent ('Are you sure it wasn't you what done it?') and the subtle ('It was you what done it, wasn't it?'). Although they were not the most cunning questions ever devised, Detritus's talent was to go on patiently asking them for hours on end, until he got the right answer, which was generally something like: 'Yes! Yes! I did it! I did it!

Now please tell me what it was I did!'

It is a pervasive and beguiling myth that the people who design instruments of death end up being killed by them. There is *almost* no foundation in fact. Colonel Shrapnel wasn't blown up, M. Guillotin died with his head on, Colonel Gatling wasn't shot. If it hadn't been for the murder of cosh and blackjack maker Sir William Blunt-Instrument in an alleyway, the rumour would never have got started.

The Ankh-Morpork view of crime and punishment

was that the penalty for the first offence should prevent the possibility of a second offence.

HOGFATHER

IT'S the night before Hogswatch. And it's too quiet.

Where is the big jolly fat man? Why is *Death* creeping down chimneys and trying to say Ho Ho Ho? The darkest night of the year is getting a lot darker . . .

Susan the gothic governess has got to sort it out by morning, otherwise there won't *be* a morning. Ever again . . .

The 20th Discworld novel is a festive feast of darkness and Death (but with jolly robins and tinsel too).

As they say: You'd better watch out . . .

Everything starts somewhere, although many physicists disagree.

*

The senior wizards of Unseen University stood and looked at the door.

There was no doubt that whoever had shut it wanted it to stay shut. Dozens of nails secured it to the door frame. Planks had been nailed right across. And finally it had, up until this morning, been hidden by a bookcase that had been put in front of it.

'And there's the sign, Ridcully,' said the Dean. 'You *have* read it, I assume. You know? The sign which says "Do not, under any circumstances, open this door"?'

'Of course I've read it,' said Ridcully. 'Why d'yer think I want it opened?'

*

Lord Downey was an assassin. Or, rather, an Assassin. The capital letter was important. It separated those curs who went around murdering people for money from the gentlemen who were occasionally consulted by other gentlemen who wished to have removed, for a consideration, any inconvenient razorblades from the candyfloss of life.

*

The members of the Guild of Assassins considered themselves cultured men who enjoyed good music and food and literature. And they knew the value of human life. To a penny, in many cases.

*

It was a quiet day for Susan, although on the way to the park Gawain trod on a crack in the pavement. On purpose.

'Gawain?' she said, eyeing a nervous bear who had suddenly spotted her and was now trying to edge away nonchalantly.

'Yes?'

'You meant to tread on that crack so that I'd have to thump some poor creature whose only fault is wanting to tear you limb from limb.'

'I was just skipping—'

'Quite. Real children don't go hoppity-skip unless they are on drugs.'

He grinned at her.

'If I catch you being twee again I will knot your arms behind your head,' said Susan levelly.

*

Susan reads a bedtime story:

'. . . and then Jack chopped down the beanstalk, adding murder and ecological vandalism to the theft, enticement and trespass charges already mentioned, but he got away with it and lived happily ever after without so much as a guilty twinge about what he had done. Which proves that you can be excused just about anything if you're a hero, because no one asks inconvenient questions.'

*

Death in person did not turn up upon the cessation of every life. It was not necessary. Governments govern, but prime ministers and presidents do not personally turn up in people's homes to tell them how to run their lives, because of the mortal danger this would present. There are laws instead.

*

It was the night before Hogswatch. All through the house . . .

. . . one creature stirred. It was a mouse.

And someone, in the face of all appropriateness, had baited a trap. Although, because it was the festive season, they'd used a piece of pork crackling. The smell of it had been driving the mouse mad all day but now, with no one about, it was prepared to risk it.

The mouse didn't know it was a trap. Mice aren't good at passing on information. Young mice aren't taken up to famous trap sites and told, 'This is where your Uncle Arthur passed away.' All it knew was that, what the hey, here was something to eat. On a wooden board with some wire round it.

A brief scurry later and its jaw had closed on the rind.

Or, rather, passed through it.

The mouse looked around at what was now lying under the big spring, and thought, 'Oops . . .'

Then its gaze went up to the black-clad figure that had faded into view by the wainscoting.

'Squeak?' it asked.

SQUEAK, said the Death of Rats.

'Never say die, master. That's our motto, eh?' said Albert. I CAN'T SAY IT'S EVER REALLY BEEN MINE.

In Biers, unless you weren't choosy, it paid to order a drink that was transparent because Igor also had undirected ideas about what you could stick on the end of a cocktail stick. If you saw something spherical and green, you just had to hope that it was an olive.

*

'Did you check the list?'

YES. TWICE. ARE YOU SURE THAT'S ENOUGH?

'Definitely.'

COULDN'T REALLY MAKE HEAD OR TAIL OF IT, TO TELL YOU THE TRUTH. HOW CAN I *TELL* IF HE'S BEEN NAUGHTY OR NICE, FOR EXAMPLE?

'Oh, well . . . I don't know . . . Has he hung his clothes up, that sort of thing . . .'

AND IF HE HAS BEEN GOOD I MAY GIVE HIM THIS KLATCHIAN WAR CHARIOT WITH REAL SPINNING SWORD BLADES?

'That's right.'

AND IF HE'S BEEN BAD?

Albert scratched his head. 'When I was a lad, you got a bag of bones. 's'mazing how kids got better behaved towards the end of the year.'

OH DEAR. AND NOW?

Albert held a package up to his ear and rustled it. 'Sounds like socks.'

SOCKS.

'Could be a woolly vest.'

SERVE HIM RIGHT, IF I MAY VENTURE TO EXPRESS AN OPINION . . .

*

The guard was cowering behind an overturned cabinet. He cringed back as Teatime stepped over it. 'What're you doing here?' he shouted. 'Who *are* you?'

'Ah, I'm glad you asked. I'm your worst nightmare!' said Teatime cheerfully.

The man shuddered.

'You mean . . . the one with the giant cabbage and the sort of whirring knife thing?'

'Sorry?' Teatime looked momentarily nonplussed.

'Then you're the one about where I'm falling, only instead of ground underneath it's all—'

'No, in fact I'm—'

The guard sagged. 'Awww, *not* the one where there's all this kind of, you know, mud and then everything goes blue—'

'No, I'm—'

'Oh, *shit*, then you're the one where there's this door only there's no floor beyond it and then there's these claws—'

'No,' said Teatime. 'Not that one.' He withdrew a dagger from his sleeve. 'I'm the one where this man comes out of nowhere and kills you stone dead.'

The guard grinned with relief. 'Oh, *that* one,' he said. 'But that one's not very—'

*

The snow had done what even wizards and the Watch couldn't do, which was clean up Ankh-Morpork. It hadn't had time to get dirty. In the morning it'd probably look as though the city had been covered in coffee meringue, but for now it mounded the bushes and trees in pure white.

*

Susan had never been able to see the attraction in cats. They were owned by the kind of people who liked puddings. There were actual people in the world whose idea of heaven would be a chocolate cat.

*

The late (or at least severely delayed) Bergholt Stuttley Johnson was generally recognized as the worst inventor in the world, yet in a very specialized sense. Merely *bad* inventors made things that failed to operate. He wasn't among these small fry. Any fool could make something that did absolutely nothing when you pressed the button. He scorned such fumble-fingered amateurs. Everything he built worked. It just didn't do what it said on the box. If you wanted a small ground-to-air missile, you asked Johnson to design an ornamental fountain. It amounted to pretty much the same thing. But this never discouraged him, or the morbid curiosity of his clients. Music, landscape gardening, architecture – there was no start to his talents.

*

Johnson's inventiveness didn't just push the edge of the envelope but often went across the room and out through the wall of the sorting office.

*

'Amazin',' said Ridcully. 'This thing's a kind of big artificial brain, then?'

'You *could* think of it like that,' said Ponder, carefully. 'Of course, Hex doesn't actually think. Not as such. It just *appears* to be thinking.'

'Ah. Like the Dean,' said Ridcully. 'Any chance of fitting a brain like this into the Dean's head?'

'It does weigh ten tons, Archchancellor.'

'Ah. Really? Oh. Quite a large crowbar would be in order, then.'

*

'I . . . *think* my name is Bilious. I'm the . . . I'm the oh God of Hangovers.'

'I've never heard of a God of Hangovers . . .'

'You've heard of Bibulous, the God of Wine?'

'Oh, yes.'

'Big fat man, wears vine leaves round his head, always pictured with a glass in his hand . . . Ow. Well, you know *why* he's so cheerful? Him and his big face? It's because he knows he's going to feel good in the morning! It's because it's *me* that—'

'—gets the hangovers?' said Susan.

'I don't even drink!' Bilious swayed. 'You know when people say "I had fifteen lagers last night and when I woke up my head was clear as a bell"?'

'Oh, yes.'

'Bastards! That's because *I* was the one who woke up groaning in a pile of recycled chilli. Just once, I mean just *once*, I'd like to open my eyes in the morning without my head sticking to something.'

*

'How do we usually test stuff?'

'Generally we ask for student volunteers,' said the Dean.

'What happens if we don't get any?'

'We give it to them anyway.'

'Isn't that a bit unethical?'

'Not if we don't tell them, Archchancellor.'

*

'I am *not* losing my hair!' snapped the Dean. 'It is just very finely spaced.'

'Half on your head and half on your hairbrush,' said the Lecturer in Recent Runes.

'No sense in bein' bashful about goin' bald,' said Ridcully evenly. 'Anyway, you know what they say about bald men, Dean.'

'Yes, they say, "Look at him, he's got no hair."'

*

At the far end of the corridor was one of the very tall, very thin windows. It looked out on to the black gardens. Black bushes, black grass, black trees. Skeletal fish cruising in the black waters of a pool, under black water lilies.

There was colour, in a sense, but it was the kind of colour you'd get if you could shine a beam of black through a prism. There were hints of tints, here and there a black you might persuade yourself was a very deep purple or a midnight blue. But it was basically black, under a black sky, because this was the world belonging to Death and that was all there was to it.

*

'Just shut up, will you?' Ridcully said. 'It's Hogswatch! That's *not* the time for silly arguments, all right?'

'Oh, yes it is,' said the Chair of Indefinite Studies glumly. 'It's exactly the time for silly arguments. In our family we were lucky to get through dinner without a reprise of What A Shame Henry Didn't Go Into Business With Our Ron. Or Why Hasn't Anyone Taught Those Kids To Use A Knife? That was another favourite.'

'And the sulks,' said Ponder Stibbons.

'Oh, the sulks,' said the Chair of Indefinite Studies. 'Not a proper Hogswatch without everyone sitting staring at different walls.'

'The games were worse,' said Ponder.

'Worse than the kids hitting one another with their toys, do you think? Not a proper Hogswatch afternoon without wheels and bits of broken dolly everywhere and everyone whining. Assault and battery included.'

'We had a game called Hunt the Slipper,' said Ponder. 'Someone hid a slipper. And then we had to find it. And then we had a row.'

'And then later on someone'll suggest a board game,' said Ponder.

'That's right. Where no one exactly remembers all the rules.'

'Which doesn't stop someone suggesting that you play for pennies.'

'And five minutes later there's two people not speaking to one another for the rest of their lives because of tuppence.'

'And some horrible little kid—'

'I know, I know! Some little kid who's been allowed to stay up wins everyone's money by being a nasty little cut-throat swot!'

'And don't forget the presents,' said the Chair of Indefinite Studies, as if reading off some internal list of gloom. 'How . . . how full of potential they seem in all that paper, how pregnant with possibilities . . . and then you open them and basically the wrapping paper was *more* interesting and you have to say "How thoughtful, that *will* come in handy!" It's not better to give than to receive, in my opinion, it's just less embarrassing.'

'I've worked out,' said the Senior Wrangler, 'that over the years I have been a net exporter of Hogswatch presents—'

'Oh, everyone is,' said the Chair. 'You spend a fortune on other people and what you get when all the paper is cleared away is one slipper that's the wrong colour and a book about ear wax.'

*

'You didn't get *that* stuff out of the sack! Not cigars and peaches in brandy and grub with fancy foreign names!'

YES, IT CAME OUT OF THE SACK.

Albert gave him a suspicious look.

'But you put it in the sack in the first place, didn't you?'

NO.

'You did, didn't you?' Albert stated.

NO.

'You put all those things in the sack.'

NO.

'You got them from somewhere and put them in the sack.'

NO.

'You *did* put them in the sack, didn't you?'

NO.

'You put them in the sack.'

YES.

*

'They're title deeds,' said Medium Dave. 'And they're better than money.'

'Paper's better'n money?' said Catseye.

'If we steal them, do they become ours?' said Chickenwire.

'Is that a trick question?' said Catseye, smirking.

'I know people say I'd kill them as soon as look at them,' whispered Teatime. 'And in fact I'd *much* rather kill you than look at you, Mr Lilywhite.'

'And what'll you do when he comes after you?'

'He can't look everywhere.'

Medium Dave shook his head. You only had to look into Teatime's mismatched eyes to know one thing, which was this: that if Teatime wanted to find you he would *not* look everywhere. He'd look in only one place, which would be the place where you were hiding.

'They've piled the teeth up in a magic circle downstairs,' said Susan.

Violet's eyes and mouth formed three Os. It was like looking at a pink bowling ball.

'What for?'

'I think they're using them to control the children. By magic.'

Violet's mouth opened wider.

'That's *horrid*.'

Horrible, thought Susan. The word is 'horrible'. 'Horrid' is a childish word selected to impress nearby males with one's fragility, if I'm any judge.

It is said that the prospect of hanging concentrates the mind wonderfully, but it was Valium compared to being watched by Mister Teatime.

*

'I could certainly run a marvellous university here if only we didn't have to have these damn students underfoot all the time.'

*

'All right,' said Susan. 'I'm not stupid. You're saying humans need . . . *fantasies* to make life bearable.'

REALLY? AS IF IT WAS SOME KIND OF PINK PILL? NO. HUMANS NEED FANTASY TO BE HUMAN. TO BE THE PLACE WHERE THE FALLING ANGEL MEETS THE RISING APE.

'Tooth fairies? Hogfathers? Little—'

YES. AS PRACTICE. YOU HAVE TO START OUT LEARNING TO BELIEVE THE *LITTLE* LIES.

'So we can believe the big ones?'

YES. JUSTICE. MERCY. DUTY. THAT SORT OF THING.

'They're not the same at all!'

YOU THINK SO? THEN TAKE THE UNIVERSE AND GRIND IT DOWN TO THE FINEST POWDER AND SIEVE IT THROUGH THE FINEST SIEVE AND THEN *SHOW* ME ONE ATOM OF JUSTICE, ONE MOLECULE OF MERCY. AND YET— Death waved a hand. AND YET YOU ACT AS IF THERE IS SOME IDEAL ORDER IN THE WORLD, AS IF THERE IS SOME . . . SOME *RIGHTNESS* IN THE UNIVERSE BY WHICH IT MAY BE JUDGED.

'Yes, but people have *got* to believe that, or what's the *point*—'

MY POINT EXACTLY.

*

Death fumbled inside his robe.

I HAVE MADE THIS FOR YOU.

Susan reached out and took a square of damp cardboard. Water dripped off the bottom. Somewhere in the middle, a few brown feathers seemed to have been glued on.

'Thank you. Er . . . what is it?'

ALBERT SAID THERE OUGHT TO BE SNOW ON IT, BUT IT APPEARS TO HAVE MELTED, said Death. IT IS, OF COURSE, A HOGSWATCH CARD.

'Oh . . .'

THERE SHOULD HAVE BEEN A ROBIN ON IT AS WELL, BUT I HAD CONSIDERABLE DIFFICULTY IN GETTING IT TO STAY ON.

'Ah . . .'

IT WAS NOT AT ALL CO-OPERATIVE.

'Really . . .?'

IT DID NOT SEEM TO GET INTO THE HOGSWATCH SPIRIT AT ALL.

JINGO

DISCWORLD goes to war, with armies of sardines, warriors, fishermen, squid and at least one very camp follower.

As two armies march, Commander Vimes of Ankh-Morpork City Watch faces unpleasant foes who are out to get him . . . and that's just the people on *his* side. The enemy might be even worse.

Jingo makes the World Cup look like a friendly five-a-side.

As every student of exploration knows, the prize goes not to the explorer who first sets foot upon the virgin soil but to the one who gets that foot home first. If it is still attached to his leg, this is a bonus.

*

Detritus's intelligence wasn't too bad for a troll, falling somewhere between a cuttlefish and a line-dancer.

*

Lord Vetinari looked attentive, because he'd always found that listening keenly to people tended to put them off.

'Oh, *history*,' said Lord Selachii. 'That's all in the past!'

'Gentlemen, please,' said the Patrician. 'Let's have no fighting, please. This is, after all, a council of war.'

*

'A Klatchian bigwig is coming *here*?' said Vimes. 'No one told me!'

'Strange as it may seem, Sir Samuel, I am occasionally capable of governing this city for minutes at a time without seeking your advice and guidance.'

*

'My mum's uncle was a sailor,' said Nobby. 'But after the big plague he got press-ganged. Bunch of farmers got him drunk, he woke up next morning tied to a plough.'

*

Sergeant Colon had had a broad education. He'd been to the School of My Dad Always Said, the College of It Stands to Reason, and was now a post-graduate student at the University of What Some Bloke In the Pub Told Me.

*

Technically they were all in uniform, too, except that mostly they weren't wearing the same uniform as anyone else. Everyone had just been sent down to the armoury to collect whatever fitted, and the result was a walking historical exhibit: Funny-Shaped Helmets Through the Ages.

*

'Dad?'

'Yes, lad?'

'Who was Mr Hong?'

'How should I know?'

'Only, when we was all heading back for the boats one of the other men said, "We all know what happened to Mr Hong when he opened the Three Jolly Luck Take-Away

Fish Bar on the site of the old fish-god temple in Dagon Street on the night of the full moon, don't we . . .?" Well, *I* don't know.'

'Ah . . .' Solid Jackson hesitated. Still, Les was a big lad now . . .

'He . . . closed up and left in a bit of a hurry, lad. So quick he had to leave some things behind.'

'Like what?'

'If you must know . . . half an ear-hole and one kidney.'

*

A few moments later Sergeant Colon walked carefully down to the main office. He toyed with some paper for a while and then said:

'You don't mind what people call *you*, do you, Nobby?'

'I'd be minding the whole time if I minded that, sarge,' said Corporal Nobbs cheerfully.

'Right. Right! And *I* don't mind what people call *me*, neither.' Colon scratched his head. 'Don't make sense, really. I reckon Sir Sam is missing too much sleep.'

'He's a very busy man, Fred.'

'Trying to do everything, that's his trouble. And . . . Nobby?'

'Yes?'

'It's Sergeant Colon, thanks.'

*

There was sherry. There was always sherry at these occasions. Sam Vimes had heard they made sherry by letting wine go rotten. He couldn't see the *point* of sherry.

*

Vimes stood up. 'You know what I always say,' he said.

Carrot removed his helmet and polished it with his sleeve. 'Yes, sir. "Everyone's guilty of something, especially the ones that aren't," sir.'

'No, not that one . . .'

'Er . . . "Always take into consideration the fact that you might be dead wrong," sir?'

'No, nor that one either.'

'Er . . . "How come Nobby ever got a job as a watchman?", sir? You say that a lot.'

'No! I meant "Always act stupid," Carrot.'

'Ah, right, sir. From now on I shall remember that you always said that, sir.'

*

'Colon and Nobbs are investigating this?' said the Patrician. 'Really?'

'Yes, sir.'

'If I were to ask you why, you'd pretend not to understand?'

Vimes let his forehead wrinkle in honest perplexity. 'Sir?'

'If you say "Sir?" again in that stupid voice, Vimes, I swear there will be trouble.'

'They're good men, sir.'

'However, some people might consider them to be unimaginative, stolid and . . . how can I put this? . . . possessed of an inbuilt disposition to accept the first explanation that presents itself and then bunk off somewhere for a quiet smoke? A certain lack of imagination? An ability to get out of their depth on a wet pavement?'

*

Vetinari peered at a small heap of bent and twisted metal.

'What was it, Leonard?' he said.

'An experimental device for turning chemical energy into rotary motion,' said Leonard. 'The problem, you see, is getting the little pellets of black powder into the combustion chamber at exactly the right speed and one at a time. If two ignite together, well, what we have is the *external* combustion engine.'

'And, er, what would be the purpose of it?' said the Patrician.

'I believe it could replace the horse,' said Leonard proudly.

They looked at the stricken thing.

'One of the advantages of horses that people often point out,' said Vetinari, after some thought, 'is that they very seldom explode.'

*

Leonard's incredible brain sizzled away alarmingly, an overloaded chip pan on the Stove of Life. It was impossible to know what he would think of next, because he was constantly reprogrammed by the whole universe. The sight of a waterfall or a soaring bird would send him spinning down some new path of practical speculation that invariably ended in a heap of wire and springs and a cry of 'I think I know what I did wrong.' He'd been a member of most of the craft guilds in the city but had been thrown out for getting impossibly high marks in the exams or, in some cases, correcting the questions. It was said that he'd accidentally blown up the Alchemists' Guild using nothing more than a glass of water, a spoonful of acid, two lengths of wire and a ping-pong ball.

*

Nobby and Colon go on a call – in plain clothes:

'Come on, open up! Watch business!'

Corporal Nobbs pulled at Sergeant Colon's sleeve and whispered in his ear.

'*Not* Watch business!' said Colon, pounding the door again. 'Nothing to do with the Watch at all! We are just civilians, all right?'

The door opened a crack.

'*Are* you the Watch?' said a voice.

'No! I think I just made that clear—'

'Piss off, copper!'

The door slammed.

'You sure this is the right place, sarge?'

'Don't call me sarge when we're in plain clothes!'

'Right you are, Fred.'

'That's—' Colon hesitated in an agony of status. 'Well, that's *Frederick* to you, Nobby.'

'Right, Frederick. And that's Cecil, thank you.'

'Cecil?'

'That is my name,' said Nobby coldly.

'Have it your way,' said Colon. 'Just remember who's the superior civilian around here, all right?'

He hammered on the door again.

'We hear you've got a room to let, missus!' he yelled.

'Brilliant, Frederick,' said Nobby. 'That was bloody *brilliant*!'

'Well, I *am* the sergeant, right?' Colon whispered.

'No.'

'Er . . . yeah . . . right . . . well, just you remember that, right?'

*

'*Sam?*'

Vimes looked up from his reading.

'Your soup will be cold,' said Lady Sybil from the far end of the table. 'You've been holding that spoonful in the air for the last five minutes by the clock.'

'Sorry, dear.'

Belatedly, his nuptial radar detected a certain chilliness from the far side of the cruet.

'Is, er, there something wrong, dear?' he said.

'Can you remember when we last had dinner together, Sam?'

'Tuesday, wasn't it?'

'That was the Guild of Merchants' annual dinner, Sam.'

Vimes's brow wrinkled. 'But you were there too, weren't you?'

*

Ankh-Morpork no longer had a fire brigade. The citizens had a rather disturbingly direct way of thinking at times, and it did not take long for people to see the rather obvious flaw in paying a group of people by the number of fires they put out. The penny really dropped shortly after Charcoal Tuesday.

Since then they had relied on the good old principle of enlightened self-interest. People living close to a burning building did their best to douse the fire, because the thatch they saved might be their own.

'Mr Vimes saved the day!' said Sergeant Colon excitedly.

'Just went straight in and saved everyone, in the finest tradition of the Watch!'

'Fred?' said Vimes, wearily.

'Yessir?'

'Fred, the finest tradition of the Watch is having a quiet smoke somewhere out of the wind at 3 a.m. Let's not get carried away, eh?'

Colon rummaged in a pocket and produced a very small book, which he held up for inspection.

'This belonged to my great-grandad,' he said. 'He was in the scrap we had against Pseudopolis and my great-gran gave him this book of prayers for soldiers, 'cos you need all the prayers you can get, believe you me, and he stuck it in the top pocket of his jerkin, 'cos he couldn't afford armour, and next day in battle – whoosh, this arrow came out of nowhere, wham, straight into this book and it went all the way through to the last page before stopping, look. You can see the hole.'

'Pretty miraculous,' Carrot agreed.

'Yeah, it was, I s'pose,' said the sergeant. He looked ruefully at the battered volume. 'Shame about the other seventeen arrows, really.'

Another little memory burst open as silently as a mouse passing wind in a hurricane.

'He is a D'reg!'

'Dreg?' said Angua.

'A warlike desert tribe,' said Carrot. 'Very fierce. Honourable, though. They say that if a D'reg is your friend he's your friend for the rest of your life.'

'And if he's *not* your friend?'

'That's about five seconds.'

*

'Everything's gone all to pot these days.'

'Not like when we were kids, sarge.'

'Not like when we were kids indeed, Nobby.'

'People trusted one another in them days, didn't they, sarge?'

'People trusted one another, Nobby.'

'Yes, sarge. I know. And people didn't have to lock their doors, did they?'

'That's right, Nobby. And people were always ready to help. They were always in and out of one another's houses.'

''sright, sarge,' said Nobby vehemently. 'I know no one ever locked their houses down *our* street.'

'That's what I'm talking about. That's my point.'

'It was 'cos the bastards even used to steal the locks.'

Colon considered the truth of this.

'Yes, but at least it was *each other's* stuff they were nicking, Nobby.'

*

Lord Rust's expression would have preserved meat for a year.

'You, Vimes, certainly are no knight. Before a knight is created he must spend a night's vigil watching his armour—'

'Practically every night of my life,' said Vimes. 'A man doesn't keep an eye on his armour round here, that man's got no armour in the morning.'

'In *prayer*,' said Rust sharply.

'That's me,' said Vimes. 'Not a night has gone by without me thinking, "Ye gods, I hope I get through this alive." '

'—and he must have proved himself on the field of combat. Against other trained men, Vimes. Not vermin and thugs.'

Vimes started to undo the strap of his helmet.

'Well, this isn't the best of moments, my lord, but if someone'll hold your coat I can spare you five minutes . . .'

*

'It is always useful to face an enemy who is prepared to die for his country. This means that both you and he have exactly the same aim in mind.'

*

The Engravers' Guild was against printing. There was something pure, they said, about an engraved page of text. It was there, whole, unsullied. Their members could do very fine work at very reasonable rates. Allowing unskilled people to bash lumps of type together showed a disrespect for words and no good would come of it.

The only attempt ever to set up a printing press in Ankh-Morpork had ended in a mysterious fire and the death by suicide of the luckless printer. Everyone knew it was suicide because he'd left a note. The fact that this had been engraved on the head of a pin was considered an irrelevant detail.

*

71-hour Ahmed was not *super*stitious. He *was* substitious, which put him in a minority among humans. He didn't believe in the things everyone believed in but which nevertheless weren't true. He believed instead in the things that were true in which no one else believed. There are many such substitions, ranging from 'It'll get better if you don't pick at it' all the way up to 'Sometimes things just happen.'

'So what're you going to do when we catch the other ship?'

'Er . . .' Vimes hadn't given this a lot of thought. But he recalled a very bad woodcut he'd once seen in a book about pirates.

'We'll swing across on to them with our cutlasses in our teeth?' he said.

'Really?' said Jenkins. 'That's good. I haven't seen that done in years. Only ever seen it done once, in fact.'

'Oh, yes?'

'Yes, this lad'd seen the idea in a book and he swung across into the other ship's rigging with his cutlass clenched, as you say, between his teeth.'

'Yes?'

'Topless Harry, we wrote on his coffin.'

Angua was aware that she had a slight advantage over male werewolves in that naked women caused fewer complaints, although the downside was that they got some pressing invitations. Some kind of covering was essential, for modesty and the prevention of inconvenient bouncing, which was why fashioning impromptu clothes out of anything to hand was a lesser-known werewolf skill.

*

'It's the waiting that's the worst part,' said his sergeant, next to him.

'It *might* be the worst part,' said the commander. 'Or, there again, the bit where they suddenly rise out of the desert and cut you in half might be the worst part.'

*

Lord Vetinari helped him up. 'Our very lives depend on your appearing to be a stupid fat idiot,' he hissed, putting Colon's fez back on his head.

'I ain't very good at acting, sir—'

'Good!'

*

'Your predecessor, Lord Snapcase, now he *was* mental. But, like I've always said, people know where they stand with Lord Vetinari . . .'

'Well done.'

'They might not *like* where they're standing of course . . .'

THE LAST CONTINENT

IT'S the Discworld's last continent and it's going to die in a few days, except . . .

Who is this hero striding across the red desert? Sheep shearer, beer drinker, bush ranger, and someone who'll even eat a Meat Pie Floater when he's *sober*.

A man in a hat whose Luggage follows him on little legs. Yes, it's Rincewind, the inept wizard who can't even *spell* wizard. He's the only hero left.

Still . . . no worries, eh?

There are some people who have a legend that the whole universe is carried in a leather bag by an old man.

Other people say: hold on, if he's carrying the entire universe in a sack, right, that means he's carrying himself and the sack *inside* the sack, because the universe contains everything. Including him. And the sack, of course. Which contains him and the sack already. As it were.

To which the reply is: well?

All tribal myths are true, for a given value of 'true'.

*

The Ceremony of the Keys went on every night in every season. Mere ice, wind and snow had never stopped it. You couldn't stop Tradition. You could only add to it.

McAbre, Head Bledlow, with his two escorts, reached the shadows by the main gate. The bledlow on duty was waiting for them.

'Halt! Who Goes There?' he shouted.

McAbre saluted. The Archchancellor's Keys!'

'Pass, The Archchancellor's Keys!'

The Head Bledlow took a step forward, extended both arms in front of him with his palms bent back towards him, and patted his chest at the place where some bledlow long buried had once had two breast pockets. Pat, pat. Then he extended his arms by his sides and stiffly patted the sides of his jacket. Pat, pat.

'Damn! Could Have Sworn I Had Them A Moment Ago!' he bellowed, enunciating each word with a sort of bulldog carefulness.

The gatekeeper saluted. McAbre saluted.

'Have You Looked In All Your Pockets?'

McAbre saluted. The gatekeeper saluted.

'I Think I Must Have Left Them On The Dresser. It's Always The Same, Isn't It?'

'You Should Remember Where You Put Them Down!'

'Hang On, Perhaps They're In My Other Jacket!'

The young bledlow who was this week's Keeper of the Other Jacket stepped forward. Each man saluted the other two. The youngest cleared his throat and managed to say:

'No, I Looked In . . . There This . . . Morning!'

McAbre gave him a slight nod to acknowledge a difficult job done well, and patted his pockets again.

'Hold On, Stone The Crows, They Were In This Pocket After All! What A Muggins I Am!'

'Don't Worry, I Do The Same Myself!'

'Is My Face Red! Forget My Own Head Next! . . . Here's The Keys, Then!' said McAbre.

'Much Obliged!' . . .

'All Safe And Secure!' shouted the gatekeeper, handing the keys back.

'Gods Bless All Present!'

'Careful Where You Put Them This Time. Ha! Ha! Ha!'

'Ho! Ho! Ho!' yelled McAbre. He saluted stiffly, went About Turn with a large amount of foot stamping and, the ancient exchange completed, marched back to the bledlows' lodge.

*

Light travels slowly on the Disc and is slightly heavy, with a tendency to pile up against high mountain ranges. Research wizards have speculated that there is another, much speedier type of light which allows the slower light to be seen, but since this moves too fast to see they have been unable to find a use for it.

*

Ponder Stibbons was one of those unfortunate people cursed with the belief that if only he found out enough things about the universe it would all, somehow, make sense. The goal is the Theory of Everything, but Ponder would settle for the Theory of Something and, late at night, he despaired of even a Theory of Anything.

*

Any true wizard, faced with a sign like 'Do not open this door. Really. We mean it. We're not kidding. Opening this door will mean the end of the universe,' would *automatically* open the door in order to see what all the fuss was about.

*

'Hah, I remember when I was a student,' said the Lecturer in Recent Runes. 'Old "Bogeyboy" Swallett took us on an expedition to find the Lost Reading Room. Three weeks we were wandering around. Had to eat our own boots.'

'Did you find it?' said the Dean.

'No, but we found the remains of the previous year's expedition.'

'What did you do?'

'We ate their boots, too.'

*

'We're a university! We *have* to have a library!' said Ridcully. 'What sort of people would we be if we didn't go into the Library?'

'Students,' said the Senior Wrangler morosely.

...a man whose ability to find water was limited to checking if his feet were wet...

Ridcully was good at doing without other people's sleep.

*

Unseen University was much bigger on the inside. Thousands of years as the leading establishment of practical magic in a world where dimensions were largely a matter of chance in any case had left it bulging in places where it shouldn't have places. There were rooms containing rooms which, if you entered them, turned out to contain the room you'd started with, which can be a problem if you are in a conga line.

*

Rincewind had always been happy to think of himself as a racist. The One Hundred Metres, the Mile, the Marathon – he'd run them all. Later, when he'd learned with some surprise what the word actually *meant*, he'd been equally certain he wasn't one. He was a person who divided the world quite simply into people who were trying to kill him and people who weren't.

*

'When you've been a wizard as long as I have, my boy [said the Senior Wrangler], you'll learn that as soon as you find anything that offers amazing possibilities for the improvement of the human condition it's best to put the lid back on and pretend it never happened.'

*

Droit de mortis: broadly speaking, the acceleration of a wizard through the ranks of wizardry by killing off more senior wizards. It is a practice currently in abeyance, since a few enthusiastic attempts to remove Mustrum Ridcully resulted in one wizard being unable to hear properly for two weeks. Ridcully felt that there was indeed room at the top, and he was occupying all of it.

*

It is a simple universal law. People always expect to use a holiday in the sun as an opportunity to read those books they've always meant to read, but an alchemical combination of sun, quartz crystals and coconut oil will somehow metamorphose any improving book into a rather thicker one with a name containing at least one Greek word or letter (*The Gamma Imperative*, *The Delta Season*, *The Alpha Project* and, in the more extreme cases, even *The Mu Kau Pi Caper*). Sometimes a hammer and sickle turn up on the cover. This is probably caused by sunspot activity, since they are invariably the wrong way round.

*

Any seasoned traveller soon learns to avoid anything wished on them as a 'regional speciality', because all the term means is that the dish is so unpleasant the people living everywhere else will bite off their own legs rather than eat it. But hosts still press it upon distant guests anyway: 'Go on, have the dog's head stuffed with macerated cabbage and pork noses – it's a *regional speciality*.'

*

The University's housekeeper [it had been unkindly said] had a face full of chins; there *was* a glossiness about her that put some people in mind of a candle that had been kept in the warm for too long. There wasn't anything approaching a straight line anywhere on Mrs Whitlow, until she found that something hadn't been dusted properly, when you could use her lips as a ruler.

*

The wizards were civilized men of considerable education and culture. When faced with being inadvertently marooned on a desert island they understood immediately that the first thing to do was place the blame.

*

'Remember what we'd say in those days?' said the Senior Wrangler. '"Never trust a wizard over sixty-five"? Whatever happened?'

'We got past the age of sixty-five, Senior Wrangler.'

*

The Bursar was, as he would probably be the first to admit, not the most mentally stable of people. He would probably be the first to admit that he was a tea-strainer.

*

Once a moderately jolly wizard camped by a dried-up waterhole under the shade of a tree that he was completely unable to identify. And he swore as he hacked and hacked at a can of beer, saying, 'What kind of *idiots* put beer in *tins*?'

*

Beer! It was only water, really, with stuff in it. Wasn't it? And most of what was in it was yeast, which was practically a medicine and definitely a food. In fact, when you thought about it, beer was only a kind of runny bread.

*

'Is it true that your life passes before your eyes before you die?'

YES.

'Ghastly thought, really.' Rincewind shuddered. 'Oh, *gods*, I've just had another one. Suppose I *am* just about to die and *this* is my whole life passing in front of my eyes?'

I THINK PERHAPS YOU DO NOT UNDERSTAND. PEOPLE'S WHOLE LIVES *DO* PASS IN FRONT OF THEIR EYES BEFORE THEY DIE. THE PROCESS IS CALLED 'LIVING'.

CARPE JUGULUM

MIGHTILY Oats has not picked a good time to be a priest. He thought he'd come to Lancre for a simple ceremony. Now he's caught up in a war between vampires and witches.

There's Young Agnes, who is *really* in two minds about everything. Magrat, who is trying to combine witchcraft and nappies, Nanny Ogg . . . and Granny Weatherwax, who is big trouble.

And the vampires are intelligent. They've got style and fancy waistcoats. They're out of the casket, and want a bite of the future. Mightily Oats knows he has a prayer, but he wishes he had an axe.

In Lancre the only truly flat places were tables and the top of some people's heads.

*

Those who are inclined to casual cruelty say that inside a fat girl is a thin girl and a lot of chocolate.

*

Agnes thought that a dumpy girl should not wear a tall hat, especially with black. It made her look as though someone had dropped a liquorice-flavoured ice-cream cone.

*

The Lancrastian idea of posh sanitation was a non-slippery path to the privy and a mail-order catalogue with really soft pages.

*

Sometimes witches have to be the ones that make the difficult decisions for people. Life and death. Choosing between saving a mother or her new-born son.

'You got to come to Mrs Ivy and her baby missus!'

'I thought old Mrs Patternoster was seeing to her,' said Granny, ramming her hatpins into place with the urgency of a warrior preparing for sudden battle.

'She says it's all gone wrong miss!'

. . .

Slice was perched along the sides of a cleft in the mountains that couldn't be dignified by the name of valley. In the moonlight Granny saw the pale upturned face waiting in the shadows of the garden as she came in to land.

'Evening, Mr Ivy,' she said, leaping off. 'Upstairs, is she?'

'In the barn,' said Ivy flatly. 'The cow kicked her . . . hard.'

Granny's expression stayed impassive.

'We shall see,' she said, 'what may be done.'

In the barn, one look at Mrs Patternoster's face told her how little that might now be.

'It's bad,' she whispered, as Granny looked at the moaning figure on the straw. 'I reckon we'll lose both of them . . . or maybe just one . . .'

There was, if you were listening for it, just the suggestion of a question in that sentence. Granny focused her mind.

'It's a boy,' she said.

Mrs Patternoster didn't bother to wonder how Granny knew, but her expression indicated that a little more weight had been added to a burden.

'I'd better go and put it to John Ivy, then,' she said.

She'd barely moved before Granny Weatherwax's hand locked on her arm.

'He's no part in this,' she said.

'But after all, he *is* the—'

'He's no part in this.'

Mrs Patternoster looked into the blue stare and knew two things. One was that Mr Ivy had no part in this, and the other was that anything that happened in this barn was never, ever, going to be mentioned again.

'I think I can bring 'em to mind,' said Granny, letting go and rolling up her sleeves. 'Pleasant couple, as I recall. He's a good husband, by all accounts.' She poured warm water from its jug into the bowl that the midwife had set up on a manger.

Mrs Patternoster nodded.

'Of course, it's difficult for a man working these steep lands alone,' Granny went on, washing her hands. Mrs Patternoster nodded again, mournfully.

'Well, I reckon you should take him into the cottage, Mrs Patternoster, and make him a cup of tea,' Granny commanded. 'You can tell him I'm doing all I can.'

This time the midwife nodded gratefully.

When she had fled, Granny laid a hand on Mrs Ivy's damp forehead.

'Well now, Florence Ivy,' she said, 'let us see what might be done. But first of all . . . no pain . . .'

INDEED.

Granny didn't bother to turn round.

'I thought you'd be here,' she said, as she knelt down in the straw.

WHERE ELSE? said Death.

'Do you know who you're here for?'

THAT IS NOT MY CHOICE. ON THE *VERY* EDGE YOU WILL ALWAYS FIND SOME UNCERTAINTY.

Granny felt the words in her head for several seconds, like little melting cubes of ice. On the very, very edge, then, there had to be . . . judgement.

'There's too much damage here,' she said, at last. 'Too much.'

A few minutes later she felt the life stream past her. Death had the decency to leave without a word.

When Mrs Patternoster tremulously knocked on the door and pushed it open, Granny was in the cow's stall. The midwife saw her stand up, holding a piece of thorn.

'Been in the beast's leg all day,' she said. 'No wonder it was fretful. Try and make sure he doesn't kill the cow, you understand? They'll need it.'

Mrs Patternoster glanced down at the rolled-up blanket in the straw. Granny had tactfully placed it out of sight of Mrs Ivy, who was sleeping now.

'I'll tell him,' said Granny, brushing off her dress. 'As for her, well, she's strong and young and you know what to do. You keep an eye on her, and me or Nanny Ogg will drop in when we can.'

It was doubtful that anyone in Slice would defy Granny Weatherwax, but Granny saw the faintest grey shadow of disapproval in the midwife's expression.

'You still reckon I should've asked Mr Ivy?' she said.

'That's what I would have done . . .' the woman mumbled.

'You don't like him? You think he's a bad man?' said Granny, adjusting her hatpins.

'No!'

'Then what's he ever done to *me*, that I should hurt him so?'

*

The people of Lancre wouldn't dream of living in anything other than a monarchy. They'd done so for thousands of years and knew that it worked. But they'd also found that it didn't do to pay too much attention to what the King wanted, because there was bound to be another king along in forty years or so and he'd be certain to want something different and so they'd have gone to all that trouble for nothing. In the meantime, his job as they saw it was to mostly stay in the palace, practise the waving, have enough sense to face the right way on coins and let them get on with the ploughing, sowing, growing and harvesting. It was, as they saw it, a social contract. They did what they always did, and he let them.

*

'I used to know an Igor from Uberwald,' said Nanny. 'Walked with a limp. One eye a bit higher than the other. Had the same manner of . . . speaking. Very good at brain juggling, too.'

'That thoundth like my Uncle Igor,' said Igor. 'He worked for the mad doctor at Blinz. Ha, an' he wath a *proper* mad doctor, too, not like the mad doctorth you get thethe dayth. And the thervantth? Even worthe. No pride thethe dayth.' He tapped the brandy flask for emphasis. 'When Uncle Igor wath thent out for a geniuth'th brain, that'th what you damn well got. There wath none of thith fumble-finger thtuff and then pinching a brain out of the "Really Inthane" jar and hopin' no one'd notithe. They alwayth do, anyway.'

Nanny took a step back. The only sensible way to hold a conversation with an Igor was when you had an umbrella.

*

Not many people ever *tasted* Nanny Ogg's home-made brandy; it was technically impossible. Once it encountered the warmth of the human mouth it immediately turned into fumes. You drank it via your sinuses.

*

'The trouble is that people always think of vampires in terms of their diet,' said the Count, as Nanny hurried away. 'It's really rather insulting. *You* eat animal flesh and vegetables, but it hardly defines you, does it?'

*

'How does Perdita work, then?' said Nanny.

Agnes sighed. 'Look, you know the part of you that wants to do all the things you don't dare do, and thinks the thoughts you don't dare think?'

Nanny's face stayed blank. Agnes floundered. 'Like . . . maybe . . . rip off all your clothes and run naked in the rain?' she hazarded.

'Oh, *yes*. Right,' said Nanny.

'Well . . . I suppose Perdita is that part of me.'

'Really? I've always been that part of me,' said Nanny. 'The important thing is to remember where you left your clothes.'

*

'People have quite the wrong idea about vampires, you see. Are we fiendish killers?' He beamed at them. 'Well, yes, of course we are. But only when necessary.'

*

They were listening quite contentedly to the worst music since Shawn Ogg's bagpipes had been dropped down the stairs.

*

They watched the servant limp off. The Count shook his head.

'He'll never retire,' said Vlad. 'He'll never take a hint.'

'And it's so old fashioned having a servant called Igor,' said the Countess. 'He really is too much.'

'Look, it's simple,' said Lacrimosa. 'Just take him down to the cellars, slam him in the Iron Maiden, stretch him on the rack over a fire for a day or two, and then slice him thinly from the feet upwards, so he can watch. You'll be doing him a kindness, really.'

'I suppose it's the best way,' said the Count sadly.

*

There was more to Mr Oats than met the eye. There had to be.

*

Books that were all about the world tended to be written by people who knew all about books rather than all about the world.

*

'Look, you said you've studied vampires, didn't you? What's good for vampires?'

Oats thought for a moment. 'Er . . . a nice dry coffin, er, plenty of fresh blood, er, overcast skies . . .' His voice trailed off when he saw her expression. 'Ah . . . well, it depends exactly where they're from, I remember. Uberwald is a very big place. Er, cutting off the head and staking them in the heart is generally efficacious.'

'But that works on everyone,' said Nanny.

*

'You don't know what he's like,' said Agnes. 'He looks at me as if he's undressing me with his eyes.'

'Eyes is allowed,' said Nanny.

*

Agnes's arm whirled. The holy water spiralled out of the bottle and hit Vlad full in the chest.

He threw his arms wide and screamed as water cascaded down and poured into his shoes.

'*Look* at this waistcoat! Will you *look* at this waistcoat? Do you know what water does to silk? You just never get it out! No matter what you do, there's always a mark.'

*

Few birds could sit more meekly than the Lancre wowhawk, or lappet-faced worrier, a carnivore permanently on the lookout for the vegetarian option.

The Count blew a smoke ring.

'Good evening,' he said, as it drifted away. 'You must be the mob.'

'May I introduce you to Sergeant Kraput, and this gentleman here picking his teeth with his knife is Corporal Svitz. They and their men will be going on duty in, oh, about an hour. Purely for reasons of security, you understand.'

'An' then we'll gut yer like a clam and stuff yer with straw,' said Corporal Svitz.

'Ah. This is technical military language of which I know little,' said the Count. 'I do so hope there is no unpleasantness.'

'I don't,' said Sergeant Kraput.

'What scamps they are,' said the Count.

*

'It'th a pleathure to be commanded in a clear, firm authoritative voithe, mithtreth,' said Igor, lurching over to the bridles. 'None of thith "Would you mind . . ." rubbith. An Igor liketh to know where he thtandth.'

'Slightly lopsidedly?' said Magrat.

*

'The Prophet Brutha said that Om helps those who help one another.'

'And does he?'

'To be honest, there are a number of opinions of what was meant.'

'How many?'

'About one hundred and sixty, since the Schism of 10.30 a.m., February 23. That was when the Re-United Free Chelonianists (Hubwards Convocation) schismed from the Re-United Free Chelonianists (Rimwards Convocation). It was rather serious.'

'Blood spilled?' said Agnes. She wasn't really interested, but it took her mind off whatever might be waking up in a minute.

'No, but there were fisticuffs and a deacon had ink spilled on him.'

*

'The Omnians used to burn witches . . .'

'They never did,' said Granny.

'I'm afraid I have to admit that the records show—'

'They never burned witches,' said Granny. 'Probably they burned some old ladies who spoke up or couldn't run away. I wouldn't look for witches bein' burned,' she added, shifting position. 'I might look for witches doin' the burning, though. We ain't *all* nice.'

*

'There is a very interesting debate raging at the moment [among Omnians] about the nature of sin, for example.'

'And what do they think? Against it, are they?' [said Granny.]

'It's not as simple as that. It's not a black and white issue. There are so many shades of grey.'

'There's no greys, only white that's got grubby. I'm surprised you don't know that. And sin, young man, is when you treat people as things. Including yourself. That's what sin is.'

'It's a lot more complicated than that—'

'No. It ain't. When people say things are a lot more complicated than that, they means they're getting worried that they won't like the truth. People as things, that's where it starts.'

'Oh, I'm sure there are worse crimes—'

'But they *starts* with thinking about people as things . . .'

*

Scraps tried to lick Igor. He was a dog with a lot of lick to share.

'Thcrapth, play dead,' said Igor. The dog dropped and rolled over with his legs in the air.

'Thee?' said Igor. 'He rememberth!'

*

Agnes indicated the headless vampire. 'Er . . . is that one Vlad?' she said.

'We can check. Piotr, show her the head.'

A young man obediently went to the fireplace, pulled on a glove, lifted the lid of a big saucepan and held up a head by its hair.

'That's not Vlad,' said Agnes, swallowing. *No*, said Perdita, *Vlad was taller*.

*

The Countess clutched his arm.

'Oh, this does so remind me of our honeymoon,' she said. 'Don't you remember those wonderful nights in Grjsknvij?'

'Oh, fresh morning of the world indeed,' said the Count solemnly.

'Such romance . . . and we met such lovely people, too. Do you remember Mr and Mrs Harker?'

'Very fondly. I recall they lasted nearly all week.'

*

Vampires are not naturally co-operative creatures. It's not in their nature. Every other vampire is a rival for the next meal. In fact, the ideal situation for a vampire is a world in which every other vampire has been killed off and no one seriously believes in vampires any more.

THE FIFTH ELEPHANT

SAM Vimes is a man on the run.

Yesterday he was a duke, a chief of police and the ambassador to the mysterious, fat-rich country of Uberwald.

Now he has nothing but his native wit and the gloomy trousers of Uncle Vanya (don't ask). It's snowing. It's freezing. And if he can't make it through the forest to civilization there's going to be a terrible war.

But there are monsters on his trail. They're bright. They're fast. They're werewolves – and they're catching up.

Starring dwarfs, diplomacy, intrigue and big lumps of fat.

All Jolson was a man who'd show up on an atlas and change the orbit of small planets. Paving stones cracked under his feet. He combined in one body – and there was plenty of room left over – Ankh-Morpork's best chef and its keenest eater, a circumstance made in mashed potato heaven. He'd picked up the nickname by general acclaim, since no one seeing him in the street for the first time could believe that it was *all* Jolson.

*

It is in the nature of the universe that the person who always keeps you waiting ten minutes will, on the day you are ten minutes tardy, have been ready ten minutes early and will make a point of *not mentioning this*.

*

Uberwald was so thickly forested, so creased by little mountain ranges and beset by rivers, that it was largely unmapped. It was mostly unexplored, too.

(At least by proper explorers. Just living there doesn't count.)

'I could've *bin* a wolf, you know,' said Gaspode.

'With diff'rent parents, of course.'

'Someone said something blotto voice,' said Captain Colon.

'I'm sure they didn't, captain,' said Nobby.

'And I won't be eyeballed like that, neither!'

'No one's looking at you!' wailed Nobby.

'Aha, you think I don't know that one?' Colon shouted. 'There's plenty of ways to eyeball someone without lookin' at 'em, corporal. That man over there is earlobing me!'

*

Gaspode settled down in the pose he almost unconsciously categorized as Faithful Companion Keeping Watch, got bored, scratched himself absent-mindedly, curled up in the pose known as Faithful Companion Curled Up With His Nose Pressed On His Bottom, and fell asleep.

*

Lord Vetinari paused. He found it difficult to talk to Frederick Colon. He dealt on a daily basis with people who treated conversation as a complex game, and with Colon he had to keep on adjusting his mind in case he overshot.

*

Gaspode wasn't sure of his own ancestry. There was some terrier, and a touch of spaniel, and probably someone's leg, and an awful lot of mongrel.

*

'I believe you were an alcoholic, Sir Samuel.' 'No,' said Vimes. 'I was a drunk. You have to be richer than I was to be an alcoholic.'

'Everyone's heard of Commander Vimes. I mean no offence, of course, but we were a little surprised when the Patrician said that you would be coming. We were expecting one of the more . . . experienced . . . diplomats.'

'Oh, I can hand around the thin cucumber sandwiches like anything,' said Vimes. 'And if you want little golden balls of chocolate piled up in a heap, I'm your man.'

*

'Igors heal very fast,' said Lady Sybil.

'They'd have to.'

'Mister Skimmer said they're very gifted surgeons, Sam.'

'Except cosmetically, perhaps.'

*

'This stuff . . . this stuff is *spying*. I wondered how Vetinari always seems to know so much!'

'Did you think it came to him in dreams, dear?'

'But there's loads of details here . . . I didn't know we did this sort of thing!'

'You use spies all the time, dear,' said Sybil.

'I do not!'

'Well, what about people like Foul Ole Ron and No Way José and Cumbling Michael?'

'That is *not* spying, that is *not* spying! That's just "information received". We couldn't do the job if we didn't know what's happening on the street!'

'Well, perhaps Havelock just thinks in terms of . . . a bigger street, dear.'

*

Vimes had once discussed the Ephebian idea of 'democracy' with Carrot, and had been rather interested in the idea that everyone had a vote until he found out that while he, Vimes, would have a vote, there was no way in the rules that anyone could prevent Nobby Nobbs from having one as well. Vimes could see the flaw there straight away.

*

The Marquis of Fantailler got into many fights in his youth, most of them as a result of being known as the Marquis of Fantailler, and wrote a set of rules for what he termed 'the noble art of fisticuffs', which mostly consisted of a list of places where people weren't allowed to hit him. Many people were impressed with his work and later stood with noble chest out-thrust and fists balled in a spirit of manly aggression against people who hadn't read the Marquis's book but *did* know how to knock people senseless with a chair. The last words of a surprisingly large number of people were 'Stuff the bloody Marquis of Fantailler—'

*

Vimes is being pursued through an unfriendly landscape.

So, what were his options? Well, he could stay in the tree and die, or run for it and die. Of the two, dying in one piece seemed better.

YOU'RE DOING VERY WELL FOR A MAN OF YOUR AGE.

Death was sitting on a higher branch of the tree.

'Are you following me or what?'

ARE YOU FAMILIAR WITH THE WORDS 'DEATH WAS HIS CONSTANT COMPANION'?

Lady Sybil wasn't a good cook.

She'd never been taught proper cookery; at her school it had always been assumed that other people would be doing the cooking and that in any case it would be for fifty people using at least four types of fork.

THE TRUTH

WILLIAM just wants to get at the truth.

Unfortunately, everyone else wants to get at William. And it's only the third edition . . .

William de Worde is the accidental editor of the Discworld's first newspaper. Now he must cope with the traditional perils of a journalist's life – people who want him dead, a recovering vampire with a suicidal fascination for flash photography, some more people who want him dead in a different way and, worst of all, the man who keeps begging him to publish pictures of his humorously shaped potatoes.

The rumour spread through the city like wildfire (which had quite often spread through Ankh-Morpork since its citizens had learned the words 'fire insurance').

*

Selling hot sausages from a tray was by way of being the ground state of Dibbler's existence, from which he constantly sought to extricate himself and back to which he constantly returned when his latest venture went all runny. Which was a shame, because Dibbler was an extremely good hot sausage salesman. He had to be, given the nature of his sausages.

*

As for Mr Pin and Mr Tulip, all that need be known about them at this point is that they are the kind of people who call you 'friend'. People like that aren't friendly.

'You know I've always wanted a paperless office—'

'Yes, Archchancellor, that's why you hide it all in cupboards and throw it out of the window at night.'

There are, it has been said, two types of people in the world. There are those who, when presented with a glass that is exactly half full, say: this glass is half full. And then there are those who say: this glass is half empty.

The world *belongs*, however, to those who can look at the glass and say: 'What's up with this glass? Excuse me? Excuse *me*? *This* is my glass? I don't *think* so. *My* glass was full! *And* it was a bigger glass!'

*

Hugglestones was a boarding school so bleak and spartan that only the upper classes would dream of sending their sons there.

It was a granite building on a rain-soaked moor, and its stated purpose was to make men from boys. The policy employed involved a certain amount of wastage, and consisted of very simple and violent games in the healthy outdoor sleet. The small, slow, fat or merely unpopular were mown down, as nature intended.

*

'Ah,' said Mr Pin. 'Right. You are concerned citizens.' He knew about *concerned citizens*. Wherever they were, they all spoke the same private language, where 'traditional values' meant 'hang someone'.

*

'Clear my appointments this morning, will you? I will see the Guild of Towncriers at nine o'clock and the Guild of Engravers at ten past.'

'I wasn't aware they had appointments, sir.'

'They will have,' said Lord Vetinari.

*

'I am looking for Mister William der Worde,' rumbled a voice.

'That's me,' said William.

'Der Patrician will see you now,' said the troll.

'I don't have an appointment with Lord Vetinari!'

'Ah, well,' said the troll, 'you'd be amazed at how many people has appointments wid der Patrician an' dey don't know it.'

*

Dibbler opened the *special* section of his tray, the high-class one that contained sausages whose contents were 1) meat, 2) from a known four-footed creature, 3) probably land-dwelling.

*

' . . . a naked man, hotly pursued by Members of the Watch, burst through the Window and ran around the Room, causing much Disarray of the Tarts before being Apprehended by the Trifles.'

An innocent young reporter writes.

*

William wondered why he always disliked people who said 'no offence meant'. Maybe it was because they found it easier to say 'no offence meant' than actually refrain from giving offence.

*

William felt predisposed to like Vimes, if only because of the type of enemies he made, but as far as he could see everything about the man could be prefaced by the word 'badly', as in -spoken, -educated and -in need of a drink.

*

'Ah, just the man I was looking for!' said William.

'Am I?' wheezed Nobbs, smoke curling out of his ears.

'Yes, I've been talking to Commander Vimes, and now I would like to see the room where the crime was committed.' William had great hopes of that sentence. It *seemed* to contain the words 'and he gave me permission to' without actually doing so.

*

One of the strange things about eating at Mrs Arcanum's was that you got more leftovers than you got original meals. That is, there were far more meals made up from what were traditionally considered the prudently usable remains of earlier meals – stews, bubble-and-squeak, curry – than there were meals at which those remains could have originated.

The curry was particularly strange, since Mrs Arcanum considered foreign parts only marginally less unspeakable than private parts and therefore added the curious yellow curry powder with a very small spoon, lest everyone should suddenly tear their clothes off and do foreign things. The main ingredients appeared to be swede and gritty rainwater tasting sultanas and the remains of some cold mutton.

*

The best way to describe Mr Windling would be like this: you are at a meeting. You'd like to be away early. So would everyone else. There really isn't very much to discuss, anyway. And just as everyone can see Any Other Business coming over the horizon and is already putting their papers neatly together, a voice says 'If I can raise a minor matter, Mr Chairman . . .' and with a horrible wooden feeling in your stomach you *know*, now, that the evening will go on for twice as long with much referring back to the minutes of earlier meetings. The man who has just said that, and is now sitting there with a smug smile of dedication to the committee process, is as near Mr Windling as makes no difference. And something that distinguishes the Mr Windlings of the universe is the term 'in my humble opinion', which they think *adds* weight to their statements rather than indicating, in reality, 'these are the mean little views of someone with the social grace of duckweed'.

*

Classically, very few people have considered that cleanliness is next to godliness, apart from in a very sternly abridged dictionary. A rank loincloth and hair in an advanced state of matted entanglement have generally been the badges of office of prophets whose injunction to disdain earthly things starts with soap.

*

'You don't think a dress like this would be a bit . . . forward, do you?' said Sacharissa, holding the dress against herself.

Rocky looked worried.

'You're quite a lot forward already,' he opined.

Sacharissa's knowledge of vintages extended just as far as knowing that Chateau Maison was a very popular wine.

Sacharissa pulled a brown leather wallet out of the jacket.

'Any clue to who he is?' said William.

'Er . . . there's something done on the leather in pokerwork,' said Sacharissa.

'What does it say?'

'"Not A Very Nice Person At All",' she read. 'I wonder what kind of person would put *that* on a wallet?'

'Someone who wasn't a very nice person,' said William.

Death sighed and shook his head.

WHO KNOWS WHAT EVIL LURKS IN THE HEART OF MEN?

The Death of Rats looked up.

SQUEAK, he said.

Death waved a hand dismissively. WELL, YES, OBVIOUSLY *ME*, he said. I JUST WONDERED IF THERE WAS ANYONE ELSE.

*

'Oh, I see,' said Lord Vetinari. 'You mean you should be free to print what you like?'

'Well . . . broadly, yes, sir.'

'Because that's in the public interest?'

'I think so, sir.'

'Stories about man-eating goldfish and people's husbands disappearing in big silver dishes?'

'No, sir. That's what the public is interested in. We do the other stuff, sir.'

'Amusingly shaped vegetables?'

'Well, a *bit* of that, sir. Sacharissa calls them human interest stories.'

'About vegetables and animals?'

'Yes, sir.'

'So . . . we have what the people are interested in, and human interest stories, which is what humans are interested in, and the public interest, which no one is interested in.'

'Except the public, sir,' said William, trying to keep up.

'Which isn't the same as people and humans?'

'I think it's more complicated than that, sir.'

'Obviously. Do you mean that the public is a different thing from the people you just see walking about the place? The public thinks big, sensible, measured thoughts while *people* run around doing silly things?'

'I think so. I may have to work on that idea too, I admit.'

*

'I'm sure we can pull together, sir.'

Lord Vetinari raised his eyebrows. 'Oh, I do hope not, I really do hope not. Pulling together is the aim of despotism and tyranny. Free men pull in all kinds of directions.' He smiled. 'It's the only way to make progress.'

*

'You think that's really true?' William said.

Sacharissa shrugged. 'Really true? Who knows? This is a newspaper, isn't it? It just has to be true until tomorrow.'

THIEF OF TIME

TIME is a resource. Everyone knows it has to be managed.

And on Discworld that is the job of the Monks of History, who store it and pump it from the places where it's wasted (like underwater – how much time does a codfish need?) to places like cities, where there's never enough time.

But the construction of the world's first truly accurate clock starts a race against, well, time for Lu-Tze and his apprentice Lobsang Ludd. Because it will stop time. And that will only be the start of everyone's problems.

Complete with a full supporting cast of heroes and villains, yetis, martial artists and Ronnie, the fifth Horseman of the Apocalypse (who left before they became famous).

'She has told me everything,' said Wen. 'I know that time was made for men, not the other way round. I have learned how to shape it and bend it. I know how to make a moment last for ever, because it already has. And I can teach these skills even to you, Clodpool. I have heard the heartbeat of the universe. I know the answers to many questions. Ask me.'

The apprentice gave him a bleary look.

'Er . . . what does master want for breakfast?' he said.

Wen looked down from their camp and across the snowfields and purple mountains to the golden daylight creating the world, and mused upon certain aspects of humanity.

'Ah,' he said. 'One of the *difficult* ones.'

*

This is the desk of a professional. It is clear that their job is their life. There are . . . human touches, but these are the human touches that strict usage allows in a chilly world of duty and routine.

Mostly they're on the only piece of real colour in this picture of blacks and greys. It's a coffee mug. Someone somewhere wanted to make it a *jolly* mug. It bears a rather unconvincing picture of a teddy bear, and the legend 'To The World's Greatest Grandad' and the slight change in the style of lettering on the word 'Grandad' makes it clear that this has come from one of those stalls that have *hundreds* of mugs like this, declaring that they're for the world's greatest Grandad/Dad/Mum/Granny/Uncle/Aunt/Blank. Only someone whose life contains very little else, one feels, would treasure a piece of gimcrackery like this.

*

They were not lifeforms. They were . . . non-lifeforms. They were the observers of the operation of the universe, its clerks, its *auditors*. They saw to it that things spun and rocks fell.

And they believed that for a thing to exist it had to have a position in time and space. Humanity had arrived as a nasty shock. Humanity practically *was* things that didn't have a position in time and space, such as imagination, pity, hope, history and belief. Take those away and all you had was an ape that fell out of trees a lot.

Intelligent life was, therefore, an anomaly. It made the filing untidy. The Auditors *hated* things like that.

*

Wen considered the nature of time and understood that the universe is, instant by instant, recreated anew. Therefore, he understood, there is in truth no past, only a memory of the past. Blink your eyes, and the world you see next did not exist when you closed them. Therefore, he said, the only appropriate state of the mind is surprise. The only appropriate state of the heart is joy. The sky you see now, you have never seen before. The perfect moment is now. Be glad of it.

*

Lobsang heard the dojo master say: 'Dojo! What is Rule One?'

'Do not act incautiously when confronting little bald wrinkly smiling men!'

*

If children were weapons, Jason would have been banned by international treaty. Jason had doting parents and an attention span of minus several seconds, except when it came to inventive cruelty to small furry animals, when he could be quite patient. Jason kicked, punched, bit and spat. His artwork had even frightened the life out of Miss Smith, who could generally find something nice to say about any child. He was definitely a boy with special needs. In the view of the staffroom, these began with an exorcism.

Madam Frout had stooped to listening at the keyhole. She had heard Jason's first tantrum of the day, and then silence. She couldn't quite make out what Miss Susan said next.

When she found an excuse to venture into the classroom half an hour later, Jason was helping two little girls to make a cardboard rabbit.

Later his parents said they were amazed at the change, although apparently now he would only go to sleep with the light on.

*

'What precisely was it you wanted, madam?' she said. 'It's just that I've left the class doing algebra, and they get restless when they've finished.'

'Algebra?' said Madam Frout, perforce staring at her own bosom, which no one else had ever done. 'But that's far too difficult for seven-year-olds!'

'Yes, but I didn't tell them that and so far they haven't found out,' said Susan.

The class had built a full-size white horse out of cardboard boxes,

during which time they'd learned a lot about horses and Susan learned about Jason's remarkably accurate powers of observation. She'd had to take the cardboard tube away from him and explain that this was a *polite* horse.

The Stationery Cupboard! That was one of the great battlegrounds of classroom history, that and the playhouse. But the ownership of the playhouse usually sorted itself out without Susan's intervention, so that all she had to do was be ready with ointment, a nose-blow and mild sympathy for the losers, whereas the Stationery Cupboard was a war of attrition. It contained pots of powder paint and reams of paper and boxes of crayons and more idiosyncratic items like a spare pair of pants for Billy, who did his best. It also contained The Scissors, which under classroom rules were treated as some kind of Doomsday Machine, and, of course, the boxes of stars. The only people allowed in the cupboard were Susan and, usually, Vincent. Despite everything Susan had tried, short of actual deception, he was always the official 'best at everything' and won the coveted honour every day, which was to go into the Stationery Cupboard and fetch the pencils and hand them out. For the rest of the class, and especially Jason, the Stationery Cupboard was some mystic magic realm to be entered whenever possible.

Honestly, thought Susan, once you learn the arts of defending the Stationery Cupboard, outwitting Jason and keeping the class pet alive until the end of term, you've mastered at least half of teaching.

*

According to the Second Scroll of Wen the Eternally Surprised, Wen the Eternally Surprised sawed the first Procrastinator from the trunk of a *wamwam* tree, carved certain symbols on it, fitted it with a bronze spindle and summoned the apprentice, Clodpool.

'Ah. Very nice, master,' said Clodpool. 'A prayer wheel, yes?'

'No, this is nothing like as complex,' said Wen. 'It merely stores and moves time.'

'That simple, eh?'

'And now I shall test it,' said Wen. He gave it a half-turn with his hand.

'Ah. Very nice, master,' said Clodpool. 'A prayer wheel, yes?'

'No, this is nothing like as complex,' said Wen. 'It merely stores and moves time.'

'That simple, eh?'

'And now I shall test it,' said Wen. He moved it a little less this time.

'That simple, eh?'

'And now I shall test it,' said Wen.

*

Lu-Tze bent down, picked up a fallen cork helmet, and solemnly handed it to Lobsang.

'Health and safety at work,' he said. 'Very important.'

'Will it protect me?' said Lobsang, putting it on.

'Not really. But when they find your head, it may be recognizable.'

*

'All roads lead to Ankh-Morpork.'

'I thought all roads led *away* from Ankh-Morpork.'

'Not the way we're going.'

*

Now the cold crept in, slowly, like a sadist's knife.

Lu-Tze strode on ahead, seemingly oblivious of it.

Lu-Tze, it was said, would walk for miles during weather when the clouds themselves would freeze and crash out of the sky. Cold did not affect him, they said.

'Sweeper!'

Lu-Tze stopped and turned. 'Yes, lad?'

'I don't know how you can stand this cold!'

'Ah, you don't know the secret?'

'Is it the Way of Mrs Cosmopilite that gives you such power?'

Lu-Tze hitched up his robe and did a little dance in the snow, revealing skinny legs encased in thick, yellowing tubes.

'Very good, very good,' he said. 'She still sends me these double-knit combinations, silk on the inside, then three layers of wool, reinforced gussets and a couple of handy trapdoors. Very reasonably priced at six dollars a pair because I'm an old customer. For it is written, "Wrap up warm or you'll catch your death." '

*

The Auditors *hated* questions. They hated them almost as much as they hated decisions, and they hated decisions almost as much as they hated the idea of the individual personality. But what they hated most was things moving around randomly.

*

The apprentice Clodpool, in a rebellious mood, approached Wen and spake thusly:

'Master, what is the difference between a humanistic, monastic system of belief in which wisdom is sought by means of an apparently nonsensical system of questions and answers, and a lot of mystic gibberish made up on the spur of the moment?'

Wen considered this for some time, and at last said: 'A fish!'

And Clodpool went away, satisfied.

*

The Code of the Igors was very strict.

Never Contradict: it was no part of an Igor's job to say things like 'No, thur, that'th an artery.' The marthter was always right.

Never Complain: an Igor would never say 'But that'th a thouthand mileth away!'

Never Make Personal Remarks: no Igor would dream of saying anything like 'I thould have thomething done about that laugh, if I wath you.'

And never, ever Ask Questions. Admittedly, Igor knew, that meant never ask BIG questions. 'Would thur like a cup of tea around now?' was fine, but 'What do you need a hundred virginth for?' or 'Where do you ecthpect me to find a brain at thith time of night?' was not.

*

Death found Pestilence in a hospice in Llamedos. Pestilence liked hospitals. There was always something for him to do.

Currently he was trying to remove the 'Now Wash Your Hands' sign over a cracked basin.

*

And what is this?

'It is a cat. It arrived. It does not appear to wish to depart.'

And the reason for its presence?

'It appears to tolerate the company of humans, asking nothing in return but food, water, shelter and comfort.'

*

'Look at the bird.'

It was perched on a branch by a fork in the tree, next to what looked like a birdhouse.

'Looks like some kind of old box to me,' said Lobsang. He squinted to see better. 'Is it an old . . . clock?' he added.

'Look at what the bird is nibbling,' suggested Lu-Tze.

'Well, it looks like . . . a crude gear-wheel? But why—'

'Well spotted. That, lad, is a clock cuckoo. A young one, by the look of it, trying to build a nest that'll attract a mate. Not much chance of that . . . See? It's got the numerals all wrong and it's stuck the hands on crooked.'

'A bird that *builds* clocks? I thought a cuckoo clock was a clock with a mechanical cuckoo that came out when—'

'And where do you think people got such a strange idea from?'

'But that's some kind of miracle!'

'Why?' said Lu-Tze. 'They barely go for more than half an hour, they keep lousy time and the poor dumb males go frantic trying to keep them wound.'

*

Of the very worst words that can be heard by anyone high in the air, the pair known as 'Oh-oh' possibly combine the maximum of bowel-knotting terror with the minimum wastage of breath.

*

'We're having rabbit,' Mrs War said. 'I'm *sure* I can make it stretch to three.'

War's big red face wrinkled. 'Do I like rabbit?'

'Yes, dear.'

'I thought I liked beef.'

'No, dear. Beef gives you wind.'

'Oh.' War sighed. 'Any chance of onions?'

'You don't like onions, dear.'

'I don't?'

'Because of your stomach, dear.'

'Oh.'

War smiled awkwardly at Death. 'It's rabbit,' he said.

Despite himself, Death was fascinated. He had never come across the idea of keeping your memory inside someone else's head.

'Perhaps I would like a beer?' War ventured.

'You don't like beer, dear.'

'I don't?'

'No, it brings on your trouble.'

'Ah. Uh, how do I feel about brandy?'

'You don't like brandy, dear. You like your special oat drink with the vitamins.'

'Oh, yes,' said War mournfully. 'I'd forgotten I liked that.'

*

'The poet Hoha once dreamed he was a butterfly, and then he awoke and said, "Am I a man who dreamed he was a butterfly, or am I a butterfly dreaming he is a man?" ' said Lobsang.

'Really?' said Susan briskly. 'And which was he?'

'What? Well . . . who knows?'

'How did he write his poems?' said Susan.

'With a brush, of course.'

'He didn't flap around making information-rich patterns in the air or laying eggs on cabbage leaves?'

'No one ever mentioned it.'

'Then he was probably a man.'

Lu-Tze had long considered that everything happens for a reason, except possibly football.

Ankh-Morpork had not had a king for many centuries, but palaces tend to survive. A city might not need a king, but it can always use big rooms and some handy large walls, long after the monarchy is but a memory and the building is renamed the Glorious Memorial to the People's Industry.

*

Wienrich and Boettcher were foreigners, and according to Ankh-Morpork's Guild of Confectioners they did not understand the peculiarities of the city's tastebuds.

Ankh-Morpork people, said the Guild, were hearty, no-nonsense folk who did not *want* chocolate that was stuffed with cocoa liquor, and were certainly not like effete la-di-dah foreigners who wanted cream in everything. In fact they actually *preferred* chocolate made mostly from milk, sugar, suet, hooves, lips, miscellaneous squeezings, rat droppings, plaster, flies, tallow, bits of tree, hair, lint, spiders and powdered cocoa husks. This meant that according to the food standards of the great chocolate centres in Borogravia and Quirm, Ankh-Morpork chocolate was formally classed as 'cheese' and only escaped, through being the wrong colour, being defined as 'tile grout'.

*

The Quirm College for Young Ladies had been very advanced in that respect, and its teachers took the view that a girl who couldn't swim two lengths of the pool with her clothes on wasn't making an effort.

Her one chocolate today and it was damn artificial damn pink-and-white damn sickly damn stupid *nougat*!

Well, no one could be expected to believe *that* counted.†

The yeti of the Ramtops, where the Discworld's magical field is so intense that it is part of the very landscape, are one of the few creatures to utilize control of personal time for genetic advantage. The result is a kind of physical premonition — you find out what is going to happen next by allowing it to happen. Faced with danger, or any kind of task that involves risk of death, a yeti will *save* its life up to that point and then proceed with all due caution, yet in the comfortable knowledge that, should everything go pancake-shaped, it will wake up at the point where it saved itself with, and this is the important part, *knowledge of the events which have just happened but which will not now happen because it's not going to be such a damn fool next time*. This is not quite the paradox it appears because, after it has taken place, it hasn't happened. All that actually remains is a memory in the yeti's head, which merely turns out to be a remarkably accurate premonition. The little eddies in time caused by all this are just lost in the noise of all the kinks, dips and knots put in time by every other living creature.

*

Susan returned to the classroom and spent the rest of the day performing small miracles, which included removing the glue from Richenda's hair, emptying the wee out of Billy's shoes and treating the class to a short visit to the continent of Fourecks.

† This is true. A chocolate you did not want to eat does not count as chocolate. This discovery is from the same branch of culinary physics that determined that food eaten while walking contains no calories.

THE LAST HERO

HE'S been a legend in his own lifetime.

He can remember the great days of high adventure.

He can remember when a hero didn't have to worry about fences and lawyers and civilization.

He can remember when people didn't tell you off for killing dragons.

But he can't always remember, these days, where he put his teeth . . .

He's really not happy about that bit.

So now, with his ancient sword and his new walking stick and his old friends – and they're very old friends – Cohen the Barbarian is going on one final quest. It's been a good life. He's going to climb the highest mountain in the Discworld and meet his gods. He doesn't like the way they let men grow old and die.

It's time, in fact, to give something back.

The last hero in the world is going to return what the first hero stole. With a vengeance. That'll mean the end of the world, if no one stops him in time.

Someone is going to try. So who knows who the last hero really is?

The place where the story happened was a world on the back of four elephants perched on the shell of a giant turtle. That's the advantage of space. It's big enough to hold practically *anything*, and so, eventually, it does.

*

People think that it is strange to have a turtle ten thousand miles long and an elephant more than two thousand miles tall, which just shows that the human brain is ill-adapted for thinking and was probably originally designed for cooling the blood. It believes mere size is *amazing*.

There's nothing amazing about size. Turtles are amazing, and elephants are quite astonishing. The fact that there's a big turtle is far less amazing than the fact that there is a turtle anywhere.

*

'Ah, well, life goes on,' people say when someone dies. But from the point of view of the person who has just died, it doesn't. It's the universe that goes on. Just as the deceased was getting the hang of everything it's all whisked away, by illness or accident or, in one case, a cucumber. Why this has to be is one of the imponderables of life, in the face of which people either start to pray . . . or become really, really angry.

*

The wizards, once they understood the urgency of a problem, and then had lunch, and argued about the pudding, could actually work quite fast.

Their method of finding a solution was by creative hubbub. If the question was, 'What is the best spell for turning a book of poetry into a frog?', then the one thing they would *not* do was look in any book with a title like *Major Amphibian Spells in a Literary Environment: A Comparison*. That would, somehow, be cheating. They would argue about it instead, standing around a blackboard, seizing the chalk from one another and rubbing out bits of what the current chalk-holder was writing before he'd finished the other end of the sentence. Somehow, though, it all seemed to work.

*

The gods play games with the fate of men. Not complex ones, obviously, because gods lack patience.

Cheating is part of the rules. And gods play hard. To lose all believers is, for a god, the *end*. But a believer who survives the game gains honour and extra belief. Who wins with the most believers, lives.

Believers can include other gods, of course. Gods *believe* in belief.

*

Lord Vetinari, despite his education, had a mind like an engineer. If you wished to open something, you found the appropriate spot and applied the minimum amount of force necessary to achieve your end. Possibly the spot was between a couple of ribs and the force was applied via a dagger, or between two warring countries and applied via an army, but the important thing was to find that one weak spot which would be the key to everything.

*

The dungeons of the Palace held a number of felons imprisoned 'at his lordship's pleasure', and since Lord Vetinari was seldom very pleased they were generally in for the long haul.

*

Leonard of Quirm was so absent-mindedly clever that he could paint pictures that didn't just follow you around the room but went home with you and did the washing-up.

*

'So how come you left the Evil Dark Lord business, Harry?' said Cohen.

'Werl, you know how it is these days,' said Evil Harry Dread.

The Horde nodded. They knew how it was these days.

'People these days, when they're attacking your Dark Evil Tower, the first thing they do is block up your escape tunnel,' said Evil Harry.

'Bastards!' said Cohen. 'You've *got* to let the Dark Lord escape. Everyone knows that.'

'That's right,' said Caleb. 'Got to leave yourself some work for tomorrow.'

*

'Anyone heard of Ning the Uncompassionate?'

'Sort of,' said Boy Willie. 'I killed him.'

'You couldn't have done! What was it he always said? "I shall revert to this vicinity!" '

'Sort of hard to do that,' said Boy Willie, pulling out a pipe and beginning to fill it with tobacco, 'when your head's nailed to a tree.'

*

'How about Pamdar the Witch Queen?' said Evil Harry. 'Now *there* was—'

'Retired,' said Cohen.

'She'd never retire!'

'Got married,' Cohen insisted.

'But she was a devil woman!'

'We all get older, Harry. She runs a shop now. Pam's Pantry. Makes marmalade,' said Cohen.

'What? She used to queen it in a throne on top of a pile of skulls!'

'I didn't say it was very *good* marmalade.'

*

Hughnon Ridcully, Chief Priest of Blind Io, shared many of the characteristics of his brother Mustrum. He also saw his job as being, essentially, one of organizer. There were plenty of people who were good at the actual *believing*, and he left them to it. It took a lot more than prayer to make sure the laundry got done and the building was kept in repair.

*

There were so many gods now . . . at least two thousand. Many were, of course, still very small. But you had to watch them. Gods were very much a fashion thing. Look at Om, now. One minute he was a bloodthirsty little deity in some mad hot country, and then suddenly he was one of the top gods. It had all been done by not answering prayers, but doing so in a sort of *dynamic* way that left open the possibility that one day he might and *then* there'd be fireworks.

*

And then, of course, you had your real newcomers like Aniger, Goddess of Squashed Animals. Who would have thought that better roads and faster carts would have led to that? But gods grew bigger when called upon at need, and enough minds had cried out, 'Oh god, what was that I hit?'

*

Death tries to come to grips with Schroedinger's Cat:

In the study of his dark house on the edge of Time, Death looked at the wooden box.

PERHAPS I SHALL TRY ONE MORE TIME, he said.

He reached down and lifted up a small kitten, patted it on the head, lowered it gently into the box, and closed the lid.

THE CAT DIES WHEN THE AIR RUNS OUT?

'I suppose it might, sir,' said Albert, his manservant. 'But I don't reckon that's the point. If I understand it right, you don't know if the cat's dead or alive until you look at it.'

THINGS WILL HAVE COME TO A PRETTY PASS, ALBERT, IF *I* DID NOT KNOW WHETHER A THING WAS DEAD OR ALIVE WITHOUT HAVING TO GO AND LOOK.

'Er . . . the way the theory goes, sir, it's the *act* of lookin' that determines if it's alive or not.'

Death looked hurt. ARE YOU SUGGESTING I WILL KILL THE CAT JUST BY LOOKING AT IT?

'It's not quite like that, sir.'

I MEAN, IT'S NOT AS IF I MAKE FACES OR ANYTHING.

'To be honest with you, sir, I don't think even the wizards understand the uncertainty business,' said Albert.

Death opened the box and took out the kitten. It stared at him with the normal mad amazement of kittens everywhere.

I DON'T HOLD WITH CRUELTY TO CATS, said Death, putting it gently on the floor.

'Some people say you achieve immortality through your children,' said the minstrel.

'Yeah?' said Cohen. 'Name one of your great-grandads, then.'

Discworld briefly discovers space travel, and Carrot, Rincewind and Leonard of Quirm look down on the Disc from its moon:

'You know, I'm not sure I ever really believed it before,' said Carrot. 'You know . . . about the turtle and the elephants and everything. Seeing it all like this makes me feel very . . . very . . .'

'Scared?' suggested Rincewind.

'No.'

'Upset?'

'No.'

'Easily intimidated?'

'No.'

Beyond the Rimfall, the continents of the world were coming into view under swirls of white cloud.

'You know . . . from up here . . . you can't see the boundaries between nations,' said Carrot, almost wistfully.

'Is that a problem?' said Leonard. 'Possibly something could be done.'

'Maybe huge, really *huge* buildings in lines, along the frontiers,' said Rincewind. 'Or . . . or very wide roads. You could paint them different colours to save confusion.'

'Should aerial travel become widespread,' said Leonard, 'it would be a useful idea to grow forests in the shape of the name of the country, or of other areas of note. I will bear this in mind.'

'I wasn't actually *sugges—*' Carrot began. And then he stopped, and just sighed.

*

On the veldt of Howondaland live the N'tuitif people, the only tribe in the world to have *no imagination whatsoever*.

For example, their story about the thunder runs something like this: 'Thunder is a loud noise in the sky, resulting from the disturbance of the air masses by the passage of lightning.' And their legend 'How the Giraffe Got His Long Neck' runs: 'In the old days the ancestors of Old Man Giraffe had slightly longer necks than other grassland creatures, and the access to the high leaves was so advantageous that it was mostly long-necked giraffes that survived, passing on the long neck in their blood just as a man might inherit his grandfather's spear. Some say, however, that it is all a lot more complicated and this explanation only applies to the shorter neck of the okapi. And so it is.'

The N'tuitif are a peaceful people, and have been hunted almost to extinction by neighbouring tribes, who have lots of imagination, and therefore plenty of gods, superstitions and ideas about how much better life would be if they had a bigger hunting ground.

Of the events on the moon that day, the N'tuitif said: 'The moon was brightly lit and from it rose another light which then split into three lights and faded. We do not know why this happened. It was just a thing.'

They were then wiped out by a nearby tribe who *knew* that the lights had been a signal from the god Ukli to expand the hunting ground a bit more. However, *they* were soon defeated entirely by a tribe who *knew* that the lights were their ancestors, who lived in the moon, and who were urging them to kill all non-believers in the goddess Glipzo. Three years later they in turn were killed by a rock falling from the sky, as a result of a star exploding a billion years ago.

What goes around, comes around. If not examined too closely, it passes for justice.

*

Few religions are definite about the size of Heaven, but on the planet Earth the Book of Revelation (ch. XXI, v.16) gives it as a cube 12,000 furlongs on a side. This is somewhat less than 500,000,000,000,000,000,000 cubic feet. Even allowing that the Heavenly Host and other essential services take up at least two thirds of this space, this leaves about one million cubic feet of space for each human occupant – assuming that every creature that could be called 'human' is allowed in, and that the human race eventually totals a thousand times the number of humans alive up until now. This is such a generous amount of space that it suggests that room has also been provided for some alien races or – a happy thought – that pets are allowed.

*

Many of the things built by the architect and freelance designer Bergholt Stuttley ('Bloody Stupid') Johnson were recorded in Ankh-Morpork, often on the line where it says 'Cause of Death'. He was, people agreed, a genius, at least if you defined the word broadly. Certainly no one else in the world could make an explosive mixture out of common sand and water. A good designer, he always said, should be capable of anything. And, indeed, he was.

NIGHT WATCH

TRUTH! Justice! Freedom! And a Hard-boiled Egg!

Commander Sam Vimes of the Ankh-Morpork City Watch had it all. But now he's back in his own rough, tough past without even the clothes he was standing up in when the lightning struck.

Living in the past is hard. Dying in the past is incredibly easy. But he must survive, because he has a job to do. He must track down a murderer, teach his younger self how to be a good copper and change the outcome of a bloody rebellion. There's a problem: if he wins, he's got no wife, no child, no future.

A Discworld Tale of One City, with a full chorus of street urchins, ladies of negotiable affection, rebels, secret policemen and other children of the revolution.

Plain old Sam Vimes had ended up with a dress uniform that at least looked as though its owner was male. But the helmet had gold decoration, and the bespoke armourers had made a new, gleaming breastplate with useless gold ornamentation on it. Sam Vimes felt like a class traitor every time he wore it. He hated being thought of as one of those people that wore stupid ornamental armour. It was gilt by association.

*

'If I had a dollar for every copper's funeral I've attended up here,' said Colon, 'I'd have . . . nineteen dollars and fifty pence.'

'Fifty pence?' said Nobby.

'That was when Corporal Hildebiddle woke up just in time and banged on the lid,' said Colon.

Privilege just means 'private law'. Two types of people laugh at the law: those that break it and those that make it.

Sweeper took a deep, long breath. 'I like building gardens,' he said. 'Life should be a garden.'

Vimes stared blankly at what was in front of them. 'Okay,' he said. 'The gravel and rocks, yes, I can see that. Shame about all the rubbish. It always turns up, doesn't it . . .'

'Yes,' said Lu-Tze. 'It's part of the pattern.'

'What? The old cigarette packet?'

'Certainly. That invokes the element of air,' said Sweeper.

'And the cat doings?'

'To remind us that disharmony, like a cat, gets everywhere.'

'The cabbage stalks? The used sonky?'†

'At our peril we forget the role of the organic in the total harmony. What arrives seemingly by chance in the pattern is part of a higher organization that we can only dimly comprehend. This is a very important fact, and has a bearing on your case.'

'And the beer bottle?'

For the first time since Vimes had met him, the monk frowned.

'Y'know, some bugger always tosses one over the wall on his way back from the pub on Friday nights. If it wasn't forbidden to do that kind of thing, he'd feel the flat of my hand and no mistake.'

† Named after Wallace Sonky, a man without whose experiments with thin rubber pressure on the housing in Ankh-Morpork would have been a good deal more pressing.

'It's not part of the higher organization?'

'Possibly. Who cares?'

*

The Night Watch. They were in the Night Watch because they were too scruffy, ugly, incompetent, awkwardly shaped or bloody-minded for the Day Watch. They were honest, in that special policeman sense of the word. That is, they didn't steal things too heavy to carry. And they had the morale of damp gingerbread.

*

'A copper doesn't keep flapping his lip. He doesn't let on what he knows. He doesn't say what he's thinking. No. He watches and listens and he learns and he bides his time. His mind works like mad but his face is a blank. Until he's ready.'

*

Dr Lawn opened his back door and Vimes brushed past, the body over his shoulders.

'You minister to all sorts, right?' said Vimes.

'Within reason, but—'

'This one's an Unmentionable,' said Vimes. 'Tried to kill me. Needs some medicine.'

'Why's he unconscious?' said the doctor.

'Didn't want to take his medicine.'

*

Apart from the curfew and manning the gates, the Night Watch didn't do a lot. This was partly because they were incompetent, and partly because no one expected them to be anything else. They walked the streets, slowly, giving anyone dangerous enough time to saunter away or melt into the shadows, and then rang the bell to announce to a sleeping world, or at any rate a world that had been asleep, the fact that all was, despite appearances, well. They also rounded up the quieter sort of drunk and the more docile kinds of stray cattle.

'What're you going to charge our man with, sarge?' said Sam.

'Attempted assault on a copper. You saw the knives.'

'You did kick him, though.'

'Right, I forgot. We'll do him for resisting arrest, too.'

Dr Lawn put the tweezers down and pinched the bridge of his nose. 'That's it,' he said, wearily. 'A bit of stitching and he'll be fine.'

'And there's some others I need you to take a look at,' said Vimes.

'You know, that comes as no surprise,' said the doctor.

'One's got a lot of holes in his feet,

one dropped through the privy roof and has got a twisted leg, and one's dead.'

'I don't think I can do much about the dead one,' said the doctor. 'How do you know he's dead? I realize that I may regret asking that question.'

'He's got a broken neck from falling off a roof and I reckon he fell off because he got a steel crossbow bolt in his brain.'

'Ah. That sounds like dead, if you want my medical opinion. Did you do it?'

'No!'

'Well, you're a busy man, sergeant. You can't be everywhere.'

*

'I understand, Havelock, that you scored zero in your examination for stealthy movement.'

'May I ask how you found that out, madam?'

'Oh, one hears things,' Madam said lightly.

'Well, it was true,' said the Assassin.

'And why was this?'

'The examiner thought I'd used trickery, madam.'

'And did you?'

'Of course. I thought that was the idea.'

'And you never attended his lessons, he said.'

'Oh, I did. Religiously.'

'He says he never saw you at any of them.'

Havelock smiled. 'And your point, madam, is . . .?'

*

Vimes turned his back and faced the crowd. He said, 'Anything's a weapon, used right. Your bell is a club. Anything that pokes the other man hard enough to give you more time is a good thing. Never, ever threaten anyone with your sword unless you really mean it, because if he calls your bluff you suddenly don't have many choices and they're all the wrong ones. Don't be frightened to use what you learned when you were kids. We don't get marks for playing fair. And for close-up fighting, as your senior sergeant I explicitly forbid you to investigate the range of coshes, black-jacks and brass knuckles sold by Mrs Goodbody at No. 8 Easy Street, at a range of prices to suit all pockets, and should any of you approach me privately I absolutely will not demonstrate a variety of specialist blows suitable for these useful yet tricky instruments.'

*

Sometimes the principles behind a glorious revolution don't stand much close examination.

'I've got a question,' said someone in the crowd of onlookers. 'Harry Supple's my name. Got a shoe shop in New Cobblers . . .'

'Yes, comrade Supple?'

'It says here in article seven of this here list—' Mr Supple ploughed on.

'—People's Declaration of the Glorious Twenty-fourth of May,' said Reg.

'Yeah, yeah, right . . . well, it says we'll seize hold of the means of production, sort of thing, so what I want to know is, how does that work out regarding my shoe shop? I mean, I'm in it anyway, right? It's not like there's room for more'n me and my lad Garbut and maybe one customer.'

'Ah, but after the revolution all property will be held in common by the people . . . er . . . that is, it'll belong to you but *also* to everyone else, you see?'

Comrade Supple looked puzzled. 'But I'll be the one making the shoes?'

'Of course. But everything will *belong* to the people.'

'So . . . who's going to pay for the shoes?' said Mr Supple.

'Everyone will pay a reasonable price for their shoes and you won't be guilty of living off the sweat of the common worker,' said Reg, shortly. 'Now, if we—'

'You mean the cows?' said Supple.

'What?'

'Well, there's only the cows, and the lads at the tannery, and frankly all they do is stand in a field all day, well, not the tannery boys, obviously, but—'

'Look,' said Reg. 'Everything will belong to the people and everyone will be better off. Do you understand?'

The shoemaker's frown grew deeper. He wasn't certain if he was part of the people.

*

The major was not a fool, even though he looked like one. He was idealistic, and thought of his men as 'jolly good chaps' despite the occasional evidence to the contrary, and on the whole did the best he could with the moderate intelligence at his disposal. When he was a boy he'd read books about great military campaigns, and visited the museums and looked with patriotic pride at the paintings of famous cavalry charges, last stands and glorious victories. It had come as rather a shock, when he later began to participate in some of these, to find that the painters had unaccountably left out the intestines. Perhaps they just weren't very good at them.

*

'What's it look like to you, Tom?' said the major.

'We've lost nearly eighty men,' said the captain.

'What? That's terrible!'

'Oh, about sixty of them are deserters, as far as I can see. As for the rest, well, as far as I can see only six or seven of them went down to definite enemy action. Three men got stabbed in alleyways, for example.'

'Sounds like enemy action to *me*.'

'Yes, Clive. But you were born in Quirm. Getting murdered in alleyways is just part of life in the big city.'

*

'Tom?'

'Yes, Clive?'

'Have you ever sung the national anthem?'

'Oh, lots of times, sir.'

'I don't mean officially.'

'You mean just to show I'm patriotic? Good gods, no. That would be a rather odd thing to do,' said the captain.

'And how about the flag?'

'Well, obviously I salute it every day, sir.'

'But you don't wave it, at all?' the major enquired.

'I think I waved a paper one a few times when I was a little boy. Patrician's birthday or something. We stood in the streets as he rode by and we shouted "Hurrah!" '

'Never since then?'

'Well, *no*, Clive,' said the captain, looking embarrassed. 'I'd be very worried if I saw a man singing the national anthem and waving the flag, sir. It's really a thing foreigners do.'

'Really? Why?'

'*We* don't need to show *we're* patriotic, sir. I mean, this is Ankh-Morpork. We don't have to make a big fuss about being the best, sir. We just *know*.'

*

'It's called Victory Stew, sergeant,' said Dibbler. 'Tuppence a bowl or I'll cut my throat, eh?'

'Close enough,' said Vimes, and looked at the strange (and, what was worse, occasionally hauntingly familiar) lumps seething in the scum. 'What's in it?'

'It's stew,' explained Dibbler. 'Strong enough to put hairs on your chest.'

'Yes, I can see that some of those bits of meat have got bristles on them already,' said Vimes.

*

There were rules. When you had a Guild of Assassins, there had to be rules which everyone knew and were never, ever broken.

An Assassin, a real Assassin, had to look like one – black clothes, hood, boots and all. If they could wear any clothes, any disguise, then what could anyone do but spend all day sitting in a small room with a loaded crossbow pointed at the door?

And they couldn't kill a man incapable of defending himself (although a man worth more than AM$10,000 a year was considered automatically capable of defending himself or at least of employing people to do it for him).

And they had to give the target a chance.

THE AMAZING MAURICE AND HIS EDUCATED RODENTS

IMAGINE a million clever rats. Rats that don't run. Rats that fight...

Maurice, a scruffy tomcat with an eye for the main chance, has the perfect fiddle going. He has a stupid-looking kid for a piper, and he has his very own plague of rats – rats who are strangely educated, so Maurice can no longer think of them as 'lunch'. And everyone knows the stories about rats and pipers – and is giving him lots of money...

Until they try the trick in the far-flung town of Bad Blintz, and the nice little con suddenly goes down the drain.

Someone there is playing a different tune. A dark, shadowy tune. Something very, very bad is waiting in the cellars. The rats must learn a new word.

Evil.

Everyone needs their little dreams. If you knew what it was that people really, *really* wanted, you very nearly controlled them.

Cats are *good* at steering people. A miaow here, a purr there, a little gentle pressure with a claw . . . Cats didn't have to think. They just had to know what they wanted. Humans had to do the thinking. That's what they were for.

*

Everyone knew about plagues of rats. There were famous stories about the rat pipers, who made their living going from town to town getting rid of plagues of rats.

And that, really, was it. You didn't need *many* rats for a plague, not if they knew their business. One rat, popping up here and there, squeaking loudly, taking a bath in the fresh cream and widdling in the flour, could be a plague all by himself.

After a few days of this, it was amazing how glad people were to see the stupid-looking kid with his magical rat pipe. And they were amazed when rats poured out of every hole to follow him out of the town. They were so amazed that they didn't bother much about the fact that there were only a few hundred rats.

They'd have been *really* amazed if they'd ever found out that the rats and the piper met up with a cat somewhere in the bushes out of town, and solemnly counted out the money.

*

There were three loud knocks from below. They were repeated. And then they were repeated again. Finally, Malicia's voice said: 'Are you two up there or not?'

Keith crawled out of the hay and looked down. 'Yes,' he said.

'Didn't you hear the secret knock?' said Malicia, staring up at him in annoyance.

'It didn't sound like a secret knock,' said Maurice.

'It *is* a secret knock!' Malicia snapped. 'I know about these things! And you're supposed to give the secret knock in return!'

'But if it's just someone knocking on the door in, you know, general high spirits, and we knock back, what are they going to think is up here?' said Maurice. 'An extremely heavy beetle?'

Malicia went uncharacteristically

silent for a moment. Then she said: 'Good point, good point. I know, I'll shout "It's me, Malicia!" and *then* give the secret knock, and that way you'll know it's me and you can give the secret knock back. Okay?'

'Why don't we just say "Hello, we're up here"?' said Keith innocently.

Malicia sighed. 'Don't you have *any* sense of drama?'

Cat singing consists of standing two inches in front of other cats and screaming at them until they give in.

'Never rush, never run. We don't want to be like the first mouse, eh?'

'No, Darktan,' the rats chorused dutifully. 'We don't want to be like the first mouse!'

'Right! What mouse do we want to be like?'

'The second mouse, Darktan!' said the rats, who'd had this lesson dinned into them many times.

'Right! And why do we want to be like the second mouse?'

'Because the second mouse gets the cheese, Darktan!'

'Good!' said Darktan.

A young rat was holding up its paw.

'Yes?'

'Er . . . can I ask a question, sir?'

'All right,' he said.

'Er . . . you said the second mouse gets the cheese, sir? But . . . doesn't the *first* mouse get something, sir?'

Darktan stared at the young rat. 'I can see you're going to be a valuable addition to the squad.' He raised his voice. 'Squad! What does the *first* mouse get?'

The roar of voices made dust fall down from the ceiling. 'The Trap!'

*

'You were stolen away at birth, I expect [said Malicia]. You probably *are* the rightful king of some country, but they found someone who looked like you and did a swap. You were probably found on a doorstep.'

'I was, yes,' said Keith.

'See? I'm always right!'

'What were you doing on a doorstep?' said Maurice.

'I don't know. Gurgling, I expect,' said Keith.

'There was a magic sword or a crown in the basket with you, probably. And you've got a mysterious tattoo or a strange-shaped birthmark, too,' said Malicia.

'I don't think so. No one ever mentioned them,' said Keith. 'There was just me and a blanket. And a note.'

'A note? But that's *important*!'

'It said "19 pints and a Strawberry Yoghurt",' said Keith.

*

'Well, you probably won't be surprised to know that I've got two dreadful step-sisters,' said Malicia. 'And I have to do all the chores!'

'Gosh, really,' said Maurice.

'Well, most of the chores,' said Malicia, as if revealing an unfortunate fact. 'Some of them, definitely. I have to clean up my own room, you know! And it's *extremely* untidy!'

'Gosh, really.'

'*And* it's very nearly the smallest bedroom. There're practically no cupboards and I'm running out of bookshelf space!'

'Gosh, really.'

'And people are incredibly cruel to me. You will note that we're here in a *kitchen*. And I'm the mayor's daughter. Should the daughter of a mayor be expected to wash up at least once a week? I think *not*!'

'Gosh, really.'

'And will you just look at these torn and bedraggled clothes I have to wear?'

Maurice looked. As far as he could tell, Malicia's dress was pretty much like any other dress.

'Here, just here,' said Malicia, pointing to a place on the hem which, to Maurice, looked no different from the rest of the dress. 'I had to sew that back myself, you know?'

*

Keith grabbed the back edge of the dresser with both hands, and braced one foot against the wall, and heaved.

Slowly, like a mighty forest tree, the dresser pitched forward. The crockery started to fall out as it tipped, plate slipping off plate in one glorious chaotic deal from a very expensive pack of cards. Even so, some of them survived the fall on to the floor, and so did some of the cups and saucers as the cupboard opened and added to the fun, but that didn't made any difference because then the huge, heavy woodwork thundered down on top of them.

One miraculously whole plate rolled past Keith, spinning round and round and getting lower on the floor with the groiyuoiyoi-*yooooinnnnggg* sound you always get in these distressing circumstances.

*

'Do you know what an aglet is?'

'Aglet? Aglet? What's an aglet got to do with anything?' snapped Malicia.

'It's those little metal bits on the end of shoelaces,' said Maurice.

'How come a cat knows a word like that?' said the girl.

'Everyone's got to know *something*,' said Maurice.

*

'They'll tell my father I've been telling stories and I'll get locked out of my room again.'

'You get locked *out* of your room as a punishment?' said Maurice.

'Yes. It means I can't get at my books. I'm rather a special person, as you may have guessed,' said Malicia, proudly.

OF COURSE THERE ARE NO CAT GODS. THAT WOULD BE TOO MUCH LIKE . . . WORK.

'When I woke up there was a rat *dancing* on my dressing-table,' said Corporal Knopf. 'Tapitty, tapitty, tap.'

'That's odd,' said Sergeant Doppelpunkt, giving his corporal a strange look.

'*And* it was humming "There's no Business like Show Business". I call that more than just "odd"!'

'No, I meant it's odd you've got a dressing-table. I mean, you're not even married.'

*

''scuse me, 'scuse me,' said a voice from beside him. He looked down at a dirty, half-scorched cat, which grinned at him.

'Did that *cat* just *speak*?' said the mayor.

Maurice looked around. 'Which one?' he said.

'You! Did you just talk?'

'Would you feel better if I said no?' said Maurice.

*

'Look, there's two types of people in the world.' said Malicia. 'There are those who have got the plot, and those that haven't.'

'The world hasn't got a *plot*,' said Maurice. 'Things just . . . happen, one after another.'

'Only if you think of it like that,' said Malicia, far too smugly in Maurice's opinion. 'There's always a plot. You just have to know where to look.' She paused for a moment and then said, 'Look! That's the word! There'll be a secret passage, of course! Everyone look for the entrance to the secret passage!'

'Er . . . how will we know it's the entrance to a secret passage?' said Keith, looking even more bewildered than normal. 'What does a secret passage *look* like?'

'It won't *look* like one, of course!'

'Oh, *well*, in that case I can see dozens of secret passages,' said Maurice. 'Doors, windows, that calendar from the Acme Poison Company, that cupboard over there, that rat hole, that desk, that—'

'You're just being sarcastic,' said Malicia, lifting up the calendar and sternly inspecting the wall behind it.

'Actually, I was just being flippant,' said Maurice. 'But I can do sarcastic if you like.'

Keith stared at the long bench which was in front of a window frosted with ancient cobwebs.

'You might try to be some help,' said Malicia, tapping the walls.

'I don't know how to look for something that doesn't look like the thing I'm looking for,' said Keith.

Malicia stood back and brushed her hair out of her eyes. 'This isn't working,' she said.

'I suppose there might not *be* a secret passage?' said Maurice. 'I know it's a rather daring idea, but perhaps this is just an ordinary shed?'

Even Maurice leaned back a little from the force of Malicia's stare.

'There *has* to be a secret passage,' she said. 'Otherwise there's no *point.*' She snapped her fingers. 'Of course! We're doing it wrong! *Everyone* knows you never find the secret passage by *looking* for it! It's when you give up and lean against the wall that you inadvertently operate the secret switch!'

Maurice looked at Keith for help. He was a human, after all. He should know how to deal with something like Malicia. But Keith was just wandering around the shed, staring at things.

Malicia leaned against the wall with incredible nonchalance. There was not a click. A panel in the floor did not slide back. 'Probably the wrong place,' she said. 'I'll just rest my arm innocently on this coat hook.' A sudden door in the wall completely failed to happen. 'Of course, it'd help if there was an ornate candlestick,' said Malicia. 'They're always a sure-fire secret passage lever. Every adventurer knows that.'

'There isn't a candlestick,' said Maurice.

'I know. Some people totally fail to have any *idea* of how to design a proper secret passage,' said Malicia. She leaned against another piece of wall, which had no effect whatsoever.

'I don't think you'll find it that way,' said Keith, who was carefully examining a trap.

'Oh? Won't I?' said Malicia. 'Well, at least I'm being *constructive* about things! Where would you look, if you're such an expert?'

'Why is there a rat hole in a rat-catchers' shed?' said Keith. 'It smells of dead rats and wet dogs and poison. I wouldn't come near this place if I was a rat.'

'Ye–es,' said Malicia. 'That usually works, in stories. It's often the stupid person who comes up with the good idea by accident.' She crouched down and peered into the hole. 'There's a sort of little lever,' she said. 'I'll just give it a little push . . .'

There was a *clonk* under the floor, part of it swung back, and Keith dropped out of sight.

'Oh, yes,' said Malicia. 'I thought something like that would probably happen . . .'

*

'Now I want to ask you a question,' said Darktan. 'You've been the leader for . . . how long?'

'Ten years,' said the mayor.

'Isn't it hard?'

'Oh, yes. Oh, yes. Everyone argues with me all the time,' said the mayor.

'Although I must say I'm expecting a little less arguing if all this works. But it's not an easy job.'

'It's ridiculous to have to shout all the time just to get things done,' said Darktan.

'That's right,' said the mayor.

'And everyone expects you to decide things,' said Darktan.

'True.'

'The last leader gave me some advice just before he died, and do you know what it was? "Don't eat the green wobbly bit"!'

'Good advice?' said the mayor.

'Yes,' said Darktan. 'But all he had to do was be big and tough and fight all the other rats that wanted to be leader.'

'It's a bit like that with the council,' said the mayor.

'What?' said Darktan. 'You bite them in the neck?'

'Not yet,' said the mayor. 'But it's a thought, I must say.'

'It's just all a lot more complicated than I ever thought it would be!' said Darktan, bewildered. 'Because after you've learned to shout you have to learn not to!'

'Right again,' said the mayor. 'That's how it works . . . See the river? See the Houses? See the people in the streets? I have to make it all work. Well, not the river, obviously, that works by itself. And every year it turns out that I haven't upset enough people for them to choose anyone else as mayor. So I have to do it again. It's a lot more complicated than I ever thought it would be.'

'What, for you too? But you're a human!' said Darktan in astonishment.

'Hah! You think that makes it easier? I thought rats were wild and free!'

'Hah!' said Darktan.

They stared out of the window.

'It's just like I always tell my daughter,' said the man. 'Stories are just stories. Life is complicated enough as it is. We have to plan for the real world. There's no room for the fantastic.'

'Exactly,' said the rat.

The thing about stories is that you have to pick the ones that last.

THE WEE FREE MEN

THERE'S trouble on the Aching farm – nightmares spreading down from the hills. And now Tiffany Aching's little brother has been stolen by the Queen of the Fairies (although Tiffany doesn't think this is entirely a bad thing).

Tiffany's got to get him back. To help her, she has a weapon (a frying pan), her granny's magic book (well, *Diseases of the Sheep*, actually) and—

'Crivens! Whut aboot us, ye daftie!'

—oh, yes. She's also got the Nac Mac Feegle, the Wee Free Men, the fightin', thievin', tiny blue-skinned pictsies who were thrown out of Fairyland for being Drunk and Disorderly . . .

Ordinary fortune-tellers tell you what you *want* to happen; witches tell you what's going to happen whether you want it to or not. Strangely enough, witches tend to be more accurate but less popular.

*

There was a small part of Tiffany's brain that wasn't too certain about the name Tiffany. She was nine years old and felt that Tiffany was going to be a hard name to live up to. Besides, she'd decided only last week that she wanted to be a witch when she grew up, and she was certain Tiffany just wouldn't work. People would laugh.

*

The teachers were useful. They went from village to village delivering short lessons on many subjects. They kept apart from the other travellers, and were quite mysterious in their ragged robes and strange square hats. They used long words, like 'corrugated iron'. They lived rough lives, surviving on what food they could earn from giving lessons to anyone who would listen. When no one would listen, they lived on baked hedgehog. They went to sleep under the stars, which the maths teachers would count, the astronomy teachers would measure and the literature teachers would name. The geography teachers got lost in the woods and fell into bear traps.

*

'I would like a question answered today,' said Tiffany. 'It's about zoology.'

'Zoology, eh? That's a big word, isn't it.'

'No, actually it isn't,' said Tiffany. 'Patronizing is a big word. Zoology is really quite short.'

*

'Are you a witch?' said Tiffany. 'I don't mind if you are.'

'What a strange question to spring on someone,' said the woman. 'Why would I be a witch?'

'You're wearing a straw hat with flowers in it.'

'Aha!' said the woman. 'That proves it, then. Witches wear tall pointy hats. Everyone knows that, foolish child.'

'Yes, but witches are also very clever,' said Tiffany calmly. 'They sneak about. Probably they often don't look like witches. And a witch coming here would know about the Baron and so she'd wear the kind of hat that everyone knows witches don't wear.'

'That was an incredible feat of reasoning,' the woman said at last. 'Whatever kind of hat I've got on, you'd say it proves I'm a witch, yes?'

'Well, the frog sitting on your hat is a bit of a clue, too,' said Tiffany.

'I'm a toad, actually,' said the creature, which had been peering at Tiffany from between the paper flowers.

'You're very yellow for a toad.'

'I've been a bit ill,' said the toad.

'And you talk,' said Tiffany.

'You only have my word for it,' said the toad, disappearing into the paper flowers. 'You can't prove anything.'

*

'Witches have animals they can talk to, called familiars. Like your toad there.'

'I'm not familiar,' said a voice from among the paper flowers. 'I'm just slightly presumptuous.'

*

'If you have a grandmother who can pass on her pointy hat to you, that saves a great deal of expense. They are incredibly hard to come by, especially ones strong enough to withstand falling farmhouses.'

*

'You might make a decent witch one day,' she said. 'But I don't teach people to be witches. They learn in a special school. I just show them the way, if they're any good. All witches have special interests, and I like children.'

'Why?'

'Because they're much easier to fit in the oven,' said Miss Tick.

*

'I will give you some free advice.'

'Will it cost me anything?'

'You could say it is priceless. Are you listening?'

'Yes.'

'Good. Now . . . if you trust in yourself . . .'

'Yes?'

'. . . and believe in your dreams . . .'

'Yes?'

'. . . and follow your star . . .'

'Yes?'

'. . . you'll still get beaten by people who spent *their* time working hard and learning things and weren't so lazy.'

*

A lot of the stories were highly suspicious, in her opinion. There was the one that ended when the two good children pushed the wicked witch into her own oven. Tiffany had worried about that after all that trouble with Mrs Snapperly. Stories like this stopped people thinking properly, she was sure. She'd read that one and thought, Excuse me? *No one* has an oven big enough to get a whole person in, and what made the children think they could just walk around eating people's houses in any case? And why does some boy too stupid to know a cow is worth a lot more than five beans have the *right* to murder a giant and steal all his gold? Not to mention commit an act of ecological vandalism? And some girl who can't tell the difference between a wolf and her grandmother must either have been as dense as teak or come from an extremely ugly family.

*

They were all about six inches tall and mostly coloured blue, although it was hard to know if that was the actual colour of their skins or just the dye from their tattoos, which covered every inch that wasn't covered with red hair. They wore short kilts, and some wore other bits of clothing too, like skinny waistcoats. A few of them wore rabbit or rat skulls on their heads, as a sort of helmet. And every single one of them carried, slung across his back, a sword nearly as big as he was.

'Whut's the plan, Rob?' said one of them.

'Okay, lads, this is what we'll do. As soon as we see somethin', we'll attack it. Right?'

This caused a cheer.

'Ach, 'tis a good plan,' said Daft Wullie.

Glint, glisten, glitter, gleam . . .

Tiffany thought a lot about words. 'Onomatopoeic', she'd discovered in the dictionary, meant words that sounded like the noise of the thing they were describing, like 'cuckoo'. But *she* thought there should be a word meaning 'a word that sounds like the noise a thing would make if that thing made a noise even though, actually, it doesn't, but would if it did'.

Glint, for example. If light made a noise as it reflected off a distant window, it'd go 'glint!' And the light of tinsel, all those little glints chiming together, would make a noise like 'glitterglitter'. 'Gleam' was a clean, smooth noise from a surface that intended to shine all day. And 'glisten' was the soft, almost greasy sound of something rich and oily.

*

'What's your name, pictsie?' she said.

'No'-as-big-as-Medium-Sized-Jock-but-bigger-than-Wee-Jock-Jock, mistress. There's no' that many Feegle names, ye ken, so we ha' to share.'

'Well, Not-as-big-as-Little-Jock—' Tiffany began.

'That'd be Medium-Sized Jock, mistress,' said Not-as-big-as-Medium-Sized-Jock-but-bigger-than-Wee-Jock-Jock.

'Well, Not-as-big-as-Medium-Sized-Jock-but-bigger-than-Wee-Jock, I can—'

'That's No'-as-big-as-Medium-Sized-Jock-but-bigger-than-Wee-Jock-*Jock*, mistress,' said Not-as-big-as-Medium-Sized-Jock-but-bigger-than-Wee-Jock-Jock. 'Ye were one jock short,' he added helpfully.

*

There was some method in the way the Nac Mac Feegle fought. For example, they always chose the biggest opponent because, as Rob Anybody said later, 'It makes them easier to hit, ye ken'. And they simply didn't *stop*. It was that which wore people down. It was like being attacked by wasps with fists.

*

'The thing about witchcraft,' said Mistress Weatherwax, 'is that it's not like school at all. *First* you get the test, and then afterwards you spend years findin' out how you passed it. It's a bit like life in that respect.'

*

'And what do you *really* do?' said Tiffany.

'We look to ... the edges,' said Mistress Weatherwax. 'There're a lot of edges, more than people know. Between life and death, this world and the next, night and day, right and wrong ... an' they need watchin'. We watch 'em, we guard the sum of things. And we never ask for any reward. That's important.'

*

'Hooses, banks, dreams, 'tis a' the same to us,' said Rob Anybody. 'There's nothing we cannae get in or oot of.'

'Except maybe pubs,' said Big Yan.

'Oh, aye,' said Rob Anybody cheerfully. 'Gettin' oot o' pubs sometimes causes us a cerrrtain amount o' difficulty, I'll grant ye that.'

MONSTROUS REGIMENT

IT began as a sudden strange fancy . . .

Polly Perks had to become a boy in a hurry. Cutting off her hair and wearing trousers was easy. Learning to fart and belch in public and walk like an ape took more time . . .

And now she's enlisted in the army, and is searching for her lost brother.

But there's a war on. There's always a war on. And Polly and her fellow recruits are suddenly in the thick of it, without any training, and the enemy is hunting them.

All they have on their side is the most artful sergeant in the army and a vampire with a lust for coffee. Well . . . they have the Secret. And as they take the war to the heart of the enemy, they have to use all the resources of . . . the Monstrous Regiment.

And then there was the young male walk. At least women swung only their *hips*. Young men swung *everything*, from the shoulders down. You have to try to occupy a lot of space. It makes you look bigger, like a tomcat fluffing his tail. The boys tried to walk big in self-defence against all those other big boys out there. I'm bad, I'm fierce, I'm cool, I'd like a pint of shandy and me mam wants me home by nine . . .

*

Polly reached the troll bridge, which crossed the river in a narrow gorge. It cost one penny to cross, or one hundred gold pieces if you had a billygoat. Trolls might not be quick thinkers but they don't forget in a hurry, either.

*

'Ever eaten scubbo? No? Nothing like a bowl of scubbo when you're hungry. You can put *anything* in scubbo. Pork, beef, mutton, rabbit, chicken, duck . . . anything. Even rats, if you've got 'em. It's food for the marching man, scubbo. Got some on the boil right now. You can have some of that, if you like.'

The squad brightened up.

'Thoundth good,' said Igor. 'What'th in it?'

'Boiling water,' said the corporal. 'It's what we call "blind scubbo".'

*

'You could try scrounging something at the inn.'

'Scrounge?' said Polly.

'Yeah. Scrounge. Scrounge, nick, have a lend of, borrow, thieve, lift, acquire, purrrr-loin. That's what you'll learn, if you're gonna survive this war.'

'We have to *steal* our food?' said Maladict.

'No, you can starve if that takes your fancy,' said the corporal. 'I've starved a few times. There's no future in it. Ate a man's leg when we were snowed up in the Ibblestarn campaign but, fair's fair, he ate mine.'

*

Lieutenant Blouse was standing in the middle of the floor in his breeches and shirtsleeves, holding a sabre. Polly was no expert in these matters, but she thought she recognized the stylish, flamboyant pose as the one beginners tend to use just before they're stabbed through the heart by a more experienced fighter.

*

'These are tricky times, sergeant. Command has never been so burdensome. The great General Tacticus says that in dangerous times the commander must be like the eagle and see the whole, and yet still be like the hawk and see every detail.'

'Yessir,' said Jackrum. 'And if he acts like a common tit, sir, he can hang upside down all day and eat fat bacon.'

*

A woman always has half an onion left over, no matter what the size of the onion, the dish or the woman.

*

Jackrum stepped back. 'We are heading for the front, lads. The war. And in a nasty war, where's the best place to be? Apart from on the moon, o' course? No one?'

Slowly, Jade raised a hand.

'Go on, then,' said the sergeant.

'In the army, sarge,' said the troll. ''cos . . .' She began to count on her fingers. 'One, you got weapons an' armour an' dat. Two, you are surrounded by other armed men. Er . . . Many, youse gettin' paid and gettin' better grub than the people in Civilian Street. Er . . . Lots, if'n you gives up, you getting taken pris'ner and dere's rules about that like Not Kicking Pris'ners Inna Head and stuff, 'cos if you kick their pris'ners inna head they'll kick your pris'ners inna head so dat's, like, you're kickin' your own head, but dere's no rule say you can't kick enemy civilians inna head. There's other stuff too, but I ran outa numbers.'

*

'You know what most of the milit'ry training is, Perks?' Jackrum went on. 'It's to turn you into a man who will, on the word of command, stick his blade into some poor sod just like him who happens to be wearing the wrong uniform. He's like you, you're like him. He doesn't really want to kill you, you don't really want to kill him. But if you don't kill him first, he'll kill you. That's the start and finish of it. It don't come easy without trainin'.'

*

Polly wondered if Jackrum ever slept. She did a spell of guard duty, and he stepped out from behind her with 'Guess who, Perks! You're on lookout. You should see the dreadful enemy before they see you. What're the four Ss?'

'Shape, shadow, silhouette and shine, sarge!' said Polly, snapping to attention.

That caused a moment's pause from the sergeant before he said: 'Just *knew* that, did yer?'

'Nosir! A little bird told me when we changed guard, sir! Said you'd asked him, sir!'

'Oh, so Jackrum's little lads are gangin' up on their kindly ol' sergeant, are they?' said Jackrum.

'Nosir. Sharing information important to the squad in a vital survival situation, sarge!'

'But I see you're not standing in a bleedin' shadow, Perks, nor have you done anything to change your bleedin' shape, you're silhouetted against the bleedin' light and your sabre's shining like a diamond in a chimney-sweep's bleedin' ear'ole! Explain!'

'It's because of the one C, sarge!' said Polly, still staring straight ahead.

'And that is?'

'Colour, sarge! I'm wearing bleedin' red and white in a bleedin' grey forest, sarge!'

She risked a sideways glance. In Jackrum's little piggy eyes there gleamed a gleam. It was the one you got when he was secretly pleased.

'Ashamed of your lovely, lovely

uniform, Perks?' he said.

'Don't want to be seen dead in it, sarge,' said Polly.

*

'General Tacticus said the fate of a battle may depend upon the actions of one man in the right place, sergeant,' said Blouse, calmly.

'*And* having a lot more soldiers than the other bugger, sir,' Jackrum insisted.

*

'Is that rum, sarge?' said Polly.

'Well done, my little bar steward. And wouldn't it be nice if it *was* rum, upon my word. Or whisky or gin or brandy. But this don't have none of those fancy names. This is the genuine stingo, this is. Pure hangman.'

'Hangman?' said Shufti.

'One drop and you're dead,' said Polly.

*

'All right,' Polly whispered. 'Remember, no swearing. No weapons, either. Anyone brought a weapon?'

There was a shaking of heads.

'Did you bring a weapon, Tonk—Magda?'

'No, Polly.'

'No item of any sort with a certain weapon-like quality?' Polly insisted.

'No, Polly,' said Tonker demurely.

'Anything, perhaps, with an edge?'

'Oh, you mean this?'

'Yes, Magda.'

'Well, a woman can carry a knife, can't she?'

'It's a *sabre*, Magda. You're trying to hide it, but it's a sabre.'

'But I'm only using it like a knife, Polly.'

'It's three feet long, Magda.'

'Size isn't important, Polly.'

'No one believes that. Leave it behind a tree, please.'

It is an established fact that, despite everything society can do, girls of seven are magnetically attracted to the colour pink.

'Sir, you know you said you were going to steal a gate key off a guard and break his neck?' said Polly.

'Indeed.'

'Do you know *how* to break a man's neck, sir?'

'I read a book on martial arts, Perks.'

'But you haven't actually *done* it, sir?'

'Well, no! I was at HQ, and you are not allowed to practise on real people, Perks.'

'Look, sir, I'm just a . . . what *is* your name, please?'

'Sam Vimes. Special envoy, which is kind of like an ambassador but without the little gold chocolates.'

*

Trying to break into a fortified and heavily guarded keep, the male Lieutenant Blouse comes up with a cunning plan, which he explains to one of his soldiers, who (unknown to him) is really female. This is the Inexorable Law of Comic Cross-Dressing:

'Astonishingly enough, Perks,' said Blouse, 'in your boyish enthusiasm you have given me a very interesting idea . . . because, of course, we only need one "washerwoman" to get us inside, do we not? And if one thinks "outside of the box", the "woman" does not in fact need to be a woman!'

Blouse beamed. Polly allowed her brow to wrinkle in honest puzzlement.

'Doesn't she, sir?' she said. 'I don't think I quite understand, sir.'

'"She", could be a man! One of us! In disguise.'

'I'll go,' said Polly quietly.

'Really, private. It would simply not work,' said Blouse. 'Oh, you're brave, certainly, but what makes you think you stand a chance of passing yourself off as a woman?'

'Well, sir . . . what?'

Blouse shook his head. 'No, they would see through you in a flash. You are a fine bunch of lads, but there is only one man here who'd stand a chance of getting away with it. Manickle?'

'Yessir?' said Shufti, rigid with instant panic.

'Can you find me a dress, do you think?'

'Sir, are you telling us . . . you're going to try to get in dressed as a woman?'

'Well, I'm clearly the only one who's had any practice,' said Blouse, rubbing his hands together. 'At my old school we were in and out of skirts all the time.'

He looked around at the circle of absolutely expressionless faces.

'Theatricals, you see?' he said brightly. 'No gels at our boarding school, of course. But we didn't let that stop us. Why, my Lady Spritely in *A Comedy of Cuckolds* is still talked about. No, if we need a woman, I'm your man.'

A HAT FULL OF SKY

ELEVEN-year-old Tiffany Aching wants to be a real witch. But a real witch doesn't casually step out of her body, leaving it empty. Tiffany does – and there's something just waiting for a handy body to take over. Something ancient and horrible, which can't die. Now Tiffany's got to learn to be a real witch really quickly, with the help of arch-witch Mistress Weatherwax and the truly amazing Miss Level.

'Crivens! And us!'

Oh, yes. And the Nac Mac Feegle – the rowdiest, toughest, smelliest bunch of fairies ever to be thrown out of Fairyland for having been drunk at two in the afternoon. They'll fight anything...

The Nac Mac Feegle are the most dangerous of the fairy races, particularly when drunk. They love drinking, fighting and stealing, and will in fact steal anything that is not nailed down. If it *is* nailed down, they will steal the nails as well.

*

The origin of the Nac Mac Feegle is lost in the famous Mists of Time. They say that they were thrown out of Fairyland by the Queen of the Fairies because they objected to her spiteful and tyrannical rule. Others say they were just thrown out for being drunk.

*

Little is known about their religion, if any, save for one fact: they think they are dead. They like our world, with its sunshine and mountains and blue skies and things to fight. An amazing world like this couldn't be open to just *anybody*, they say. It must be some kind of a heaven or Valhalla, where brave warriors go when they are dead. So, they reason, they have already been alive somewhere else, and then died and were allowed to come here because they have been so *good*.

This is a *quite* incorrect and fanciful notion because, as we know, the truth is exactly the other way around.

*

The new boots were all wrong. They were stiff and shiny. Shiny boots! That was disgraceful. Clean boots, that was different. There was nothing wrong with putting a bit of a polish on boots to keep the wet out. But boots had to work for a living. They shouldn't *shine*.

Witches were a bit like cats.

They didn't much like one another's company, but they *did* like to know where all the other witches *were*, just in case they needed them.

People in the chalk country didn't trust witches. They thought they danced around on moonlit nights without their drawers on. (Tiffany had made enquiries about this, and had been slightly relieved to find out that you didn't have to do this to be a witch. You could if you wanted to, but only if you were certain where all the nettles, thistles and hedgehogs were.)

*

If there's one thing a Feegle likes more than a party, it's a bigger party, and if there's anything better than a bigger party, it's a bigger party with someone else paying for the drink.

*

If you want to upset a witch you don't have to mess around with charms and spells, you just have to put her in a room with a picture that's hung slightly crooked and watch her squirm.

*

Rob Anybody had mastered the first two rules of writing, as he understood them.

1) Steal some paper.

2) Steal a pencil.

Unfortunately there was more to it than that.

*

Twoshirts was just a bend in the road, with a name. There was nothing there but an inn for the coaches, a blacksmith's shop, and a small store with the word SOUVENIRS written optimistically on a scrap of cardboard in the window. And that was it. Around the place, separated by fields and scraps of woodland, were the houses of people for whom Twoshirts was, presumably, the big city. Every world is full of places like Twoshirts. They are places for people to come from, not go to.

*

The wood was about half an hour's walk away. It was nothing special, as woods go, being mostly full-grown beech, although once you know that beech drips unpleasant poisons on the ground beneath it to keep it clear it's not quite the timber you thought it was.

*

First Thoughts are the everyday thoughts. Everyone has those. Second Thoughts are the thoughts you think about the *way* you think. People who enjoy thinking have those. Third Thoughts are thoughts that watch the world and think all by themselves. They're rare, and often troublesome. Listening to them is part of witchcraft.

*

She had a dobby stone, which was supposed to be lucky because it had a hole in it. (She'd been told that when she was seven, and had picked it up. She couldn't quite see how the hole made it lucky, but since it had spent a lot of time in her pocket, and then safe and sound in the box, it probably *was* more fortunate than most stones, which got kicked around and run over by carts and so on.)

*

Every kitchen drawer Tiffany had ever seen might have been *meant* to be neat but over the years had been crammed with things that didn't quite fit, like big ladles and bent bottle openers, which meant that they always stuck unless you knew the trick of opening them.

*

'Have you ever been to a circus?'

Once, Tiffany admitted. It hadn't been much fun. Things that try too hard to be funny often aren't. There had been a moth-eaten lion with practically no teeth, a tight-rope walker who was never more than a few feet above the ground, and a knife-thrower who threw a lot of knives at an elderly woman in pink tights on a big spinning wooden disc and completely failed to hit her every time. The only real amusement was afterwards, when a cart ran over the clown.

*

'He's always talking about . . . his funeral.'

'Well, it's important to him. Sometimes old people are like that. They'd hate people to think that they were too poor to pay for their own funeral. Mr Weavall'd die of shame if he couldn't pay for his own funeral.'

*

'We do what can be done,' said Miss Level. 'Mistress Weatherwax said you've got to learn that witchcraft is mostly about doing quite ordinary things.'

'And you have to do what she says?' said Tiffany.

'I listen to her advice,' said Miss Level, coldly.

'Mistress Weatherwax is the head witch, then, is she?'

'Oh no!' said Miss Level, looking shocked. 'Witches are all equal. We don't have things like head witches. That's *quite* against the spirit of witchcraft.'

'Oh, I see,' said Tiffany.

'Besides,' Miss Level added, 'Mistress Weatherwax would never allow that sort of thing.'

*

Tiffany couldn't help noticing that Petulia had jewellery everywhere; later she found that it was hard to be around Petulia for any length of time without having to unhook a bangle from a necklace or, once, an earring from an ankle bracelet (nobody ever found out how that one happened). Petulia couldn't resist occult jewellery. Most of the stuff was to magically protect her from things, but she hadn't found anything to protect her from looking a bit silly.

*

You had to remember that pictsies weren't brownies. In theory, brownies would do the housework for you if you left them a saucer of milk.

The Nac Mac Feegle . . . wouldn't.

*

In truth, most witches could get through their whole life without having to do serious, undeniable magic (making shambles and curse-nets and dreamcatchers didn't really count, being rather more like arts-and-crafts, and most of the rest of it was practical medicine, common sense and the ability to look stern in a pointy hat). But being a witch and wearing the big black hat was like being a policeman. People saw the uniform, not you. When the mad axeman was running down the street you weren't allowed to back away muttering 'Could you find someone else? Actually, I mostly just do, you know, stray dogs and road safety . . .' You were there, you had the hat, you did the job. That was a basic rule of witchery: *It's up to you.*

*

'How many fingers am I holdin' up?' he said.

'Five,' whispered Miss Level.

'Am I? Ah, well, ye could be right, ye'd have the knowin' o' the countin',' said Rob.

*

The Feegle way of reading:

'Worrds,' said Rob Anybody.

'Yes, they say—' Billy began.

'I ken weel what they say!' snapped Rob Anybody. 'I ha' the knowin' of the readin'! They say—'

He looked up again. 'OK, they say . . . that's the snake, an' that's the kinda like a gate letter, an' the comb on its side, two o' that, an' the fat man standin' still, an' the snake again, and then there's whut we calls a "space" and then there's the letter like a saw's teeth, and two o' the letters that's rooound like the sun, and the letter that's a man sittin' doon, and onna next line we ha' . . . the man wi' his arms oot, and the letter that's you, an' ha, the fat man again but noo he's walkin', an' next he's standin' still again, an' next is the comb, an' the up-an'-doon ziggy-zaggy letter, and the man's got his arms oot, and then there's me, and that ziggy-zaggy and we end the line with the comb again . . . an' on the *next* line we starts wi' the bendy hook, that's the letter rooound as the sun, them's twa men sittin' doon, there's the letter reaching ooot tae the sky, then there's a space 'cos there's nae letter, then there's the snaky again, an' the letter like a hoose frame, and then there's the letter that's me, aye, an' another fella sitting doon, an' another big rooound letter, and, ha, oor ol' friend, the fat man walkin'! The End!'

He stood back, hands on hips, and demanded: 'There! Is that readin' I just did, or wuz it no'?'

(And the words were: SHEEP'S WOOL, TURPENTINE, JOLLY SAILOR.)

*

Everyone in the mountains had heard of Mistress Weatherwax. If you didn't have respect, she said, you didn't have anything.

They were treated like royalty – not the sort who get dragged off to be beheaded or have something nasty done with a red-hot poker, but the other sort, when people walk away dazed saying, 'She actually said hello to me, very graciously! I will never wash my hand again!'

*

'Let's get moving.'

'We haven't even had anything to eat!' said Tiffany, running after her.

'I had a lot of voles last night,' said Mistress Weatherwax over her shoulder.

'Yes, but *you* didn't actually eat them, did you?' said Tiffany. 'It was the owl that *actually* ate them.'

'Technic'ly, yes,' Mistress Weatherwax admitted. 'But if you think you've been eating voles all night you'd be amazed how much you don't want to eat anything next morning.'

For an old woman Mistress Weatherwax could move quite fast. She strode over the moors as if distance was a personal insult.

There were no judges, and no prizes. The Witch Trials weren't like that, as Petulia had said. The point was to show what you could do, to show what you'd become, so that people would go away thinking things like 'That Caramella Bottlethwaite, she's coming along nicely'. It wasn't a competition, honestly. No one *won*.

And if you believed *that* you'd believe that the moon is pushed around the sky by a goblin called Wilberforce.

*

'If you don't know when to be a human being, you don't know when to be a witch. And if you're too afraid of goin' astray, you won't go anywhere.'

*

'I'm clever enough to know how you manage *not* to think of a pink rhinoceros if someone says "pink rhinoceros",' she managed to say aloud.

'Ah, that's deep magic, that is,' said Granny Weatherwax.

'No. It's not. You don't know what a rhinoceros looks like, do you?'

Sunlight filled the clearing as the old witch laughed, as clear as a downland stream.

'That's right!' she said.

GOING POSTAL

MOIST von Lipwig is a con artist . . .

. . . and a fraud and a man faced with a life choice: be hanged, or put Ankh-Morpork's ailing postal service back on its feet.

It's a tough decision.

But he's got to see that the mail gets through, come rain, hail, sleet, dogs, the Post Office Workers' Friendly and Benevolent Society, the evil chairman of the Grand Trunk Semaphore Company, and a midnight killer.

Getting a date with Adora Belle Dearheart would be nice, too.

They say that the prospect of being hanged in the morning concentrates a man's mind wonderfully; unfortunately, what the mind inevitably concentrates on is that it is in a body that, in the morning, is going to be hanged.

*

'I'd get some rest if I was you, sir, 'cos we're hanging you in half an hour,' said Mr Wilkinson.

'Hey, don't I get breakfast?'

'Breakfast isn't until seven o'clock, sir.'

*

'I'm offering you a job, Mr Lipwig, that of Postmaster General of the Ankh-Morpork Post Office. The job, Mr Lipwig, involves the refurbishment and running of the city's postal service, preparation of the international packets, maintenance of Post Office property, et cetera, et cetera—'

'If you stick a broom up my arse I could probably sweep the floor, too,' said Moist.

Lord Vetinari gave him a long, long look.

'Well, if you wish,' he said, and turned to a hovering clerk. 'Drumknott, does the housekeeper have a store cupboard on this floor, do you know?'

*

'I *believe* in freedom, Mr Lipwig. Not many people do, although they will of course protest otherwise. And no practical definition of freedom would be complete without the freedom to take the consequences. Indeed, it is the freedom upon which all the others are based.'

*

The world was blessedly free of honest men, and wonderfully full of people who believed they could tell the difference between an honest man and a crook.

He had a beard of the short bristled type that suggested that its owner had been interrupted halfway through eating a hedgehog.

A large black and white cat had walked into the room.

'That's Mr Tiddles, sir,' said Groat.

'*Tiddles?*' said Moist. 'You mean that really is a cat's name? I thought it was just a joke.'

'Not so much a name, sir, more of a description,' said Groat.

*

Before you could sell glass as diamonds you had to make people really *want* to see diamonds. That was *the* trick, the trick of all tricks. You changed the way people saw the world. You let them see it the way *they* wanted it to be . . .

*

Being an absolute ruler today was not as simple as people thought. At least, it was not simple if your ambitions included being an absolute ruler tomorrow. There were subtleties. Oh, you could order men to smash down doors and drag people off to dungeons without trial, but too much of that sort of thing lacked style and anyway was bad for business, habit-forming and very, very dangerous for your health. A thinking tyrant, it seemed to Vetinari, had a much harder job than a ruler raised to power by some idiot vote-yourself-rich system like democracy. At least they could tell the people he was their fault.

*

'Looks like you're genuine after all, then,' the old man said. 'One of the dark clerks wouldn't have [done] that. We thought you was one of his lordship's special gentlemen, see. No offence, but you've got a bit more colour than the average penpusher.'

'Dark clerks?' said Moist, and then recollection dawned. 'Oh . . . do you mean those stocky little men in black suits and bowler hats?'

'The very same. Scholarship boys at the Assassins' Guild, some of 'em. I heard that they can do some nasty things when they've a mind.'

'I thought you called them penpushers?'

'Yeah, but I didn't say where, hee-hee.'

*

Mr Pump, a golem, points out to conman Moist von Lipwig the downstream consequences of what had seemed to Moist to be harmless scams to separate fools from their money:

'You can't just go around killing people!' shouted Moist.

'Why Not? You Do.'

'What? I do not! Who told you that?'

'I Worked It Out. You Have Killed Two Point Three Three Eight People,' said the golem calmly.

'I have never laid a finger on anyone in my life, Mr Pump. I may be – all the things you know I am, but I am *not* a killer! I have never so much as drawn a sword!'

'No, You Have Not. But You Have Stolen, Embezzled, Defrauded And Swindled Without Discrimination, Mr Lipvig. You Have Ruined Businesses

And Destroyed Jobs. When Banks Fail, It Is Seldom Bankers Who Starve. Your Actions Have Taken Money From Those Who Had Little Enough To Begin With. In A Myriad Small Ways You Have *Hastened* The Deaths Of Many. You Do Not Know Them. You Did Not See Them Bleed. But You Snatched Bread From Their Mouths And Tore Clothes From Their Backs. For Sport, Mr Lipvig. For Sport. For The Joy Of The Game.'

Moist's mouth had dropped open. It shut. It opened again. It shut again. You can never find repartee when you need it.

'I Have Read The Details Of Your Many Crimes, Mr Lipvig. You Took From Others Because You Were Clever And They Were Stupid.'

'Hold on, most of the time they thought they were swindling me!'

'You Set Out To Trap Them, Mr Lipvig.'

People in Ankh-Morpork

always paid attention to people on rooftops, in case there was a chance of an interesting suicide.

By law and tradition the great Library of Unseen University is open to the public, although they aren't allowed as far as the magical shelves. They don't realize this, however, since the rules of time and space are twisted inside the Library and so hundreds of miles of shelving can easily be concealed inside a space roughly the thickness of paint.

People flock in, nevertheless, in search of answers to those questions only librarians are considered to be able to answer, such as 'Is this the laundry?' 'How do you spell surreptitious?' and, on a regular basis: 'Do you have a book I remember reading once? It had a red cover and it turned out they were twins.'

*

The hub or nerve centre of the coach business was a big shed next to the stable. It smelled – no, it stank – no, it *fugged* of horses, leather, veterinary medicine, bad coal, brandy and cheap cigars. That's what a fug was. You could have cut cubes out of the air and sold it for cheap building material.

*

Ankh-Morpork was a lot more civilized these days. Between them the Watch and the Guilds had settled things down enough to ensure that actually being attacked while going about your lawful business in Ankh-Morpork was now merely a possibility instead of, as it once was, a matter of course. And the streets were so clean now that you could sometimes even *see* the street.

*

The Mended Drum could be depended upon. If someone didn't come out of the door backwards and fall down in the street just as you passed, then there was something wrong with the world.

*

Stanley took down, from the shelf, the Book of Regulations. He turned the pages methodically until he came to the bookmark he'd put in a minute ago, on the page What To Do In Case Of Fire.

So far he'd done 1: Upon Discovery of the Fire, Remain Calm.

Now he came to 2: Shout 'Fire!' in a Loud, Clear Voice.

'Fire!' he shouted, and then ticked off 2 with his pencil.

Next was: 3: Endeavour to Extinguish Fire If Possible.

Stanley went to the door and opened it. Flames and smoke billowed in. He stared at them for a moment, shook his head, and shut the door.

Paragraph 4 said: If Trapped by Fire, Endeavour to Escape. Do Not Open Doors If Warm. Do Not Use Stairs If Burning. If No Exit Presents Itself Remain Calm and Await a) Rescue or b) Death.

This seemed to cover it.

*

. . . Anoia, a minor goddess of Things That Stick In Drawers. Often, but not uniquely, a ladle, but sometimes a metal spatula or, rarely, a mechanical egg-whisk that nobody in the house admits to ever buying. The desperate mad rattling and cries of 'How can it close on the damn thing but not open with it? Who bought this? Do we *ever* use it?' is as praise unto Anoia. She also eats corkscrews.

*

Ankh-Morpork never slept; the city never did more than doze, and would wake up around 3 a.m. for a glass of water.

Ridcully practised the First Available Surface method of filing.

'Was there something else, Mr Stibbons?'

Ponder looked at his clipboard. 'There's a polite letter from Lord Vetinari asking on behalf of the city whether the University might consider including in its intake, oh, twenty-five per cent of less able students, sir?'

'Can't have a bunch of grocers and butchers telling a university how to run itself, Stibbons!' Ridcully said firmly. 'Thank them for their interest and tell them we'll continue to take one hundred per cent of complete and utter dullards, as usual. Take 'em in dull, turn 'em out sparklin', that's always been the UU way!'

*

If there's one thing a wizard hates, it's having to wait while the person in front of them is in two minds about coleslaw. It's a salad bar, they say, it's got the kind of stuff salad bars have, if it was surprising it wouldn't *be* a salad bar, you're not here to *look* at it. What do you expect to find? Rhino chunks? Pickled coelacanth?

The Lecturer in Recent Runes ladled more bacon bits into his salad bowl, having artfully constructed buttresses of celery and breastworks of cabbage to increase its depth five times.

*

'The Grand Trunk will remain closed in the interim,' said Lord Vetinari.

'It's private property!' Greenham burst out.

'Tyrant, remember,' said Vetinari.

See a pin and pick it up, and all day long you'll have a pin.

THUD!

KOOM Valley? That was where the trolls ambushed the dwarfs, or the dwarfs ambushed the trolls. It was far away. It was a long time ago.

But if he doesn't solve the murder of just one dwarf, Commander Sam Vimes of Ankh-Morpork City Watch is going to see it fought again, right outside his office.

With his beloved Watch crumbling around him and war-drums sounding, he must unravel every clue, outwit every assassin and brave any darkness to find the solution. And darkness is *following* him.

Oh … and at six o'clock every day, without fail, with no excuses, he must go home to read *Where's My Cow?*, with all the right farmyard noises, to his little boy.

There are some things you *have* to do.

Vimes is chatting to his butler:

'Tell me, Willikins, did you fight much when you were a kid? Were you in a gang or anything?'

'I was privileged to belong to the Shamlegger Street Rude Boys, sir,' said the butler.

'Really?' said Vimes, genuinely impressed. 'They were pretty tough nuts, as I recall.'

'Thank you, sir,' said Willikins smoothly. 'I pride myself I used to give somewhat more than I got if we needed to discuss the vexed area of turf issues with the young men from Rope Street. Stevedore's hooks were their weapon of choice, as I recall.'

'And yours . . .?' said Vimes, agog.

'A cap-brim sewn with sharpened pennies, sir.'

'Ye gods, man! You could put someone's eye out with something like that.'

'With care, sir, yes,' said Willikins, meticulously folding a towel.

*

Vimes knew all the arguments for having different species in the Watch. They were good arguments. Some of the arguments against them were bad arguments. There were trolls in the Watch, *plenty* of dwarfs, one werewolf, three golems, an Igor and, not least, Corporal Nobbs† . . .

*

† This was a bit of a slur on Nobby, Vimes had to admit. Nobby was human, just like many other officers. It was just that he was the only one who had to carry a certificate to prove it.

Fred Colon was not the greatest gift to policing. He was slow, stolid and not very imaginative. But he'd plodded his way around the streets for so long that he'd left a groove and somewhere inside that stupid fat head was something very smart, which sniffed the wind and heard the buzz and read the writing on the wall, admittedly doing the last bit with its lips moving.

*

To look at Fred Colon, you'd see a man who might well, if he fell over a cliff, have to stop and ask directions on the way down.

*

'. . . that girl you're going out with . . . She's nearly six feet tall and she's got a bosom like . . . well, she's a big girl, Nobby.' Fred Colon was at a loss. 'She told me, Nobby, that she's been Miss May on the centrefold of *Girls, Giggles and Garters*! Well, I mean . . .!'

'*What* do you mean, sarge? Anyway, she wasn't just Miss May, she was the first week in June as well,' Nobby pointed out. 'It was the only way they had room.'

'Err, well, I ask you,' Fred floundered, 'is a girl who displays her body for money the right kind of wife for a copper? Ask yourself that!'

Nobby's face wrinkled up in deep thought.

'Is this a trick question, sarge?' he said, at last.

*

Corporal Nobbs attends a burglary at the Royal Art Museum.

'Hey, this must be a clue, sarge!' said Nobby. 'Look, someone dumped a load of stinking ol' rubbish here!'

'Don't touch that, please!' said Sir Reynold, rushing over. 'That's *Don't Talk to Me About Mondays!* It's Daniellarina Pouter's most controversial hwork!'

'It's only a lot of old rubbish,' Nobby protested, backing away.

'Art is greater than the sum of its mere mechanical components, corporal,' said the curator.

'What about this one, then?' said Nobby, pointing to the adjacent plinth. 'It's just a big stake with a nail in it! Is this art, too?'

'*Freedom*? If it hwas ever on the market, it hwould probableah fetch thirty thousand dollars,' said Sir Reynold.

'For a bit of wood with a nail in it?' said Fred Colon. 'Who did it?'

'After he viewed *Don't Talk to Me About Mondays!* Lord Vetinari graciously had Ms Pouter nailed to the stake by her ear,' said Sir Reynold. 'However, she did manage to pull free during the afternoon.'

'I bet she was mad!' said Nobby.

'Not after she hwon several awards for it. I believe she's planning to nail herself to several other things. It could be a very exciting exhibition.'

*

Colon knew in his heart that spinning upside down around a pole wearing a costume you could floss with definitely was not Art, and being painted lying on a bed wearing nothing but a smile and a small bunch of grapes was good solid Art, but putting your finger on why this was the case was a bit tricky.

*

'Dave said the government hushed it up.'

'Yeah, but your mate Dave says the government always hushes things up, Nobby,' said Fred.

'Well, they do.'

'Except he always gets to hear about 'em, and *he* never gets hushed up,' said Fred.

'I know you like to point the finger of scoff, sarge, but there's a lot goes on that we don't know about.'

'Like what, exactly?' Colon retorted. 'Name me one thing that's going on that you don't know about.'

*

'Don't try to put me at my ease,' said Vimes. 'It makes me nervous when people do that.'

*

Coppers stayed alive by trickery. That's how it *worked*. You had your Watch Houses with the big blue lights outside, and you made certain there were always burly watchmen visible in the big public places, and you swanked around like you owned the place. But you didn't own it. It was all smoke and mirrors. You magicked a little policeman into everyone's head. You relied on people giving in, knowing the *rules*. But in truth a hundred well-armed people could wipe out the Watch, if they knew what they were doing. Once some madman finds out that a copper taken unawares dies just like anyone else, the spell is broken.

*

Ankh-Morpork was built on Ankh-Morpork. Everyone knew that. They had been building with stone here ten thousand years ago. As the annual flooding of the Ankh brought more silt, so the city had risen on its walls until attics had become cellars. Even at basement level today, it was always said, a man with a pickaxe and a good sense of direction could cross the city by knocking his way through underground walls, provided he could also breathe mud.

*

Blackboard monitor. Well, he had been, in that little street school more than forty-five years ago. Mum had insisted. Gods knew where she'd sprung the penny a day it cost, although most of the time Dame Slightly had been happy to accept payment in old clothes and firewood. Numbers, letters, weights, measures; it was not what you'd call a rich curriculum. Vimes had attended for nine months or so, until the streets demanded he learn much harder and sharper lessons. But, for a while, he'd been trusted to hand out the slates and clean the blackboard. Oh, the heady, strutting power of it, when you're six years old!

*

Vimes carefully lifted the top of the bacon, lettuce and tomato sandwich, and smiled inwardly. Good old Cheery. She knew what a Vimes BLT was all about. It was about having to lift up quite a lot of crispy bacon before you found the miserable skulking vegetables. You might never notice them at all.

A young man of godlike proportions† was standing in the doorway.

Vimes takes parental duty seriously . . .

He'd be home in time. Would a minute have mattered? No, probably not, although Young Sam appeared to have a very accurate internal clock. Possibly even two minutes would be okay. Three minutes, even. You could go to five, perhaps. But that was just it. If you could go to five

† The better class of gods, anyway. Not the ones with the tentacles, obviously.

minutes then you'd go to ten, then half an hour, a couple of hours . . . and not see your son all evening. So that was that. Six o'clock, prompt. Every day. Read to Young Sam. No excuses. He'd promised himself that. *No excuses.* No excuses at all. Once you had a good excuse, you opened the door to bad excuses.

*

and the book he reads . . .

It was called *Where's My Cow?*

The unidentified complainant had lost their cow. That was the story, really.

Page one started promisingly:

Where's my cow?
Is that my cow?
It goes, 'Baa!'
It is a sheep!
That's not my cow!

Then the author began to get to grips with their material:

Where's my cow?
Is that my cow?
It goes, 'Neigh!'
It is a horse!
That's not my cow!

At this point the author had reached an agony of creation and was writing from the racked depths of their soul.

Where's my cow?
Is that my cow?
It goes, 'Hruuugh!'
It is a hippopotamus!
That's not my cow!

(Rest assured: the cow is found.)

*

'When did you last eat?' said Sybil.

'I had a lettuce, tomato and bacon sandwich, dear,' Vimes said, endeavouring by tone of voice to suggest that the bacon had been a mere condiment rather than a slab barely covered by the bread.

'I expect you jolly well did,' said Sybil, rather more accurately conveying the fact that she didn't believe a word of it.

Tomato ketchup is not a vegetable.

'What's the password?' Vimes said quickly.

The shadowy figure, who was cloaked and hooded, hesitated.

'Pathword? Ecthcuthe me, I've got it written down thomewhere—'

'Okay, Igor, come on in,' said Carrot.

'How did you know it wath me, thur?' said Igor.

*

'I'm going to have a look for Angua,' said Carrot. 'She hasn't slept in her bed.'

'But at this time of the month—'

'I know, sir. She hasn't slept in her basket, either.'

*

Vetinari drummed his fingers on the table. 'What would you do if I asked you an outright question, Vimes?'

'I'd tell you a downright lie, sir.'

'Then I will not do so,' said Vetinari, smiling faintly.

'Thank you, sir. Nor will I.'

*

'We need to talk to you,' said Carrot. 'Do you want a lawyer?'

'No, I ate already.'

'You *eat* lawyers?' said Carrot.

Brick gave him an empty stare until sufficient brain cells had been mustered.

'What d'y'call dem fings, dey kinda crumble when you eat dem?' he ventured.

Carrot looked at Detritus and Angua, to see if there was going to be any help there.

'*Could* be lawyers,' he conceded.

'Dey go soggy if you dips 'em in somefing,' said Brick.

'More likely to be biscuits, then?' Carrot suggested.

*

There was an old military saying that Fred Colon used to describe total bewilderment and confusion. An individual in that state, according to Fred, 'couldn't tell if it was arsehole or breakfast time'.

*

The plain fact was that while Tawneee had a body that every other woman should hate her for, she was actually very likeable. This was because she had the self-esteem of a caterpillar and, as you found out in any kind of conversation with her, about the same amount of brain. Perhaps it all balanced out, perhaps some kindly god had said to her: 'Sorry, kid, you are going to be thicker than a yard of lard, but the good news is, that's not going to matter.'

*

'It's the jerk syndrome. It means . . . sometimes a woman is so beautiful that any man with half a brain isn't going to *think* of asking her out, okay? Because it's *obvious* that she's far too grand for the likes of him. Are you with me?'

'I think so.'

'Well, that's Tawneee. And, for the purposes of this explanation, Nobby has not got half a brain. He's so used to women saying no when he asks them out that he's not afraid of being blown out. So he asks her, because he figures, why not? And *she*, who by now thinks there's something wrong with her, is so grateful she says okay.'

*

'Needs eating up.' That was a phrase of Sybil's that got to Vimes. She'd announce at lunch: 'We must have the pork tonight, it needs eating up.' Vimes never had an actual problem with this, because he'd been raised to eat what was put in front of him, and do it quickly, too, before someone else snatched it away. He was just puzzled at the suggestion that he was there to do the food a favour.

*

When *did* Lord Vetinari sleep? Presumably the man must get his head down at some point, Vimes reasoned. Everyone slept. Catnaps could get you by for a while, but sooner or later you need a solid eight hours, right?

It was almost midnight, and there was Vetinari at his desk, fresh as a daisy and chilly as morning dew.

*

Mustrum Ridcully was capable of enormous powers of concentration when absolutely no alternative presented itself.

*

'This is all rather fun,' said Sybil, as the coaches headed out of the city. 'Do you remember when we last went on holiday, Sam?'

'That wasn't really a holiday, dear,' said Vimes.

'Well, it was very interesting, all the same,' said Sybil.

'Yes, dear. Werewolves tried to eat me.'

*

Historical Re-creation. With people dressing up and running around with blunt weapons, and people selling hot dogs, and the girls all miserable because they can only dress up as wenches, wenching being the only job available to women in the olden days.

WINTERSMITH

TIFFANY Aching put one foot wrong, made one little mistake . . .

And now the spirit of winter is in love with her. He gives her roses and icebergs, says it with avalanches and showers her with snowflakes – which is tough when you're thirteen, but also just a little bit . . . cool.

And just because the Wintersmith wants to marry you is no excuse for neglecting the chores. So she must look after Miss Treason, who's 113 and has far too many eyes, learn the secret of Boffo, catch Horace the cheese, stop Annagramma

Hawkin from becoming an embarrassment to all witches, avoid Nanny Ogg giving her a lecture on sex, stop the gods from seeing her in the bath—

'Crivens!'

—oh, yes, and be helped by the Nac Mac Feegles, whether she wants it or not.

It's unfair, but as Granny Weatherwax says, no one ever said it was going to be fair. And if Tiffany doesn't work it all out, there will never be another springtime . . .

When the gods made sheep they must've left their brains in their other coat.

'Cackling', to a witch, didn't just mean nasty laughter. It meant your mind drifting away from its anchor. It meant you losing your grip. It meant loneliness and hard work and responsibility and other people's problems driving you crazy a little bit at a time, each bit so small that you'd hardly notice it, until you thought that it was normal to stop washing and wear a kettle on your head. It meant you thinking that the fact you knew more than anyone else in your village made you better than them. It meant thinking that right and wrong were negotiable. And, in the end, it meant you 'going to the dark', as the witches said. That was a bad road. At the end of that road were poisoned spinning-wheels and gingerbread cottages.

*

Everyone had something inside them that told the world they were there. That was why you could often sense when someone was behind you, even if they were making no sound at all. You were receiving their 'I am here!' signal.

Some people had a very strong one. They were the people who got served first in shops. Granny Weatherwax had an 'I am here' signal that bounced off the mountains when she wanted it to; when she walked into a forest, all the wolves and bears ran out the other side.

*

Mrs Earwig was all wrong to Granny Weatherwax. She wasn't born locally, which was almost a crime to begin with. She wrote books, and Granny Weatherwax didn't trust books. And Mrs Earwig believed in shiny wands and magical amulets and mystic runes and the power of the stars, while Granny Weatherwax believed in cups of tea, dry biscuits, washing every morning in cold water and, well, she believed mostly in Granny Weatherwax.

*

Most witches liked black, but Miss Treason even had black goats and black chickens. The walls were black. The floor was black. If you dropped a stick of liquorice, you'd never find it again. And, to Tiffany's dismay, she had to make her cheeses black, which meant painting the cheeses with shiny black wax. It did keep them moist, but

Tiffany distrusted black cheeses. They always looked as though they were plotting something.

*

'Gods, elementals, demons, spirits . . . sometimes it's hard to tell 'em apart wi'oot a map.'

*

You could hear the snow falling. It made a strange little noise, like a faint, cold sizzle.

*

The Chalk Hill Feegles were more at home with the drinkin', stealin' and fightin', and Rob Anybody was good at all three. But he'd learned to read and write because Jeannie had asked him to. He did them with a lot more optimism than accuracy. When he was faced with a long sentence he tended to work out a few words and then have a great big guess.

*

The white kitten watched the snowflakes. It was called You, as in 'You! Stop that!' and 'You! Get off there!' When it came to names, Granny Weatherwax didn't do fancy.

*

'The important thing,' said Miss Treason, 'is to stay the passage of the wind. You should avoid rumbustious fruits and vegetables. Beans are the worst, take it from me.'

'I don't think I understand—' Tiffany began.

'Try not to fart, in a nutshell.'

'In a nutshell I imagine it would be pretty unpleasant!' said Tiffany, nervously.

*

The Feegles didn't know the meaning of the word 'fear'. Sometimes Tiffany wished they'd read a dictionary. They fought like tigers, they fought like demons, they fought like giants. What they didn't do was fight like something with more than a spoonful of brain.

*

Nanny Ogg was good at listening, at least. She listened like a great big ear, and before Tiffany realized it she was telling her everything. Everything. Nanny sat on the opposite side of the big kitchen table, puffing gently at a pipe with a hedgehog carved on it. Sometimes she'd ask a little question, like 'Why was that?' or 'And then what happened?' and off they'd go again. Nanny's friendly little smile could drag out of you things you didn't know you knew.

*

From the best chair in the room of ornaments, a large grey cat watched Tiffany with a half-open eye that glinted with absolute evil. Nanny had referred to him as 'Greebo . . . don't mind him, he's just a big old softie,' which Tiffany knew enough to interpret as 'He'll have his claws in your leg if you go anywhere near him.'

It was hard to be embarrassed by Nanny Ogg, because her laugh drove it away. She wasn't embarrassed about anything.

She opened the cutlery drawer for a spoon. It stuck. She rattled it, pulled at it and swore a few times, but it stayed stuck.

'Oh, yes, go ahead,' said a voice behind her. 'See how much help that is. Don't be sensible and stick your hand under the top and carefully free up the stuck item. Oh no. Rattle and curse, that's the way!'

Tiffany turned.

There was a skinny, tired-looking woman standing by the kitchen table. She seemed to be wearing a sheet draped around her and was smoking a cigarette. Tiffany had never seen a woman smoke a cigarette before, but especially never a cigarette that burned with a fat red flame and gave off sparks.

'Who are you?' she said sharply.

'Anoia, Goddess of Things That Get Stuck In Drawers,' said the woman. 'Pleased to meet you.'

'There's a goddess just for that?' said Tiffany.

'Well, I find lost corkscrews and things that roll under furniture,' said Anoia, off-handedly. 'They want me to do stuck zips, and I'm thinking about that. But mostly I manifest whensoever people rattle stuck drawers and call upon the gods.' She puffed on her cigarette. 'Got any tea?'

'But I didn't call on anyone!'

'You did,' said Anoia. 'You cussed. Sooner or later, every curse is a prayer.' She waved the hand that wasn't holding the cigarette and something in the drawer went *pling*. 'It'll be all right now. It was the fish slice. Everyone has one, and no one knows why. Did anyone in the world ever knowingly go out one day and buy a fish slice? I don't think so.'

Annagramma was as vain as a canary in a room full of mirrors.

Roland tugged the sword out of its scabbard. It was heavy and not at all like the flying, darting silver thing that he'd imagined. It was more like a metal club with an edge.

He gripped it in both hands and managed to hurl it out into the middle of the slow, dark river.

Just before it hit the water a white arm rose and caught it. The hand waved the sword a couple of times, and then disappeared with it under the water.

'Was that supposed to happen?' he said.

'A man throwin' his sword awa'?' yelled Rob. 'No! Ye're no' supposed tae bung a guid sword intae the drinkie!'

'No, I mean the hand,' said Roland. 'It just—'

'Ach, they turn up sometimes.' Rob Anybody waved a hand as if midstream underwater sword jugglers were an everyday occurrence.

*

When the noise had died down a bit the drummer beat the drum a few times and the accordionist played a long drawn-out chord, the legal signal that a Morris Dance is about to begin, and people who hang around have only got themselves to blame.

MAKING MONEY

IT'S an offer you can't refuse.

Who would not wish to be the man in charge of Ankh-Morpork's Royal Mint *and* the bank next door?

It's a job for life. But, as former conman Moist von Lipwig is learning, life is not necessarily for long.

The Chief Cashier is almost certainly a vampire. There's something nameless in the cellar (and the cellar itself is pretty nameless), and it turns out that the Royal Mint runs at a loss. A three-hundred-year-old wizard is after his girlfriend, he's about to be exposed as a fraud, but the Assassins' Guild might get him first. In fact, lots of people want him dead.

Oh. And every day he has to take the Chairman for walkies.

Everywhere he looks he's making enemies.

What he *should* be doing is . . . Making Money!

The Guild of Thieves paid a twenty-dollar bounty fee for a non-accredited thief brought in alive, and there were oh, so many ways of still being alive when you were dragged in and poured out on the floor.

*

'You Have An Appointment Now With Lord Vetinari,' said the golem.

'I'm sure I don't.'

'There Are Two Guards Outside Who Are Sure You Do.'

*

Lord Vetinari lifted an eyebrow with the care of one who, having found a piece of caterpillar in his salad, raises the rest of the lettuce.

*

'[The bank] was built as a temple, but never used as one.'

'Really?' said Moist. 'Which god?'

'None, as it turned out. One of the kings of Ankh commanded it to be built about nine hundred years ago,' said Bent. 'I suppose it was a case of speculative building. That is to say, he had no god in mind.'

'He hoped one would turn up?'

'Exactly, sir.'

'Like bluetits?' said Moist, peering around. 'This place was a kind of celestial bird box?'

*

'It costs more than a penny to make a penny,' Moist murmured. 'Is it just me, or is that *wrong*?'

'But, you see, once you have made it, a penny keeps on being a penny,' said Mr Bent. 'That's the magic of it.'

'It is?' said Moist. 'Look, it's a copper disc. What do you expect it to become?'

'In the course of a year, just about everything,' said Mr Bent, smoothly. 'It becomes some apples, part of a cart, a pair of shoelaces, some hay, an hour's occupancy of a theatre seat. It may even become a stamp and send a letter, Mr Lipwig. It might be spent three hundred times and yet – and this is the good part – it is still one penny, ready and willing to be spent again. It is not an apple, which will go bad. Its worth is fixed and stable. It is not consumed.'

*

Mr Fusspot was the smallest and ugliest dog Moist had ever seen. It reminded him of those goldfish with the huge bulging eyes that look as though they are about to explode. Its nose, on the other hand, looked stoved in. It wheezed, and its legs were so bandy that it must sometimes trip over its own feet.

The dog gave a little yappy bark and then covered Moist's face in all that was best in dog slobber.

*

'I don't really understand how banks work.'

'How do you *think* they work?'

'Well, you take rich people's money and lend it to suitable people at interest, and give as little as possible of the interest back.'

'Yes, and what is a suitable person?'

'Someone who can prove they don't need the money?'

*

'Old money' meant that it had been made so long ago that the black deeds which had originally filled the coffers were now historically irrelevant. Funny, that: a brigand for a father was something you kept quiet about, but a slave-taking pirate for a great-great-great-grandfather was something to boast of over the port. Time turned the evil bastards into rogues, and rogue was a word with a twinkle in its eye and nothing to be ashamed of.

*

'I did not become ruler of Ankh-Morpork by understanding the city. Like banking, the city is depressingly easy to understand. I have remained ruler by getting the city to understand *me*.'

The city bleeds, Mr Lipwig, and you are the clot I need.

The lady in the boardroom was certainly an attractive woman, but since she worked for the *Times* Moist felt unable to award her total ladylike status. Ladies didn't fiendishly quote exactly what you said but didn't exactly mean, or hit you around the ear with unexpectedly difficult questions. Well, come to think of it, they did, quite often, but *she* got paid for it.

*

'The world is full of things worth more than gold. But we dig the damn stuff up and then bury it in a different hole. Where's the sense in that? What are we, magpies? Good heavens, *potatoes* are worth more than gold!'

'Surely not!'

'If you were shipwrecked on a desert island, what would you prefer, a bag of potatoes or a bag of gold?'

'Yes, but a desert island isn't Ankh-Morpork!'

'And that proves gold is only valuable because we agree it is, right? It's just a dream. But a potato is always worth a potato, anywhere. A knob of butter and a pinch of salt and you've got a meal, *anywhere*. Bury gold in the ground and you'll be worrying about thieves for ever. Bury a potato and in due season you could be looking at a dividend of a thousand per cent.'

*

'Vetinari has a dog?'

'Had. Wuffles. Died some time ago. There's a little grave in the Palace grounds. He goes there alone once a week and puts a dog biscuit on it.'

'Vetinari does that?'

'Yes.'

'Vetinari the cool, heartless, calculating tyrant?'

'Indeed.'

*

Don't let me detain you. What a wonderful phrase Vetinari had devised. The jangling double meaning set up undercurrents of uneasiness in the most innocent of minds. The man had found ways of bloodless tyranny that put the rack to shame.

*

Stamp collecting! It had started on day one, and then ballooned like some huge . . . thing, running on strange, mad rules. Was there any other field where flaws made things worth more? Would you buy a suit just because one arm was shorter than the other? Or because a bit of spare cloth was still attached?

*

Claud Maximillian Overton Transpire Dibbler, a name bigger than the man himself. Everyone knew C. M. O. T. Dibbler. He sold pies and sausages off a tray, usually to people who were the worse for drink who then became the worse for pies.

*

Moist had eaten the odd pork pie and occasional sausage in a bun and that very fact interested him. There was something about the stuff that drove you back for more. There had to be some secret ingredient, or maybe the brain just didn't believe what the taste buds told it, and wanted to feel once again that flood of hot, greasy, not entirely organic, slightly crunchy substances surfing across the tongue. So you bought another one.

And, it had to be said, there were times when a Dibbler sausage in a bun was just what you wanted. Sad, yet true. Everyone had moments like that. Life brought you so low that for a vital few seconds that charivari of strange greases and worrying textures was your only friend in all the world.

*

The Watch armour fitted like a glove. He'd have preferred it to fit like a helmet and breastplate. It was common knowledge that the Watch's approach to uniforms was one-size-doesn't-exactly-fit-anybody, and that Commander Vimes disapproved of armour that didn't have that kicked-by-trolls look. He liked it to make it clear that it had been doing its job.

'I'm an Igor, thur. We don't athk quethtionth.'

'Really? Why not?'

'I don't know, thur. I didn't athk.'

Students, eh? Love 'em or hate 'em, you're not allowed to hit 'em with a shovel.

'I'm afraid I have to close the office now, reverend.' The voice of Ms Houser broke into Cribbins's dreams . . .

Ms Houser was standing there, not gloriously naked and pink as so recently featured in the reverie, but in a plain brown coat and an unsuitable hat with feathers in it.

*

Talking to the Watch was like tap-dancing on a landslide. If you were nimble you could stay upright, but you couldn't steer and there were no brakes and you just knew that it was going to end in a certain amount of fuss.

*

The price of a good woman was proverbially above rubies, so a bad one was presumably a lot more.

*

He slapped Hubert twice across the face and pulled a jar out of his pocket.

'Mr Hubert? How many fingerth am I holding up?'

Hubert slowly focused. 'Thirteen?' he quavered.

Igor relaxed, and dropped the jar back into his pocket. 'Jutht in time. Well done, thur!'

*

All heads turned. A path [in the crowd] cleared itself for Lord Vetinari; paths do for men known to have dungeons in their basements.

*

'The law must be obeyed, Miss Dearheart [said Lord Vetinari]. Even tyrants have to obey the law.' He paused, looking thoughtful, and continued: 'No, I tell a lie, tyrants do *not* have to obey the law, obviously, but they do have to observe the niceties. At least, I do.'

*

It was 6 a.m., and the fog seemed glued to the windows, so thick that it should have contained croutons.

*

'Is he allowed to do that?'

'I think that comes under the rule of Quia Ego Sic Dico.'

'Yes, what does that mean?'

' "Because I say so", I think.'

'That doesn't sound like much of a rule!'

'Actually, it's the only one he needs.'

*

'Every problem is an opportunity,' said Moist.

'Well, if you upset Vetinari again you will have a wonderful opportunity to never have to buy a hat.'

'No, I think he likes a little opposition.'

'And are you any good at knowing how much?'

'No. It's what I enjoy. You get a wonderful view from the point of no return.'

*

Moist von Lipwig quizzes staff at the bank about the cost of making money:

'So how do you get paid?'

There was a moment's silence, and then Mr Shady said, like a man talking to a child: 'This *is* a mint, sir.'

'You make your own wages? Well, at least you're in a profitable business,' said Moist cheerfully. 'I mean, you must be making money hand over fist!'

'We manage to break even, sir, yes,' said Shady, as if it was a close-run thing.

'Break even? You're a mint!' said Moist. 'How can you not make a profit by making money?'

'Overheads, sir. There's overheads wherever you look.'

'Even underfoot?'

'There too, sir,' said Shady. 'It's ruinous, sir, it really is. Y'see, it costs a ha'penny to make a farthin' an' nearly a penny to make a ha'penny. A penny comes in at a penny farthin'. Sixpences costs tuppence farthin', so we're in pocket there. Half a dollar costs seven pence. And it's only sixpence to make a dollar, a definite improvement, but that's 'cos we does 'em here. The real buggers are the mites, 'cos they're worth half a farthin' but cost sixpence 'cos it's fiddly work, bein' so small and havin' that hole in the middle. The thrupenny bit, sir, we've only got a couple of people makin' those, a lot of work which runs out at seven pence. And don't ask me about the tuppenny piece!'

'What about the tuppenny piece?'

'I'm glad you asked me that, sir. Fine work, sir, tots up to seven and one-sixteenth pence.'

WIT & WISDOM

INDEX

E

F

G

T

U